Meet Me in Venice

ELIZABETH ADLER

ST. MARTIN'S GRIFFIN NEW YORK

This is a work of fiction. All of the characters, organizations, and events portrayed in this novel are either products of the author's imagination or are used fictitiously.

www.stmartins.com

Design by Maggie Goodman

Library of Congress Cataloging-in-Publication Data

Adler, Elizabeth (Elizabeth A.)
Meet me in Venice / Elizabeth Adler.
p. cm.
ISBN-13: 978-0-312-36448-9
ISBN-10: 0-312-36448-2
1. Antique dealers—Fiction. 2. Antiques business—Fiction. 3. Venice (Italy)—Fiction. 4. Shanghai (China)—Fiction. 5. Paris (France)—Fiction. 6. Americans—Foreign countries—Fiction. I. Title.
PR6051.D56 M44 2007
823'.914—dc22

2007012955

First St. Martin's Griffin Edition: July 2008

10 9 8 7 6 5 4 3 2 1

For my mother and father,
who would have so enjoyed reading this

ACKNOWLEDGMENTS

Of course, my thanks to my editor, Jen Enderlin. I would happily allow her to edit my entire life. And to my agent, Anne Sibbald, and her team at Janklow & Nesbit Associates, who all look after me with care and affection—which I return with gratitude. And to Sweat Pea and Sunny, my beautiful—and naughty—cats (one of whom you might recognize in this book), who keep me company in those long hours of writing.

Meet Me in Venice

PROLOGUE

ANA Yuan, a plain young woman in a summery blue dress and sandals, never felt even a hint of danger when she boarded the double-decker train from Shanghai to Suzhou on the borders of the Taihu Lake.

The landscape was dreamlike, more than sixty percent water with low hills bordering cultivated fields. Canals intersected the ancient city, framed by graceful arched bridges. There were leafy lanes and centuries-old pavilions and famous gardens dating back through four dynasties. It was no wonder Suzhou was described by Marco Polo as "the Venice of the East."

The journey took only ninety minutes, but when the train stopped Ana was dismayed to find it was raining. Still, always uncertain of the temperamental weather, she had carried an umbrella.

Regretting the summery blue dress and the sandals, she hurried into a taxi.

Arriving at her destination, Ana paid off the driver. She put up her umbrella and began to walk down the cobblestone pathway by the edge of the canal. It was late and the area was deserted. The rain was coming down hard now, and what with the clouds and the dusk, the carbon-gray water and the pathway covered by dense leafy trees, it was darker and more lonely than she would have liked. Suddenly nervous, she glanced around but no one was about.

Ana's summer sandals clattered noisily on the slick wet stones as she hurried toward her rendezvous. Head tucked under the umbrella, shivering in the damp, she did not notice the observer behind her, keeping carefully to the shadows under the trees.

She paused at the arched bridge that resembled the ones in Venice, looking around her, half-smiling. She did not hear the observer approaching on soft feet.

He struck her a vicious blow behind the knees, sending her sprawling. Her skull smacked on the stone path and her eyes rolled up in her head. She was unconscious. He dragged her to the edge of the canal and pushed her into the water. There was a splash, then the soft thud of his urgent footsteps running back along the lane. The heavy rain conveniently washed away any traces of her blood from the path. It was the perfect murder.

The next morning Ana's body in her summery blue dress was found where it had drifted, caught in the reeds further down the canal. Her death was judged an accident: a fall on the slippery stones when she must have hit her head; a tumble unconscious into the canal; a drowning.

She was buried with great ceremony in the wealthy Yuan family's plot in Shanghai. Her handsome young American husband, Bennett Yuan, sobbed, heartbroken, but despite their sorrow her Chinese family remained impassive and dignified.

Tragic, the mourners said. Such a sweet girl, happily married and with everything to live for. And what on earth was she doing in Suzhou anyway?

PART ONE

PRECIOUS

ONE

SHANGHAI

Six Months Later

LILY Song was eating breakfast at the Happybird Tea House, an open-fronted place in an alley off the Renmin Road, named for the tiny birds, the pets of the customers that accompanied them in their little bamboo cages, singing their morning songs. She ate there every morning at exactly the same time—eight o'clock—and she always had exactly the same thing: shrimp dim sum with vegetables and green tea with semolina grains that swelled up like miniature cannonballs in the hot tea and tasted like slippery bird shot. Her fellow breakfasters were all men but that did not bother her and anyway they were all too immersed in their newspapers and noodles to notice her, even though she was an attractive woman.

She was small and very slender, with a shoulder-length swing of glossy black hair and eyes so dark a brown they looked almost black too. She had the fair skin of her European mother and the delicate bridgeless nose of her Chinese father, and she wore either conservative Western clothes bought at the better boutiques on the Nanking Road, or the traditional brocade dress, the *quipao* in jewel tones, tailored specifically to her directions by an expert in his tiny storefront shop near the Bubbling Well Road. Either way, though she was not beautiful, she gave the impression of an attractive, successful woman. Which, in a sense, she was.

This morning, however, she was wearing narrow black pants with a black linen top. Her hair was pulled back and large sunglasses hid her eyes. She could have passed unnoticed in any Shanghai crowd. She glanced up as a man entered, then stood looking around him. He was a foreigner, older, smart in a lightweight beige business suit and he carried a leather document case. Lily lifted her hand, beckoning him over.

He came and sat in the chair opposite. With a gruff "good morning" he placed the document case on the table in front of him. A soft-footed server hovered nearby and Lily ordered plain green tea for her guest. She asked if he would like to eat and with a faint look of disgust he said he would not. He was Swiss and conservative and he did not like Chinese food. The teahouse was not a place he would have chosen to do business but this was Lily's call.

"My client is interested in anything you can show him," he said without wasting any time. "Provided it can be authenticated, that is."

Lily had done business with him before. His client's identity was preserved under a cloak of strict anonymity, which suited her just fine. That way she didn't have to deal with tricky, rich, artistic personalities who thought they knew more than she did. Antiques and, in particular, stolen antiques were what she had dealt in since she was sixteen and she knew what she was talking about.

"I have some things your client might be interested in," she said in a low voice, because you never knew who was listening. "I expect to take delivery of a batch of antiquities very soon. Cloisonné, famille verte, statues. . . ."

"When will you have them?" His eyes bored into her, questioning her integrity. She hated him for it but she did not show that. Instead she smiled.

"Within a few weeks. Meanwhile, here is something very special. The most important piece I have ever come across." She reached in her purse, took out a photograph and handed it to him.

The man studied it carefully. "My client doesn't care for jewelry," he said curtly.

"I think he will care for this when he hears its provenance." Lily took another sip of her green tea, meeting his eyes across the table. "Your client will no doubt have heard of the great Dragon Lady, Cixi, the Dowager Empress of China?" She spelled the name for him and told him it was pronounced *chee shee,* so that he could make his notes correctly.

"Cixi was once a concubine but eventually she ruled China and was said to have been even more powerful than her contemporary, Queen Victoria.

"The Empress lived in great splendor in the Forbidden City, and in preparation for her death she built herself a magnificent tomb, a lavish complex of temples, gates and pavilions glittering in gold and precious stones.

"Eventually, she was buried there, wearing her elaborate crown and magnificent robes, along with her wonderful jewels and precious ornaments. And before they sealed the coffin, in accordance with Imperial custom, a large and very rare pearl, the size of a robin's egg, was placed in her mouth. It was believed this would preserve the royal corpse from decay."

Lily paused in her story, studying the man opposite. He was looking at the photograph she had given him. She could tell from his body language he was interested, even though he pretended otherwise. It was all about money, she thought, cynically. But then, wasn't it always?

"Twenty years later," she said, "the revolutionary troops dynamited the entrance to Cixi's burial chamber. The soldiers stripped the temples, looted all the treasures and opened Cixi's coffin. They ripped off her Imperial robes and stole the crown from her head. Then they threw her naked corpse onto the muddy ground."

Lily paused and the man's stunned eyes met hers, waiting for what she would say next. "The body was said to be intact," she said softly. "And from her mouth, they stole that single, massive, rare pearl. A moonbeam of light and cool as death itself."

The man lowered his eyes to the photograph and she smiled; she knew she had his interest now.

"Yes," she said softly, "it's the very same one. There was, it has been said, a second pearl, this one taken from the Empress's crown. It's rumored that the second pearl came into the possession of Premier Chiang Kai-shek and ended up as an ornament, along with another fine pearl, on the party shoes of his wife, the famous Soong Mai-ling. The rest of the jewels disappeared into obscurity and into hidden collections."

She paused again, making him wait. "Until suddenly," she said, "sixty or so years ago, a necklace surfaced, embedded with emeralds and rubies, diamonds and jade, all said to be from Cixi's tomb. And at its center was the famous pearl."

Smiling, she saw him take a deep breath. Then he said, "And you are telling me you have this necklace with the pearl in your possession?"

She lowered her eyes. "Let us just say I know where to lay my hands on it." Lily understood that he knew the existence of the necklace must be kept secret, that if the authorities found out about it she would certainly be in danger.

"And the price?"

"As always, that is open to discussion. Obviously it will not be cheap. And there is, of course, always a premium on a history and provenance as sinister as this one. Many men would enjoy handling the pearl from the mouth of the dead Empress, a woman who was once a famous concubine. It would give them a special thrill, I think." She smiled at the man, gathering up her handbag. "I'm sure we can do business together," she said, offering him her hand.

The little birds trilled joyously as she left.

TWO

PARIS

SIX thousand miles away, Lily's cousin, Precious Rafferty, was sitting in a crowded café near the rue de Buci on Paris's Left Bank. It was ten o'clock on a rainy Saturday morning. She was sipping her café crème and nibbling on a slab of toasted baguette, watching the shoppers at the bustling street market putting up their umbrellas and walking a little faster past the piled displays of fruits and vegetables and the fragrant herbs and cheeses.

The shoppers were beginning to thin out; a rainy Saturday was not good for business, though fortunately her own store, Rafferty Antiques, did not depend on passersby for trade.

She finished her coffee and waved goodbye to the waiter who knew her well because she was a local and had been breakfasting there every day for years, then pushed her way out through the crowded tables. She stood for a while under the awning, wrapping her blue scarf over her hair to protect it from the rain, looking at the young couple sitting at a table, braving the elements. They were holding hands and gazing lovingly at each other. She guessed they were tourists, probably honeymooners, and she thought wistfully how happy they looked.

How, she wondered, did you go about finding that kind of happiness? Where did it come from? Was there some invisible element floating in the air that you caught hold of, unknowing, and suddenly there you were, in love and blissfully happy? A couple instead of one. Whatever it was she certainly hadn't found it yet.

Stopping at the patisserie for a raspberry napoleon to get her through the morning, she hurried back through the rain, turning onto the rue Jacob where she lived over her antiques store.

Preshy had run the business for fifteen years, ever since her grandfather Hennessy died, but it still gave her a thrill to see *"Rafferty Antiques"* written in flowing gilt script across the window. She stopped to peer inside, imagining herself a customer, seeing the once-red walls, faded over the years to a soft fuchsia, and admiring the shell-shaped alabaster sconces that added a muted glow.

The narrow room was crammed with antique pieces, bathed in a gentle aura from the special overhead lighting. There was a lovely marble head of a boy with the tight curls of youth; a small Etruscan bowl that was probably a later copy, and a life-sized marble of Aphrodite, emerging from the sea, her delicate hand outstretched.

Next to the store, tall wooden gates led into one of those charming secretive Parisian courtyards centered with an old paulownia tree, which in spring was covered in showy flowers that dropped their white petals onto the gray cobbles.

Preshy's grandfather Arthur Hennessy, who'd fought with the U.S. Army in France and fallen in love with Paris, had discovered the apartment in the secret courtyard. He'd bought it for a song and opened his antiques store specializing in artifacts from Italy and the Balkans that were easy to come by right after the conflict.

When she was six, Preshy's parents were killed in a plane crash en route to a writers' conference in a snowstorm. Her grandmother had also died young, so Grandfather Hennessy sent her Austrian aunt to San Francisco to bring her back to Paris. And it was Aunt Grizelda, the Countess von Hoffenberg, a woman of the world, eccentric, glamorous, childless and seductive, and with absolutely no clue as to the proper etiquette of child rearing, who'd brought Preshy up.

Having a small child around certainly didn't cramp Grizelda's style though. She simply hired a French governess and hauled Preshy everywhere with her, upping stakes every few months and moving her from the von Hoffenberg castle in the mountains near Salzburg, to her permanent suite at the Carlyle in New York, or the one at Paris's Ritz Hotel. In fact Preshy became a sort of international Eloise, familiar with doormen, housekeepers and waiters and spoiled by maître d's and hotel managers.

She adored Aunt Grizelda, and she also loved her grandfather, who finally became interested in her when she was old enough to attend college in Boston and visit him in Paris where she learned about the antiques trade.

Confident that she would do well, her grandfather willed her the store and the apartment over it. But within a few weeks of his death, Preshy discovered that the business was in chaos. He had let things slip in his old age and there was only the stock—and not much of that—and very little money. Gradually, with hard work and dedication, she had revamped it. She wasn't making a fortune yet, and most of what came in went out immediately, reinvested in new stock. Still, she was making a living and she was optimistic for better things to come.

Meanwhile, she suddenly seemed to have reached the age of thirty-eight without ever committing to a serious relationship. Oh sure, there had been love affairs and even a couple of men she'd thought exciting, or romantic, for a while, but somehow none of them had worked out.

"You're too picky," Aunt Grizelda complained as yet another suitor bit the dust, but Preshy just laughed. Inside though, she was beginning to wonder if she would ever meet someone she really *liked.* Someone she enjoyed and could laugh with. Someone who would sweep her off her feet. She thought it very unlikely.

There was nothing wrong with her. She was a tall, lanky, attractive woman with a cloud of curly copper-blond hair that frizzed horribly in the rain, her mother's jutting cheekbones and the wide Hennessy mouth. She didn't care much about clothes, something that drove her clotheshorse aunt crazy, but she thought she dressed reasonably well when she had to, relying on that old standby, the little black dress. But day to day it was jeans and white T-shirts.

She was educated and charming; she enjoyed good food and

was particular about her wine. She went to the latest movies and to gallery openings, concerts and the theater with her friends. In fact she enjoyed life, but she thought sadly, she might enjoy it more if she ever found a soul mate.

She let herself into the courtyard and climbed the steps to the sixteenth-century stone apartment "over the shop." Her home was a cozy refuge in winter, and in summer, with the tall windows flung open to the breeze, it was a cool city space filled with sunlight and the sound of the birds nesting in the paulownia tree.

The phone was ringing and she galloped across the room and grabbed it with a breathy "Hello."

"Hi, sweets, it's me."

Her best friend Daria's loud Boston twang bounced in her ear and she held the phone away with an exasperated frown.

"Isn't it a bit early for you to be calling?" she asked, trying to calculate the time difference.

"Yeah, well Super-Kid's been up all night. Presh, what are you supposed to do when your three-year-old has bad dreams? Take her to a shrink?"

Preshy laughed. "Stop feeding her soft drinks and candy, I'd think. Anyway, it's a cheaper solution than a shrink. And besides, I don't think she has enough vocabulary yet to talk to a psychiatrist."

She was grinning as she said it, joking around as they always did. Daria's three-year-old's name was Lauren, but she'd always been known as Super-Kid, and she was Preshy's goddaughter.

Daria was married to a physics professor, Tom, and she was always on to Preshy about finding "the right one." Today was no exception.

"So, it's Saturday," Daria began. "What are you going to do tonight?"

"Oh, you know, Daria, I'm tired. It's been a long week. I drove over to Brussels for the antiques fair there, and then when I got back my assistant went down with the flu—though personally I'm inclined to believe it's a 'man' kind of flu."

"Hmm, pity it wasn't you," Daria said smartly. "You could use a bit of a 'man-flu' yourself, Presh. I mean, how can a gal who looks like you, who is . . . well who is *you,* be staying home alone on Saturday night in Paris?"

"Because I want to, Daria. There's a gallery opening I could go to, right down the street, but I simply can't be bothered with the white wine and chatting with the artist, and besides I don't like his work. And I'm too tired for a movie."

"You've got to get a life, Presh," Daria said sternly. "Remember, we only get to go around once. Why not come on over here and let me introduce you to some nice tenured professor? You'd make an ideal academic's wife."

"*Me?* Oh yeah, sure. And he'd live in Boston and I'd live in Paris. Makes for a great marriage, huh?"

"Then have Sylvie set you up with someone."

Sylvie was their other "best friend." She was French, a chef who'd opened her own successful bistrot, Verlaine, a couple of years ago, and who was also so caught up in her work she had no time to meet men.

"Sylvie only knows other chefs, and with their hours who needs that?" Preshy replied. "Anyhow, did you ever stop to think I might be quite happy just as I am? I don't want any changes; I don't have time for them. I have my life, I go out when I want . . ."

"With whom?" Daria said, leaving her no loopholes, but Preshy just laughed.

"I mean it, sweets," Daria said with an exasperated sigh, "just leave the shop in charge of the 'man-flu' assistant for a week and come on over here. I promise we'll show you a good time."

Preshy said she'd think about it and they chatted for a while longer. When she rang off, she went to the shelf and looked at the silver-framed photo of the three best friends, aged eighteen.

Daria was in the middle, her long straight blond hair floating on the sea breeze, long slim legs firmly planted, steady blue eyes smiling as usual. Preppie personified in shorts and a polo shirt.

Sylvie was on the left, with a glossy black gamine haircut and solemn dark eyes, plump even then because she was working that summer in a local restaurant and was always tasting the food "to make sure it was okay."

Preshy was on the right, taller than the others and skinny with it, her gold hair frizzing into a halo in the humid sea air, green-blue eyes sparkling with fun, her wide mouth open in a laugh. None of them could be called great beauties but they were young and attractive and vividly alive.

As girls, the three of them had spent summer weeks at Daria's family's tumbledown gray shingled cottage on Cape Cod, idling away the hours that seemed to stretch pleasantly into infinity, lathering on the sun lotion and lying full-out, intent on getting that enviable bronze tan. They would take long walks down the beach, flirting with the college boys they met along the way, meeting up with them again as the sun went down for beer and cheese dip on the brittle peeling wooden deck. Then disco dancing as the moon came up, windswept and happy with the testosterone-high boys and themselves, sexy in short shorts and tank tops, displaying their tans.

Preshy had met Sylvie at one of the schools she occasionally attended whenever she was in Paris, and later, when she met Daria at school in Boston, she had brought Sylvie there with her because she just knew the three of them would get on. They had been best friends ever since. There was nothing they didn't know about each other and she loved them like sisters.

Overwhelmed with sudden nostalgia for the past when they had all been so carefree, so young, with all the world and the future beckoning them on to new lives, Preshy wondered if, after all, she had made the wrong choices. But that past was gone and now all she had to look forward was becoming a successful career woman. Marriage and babies were definitely not in her stars.

Telling herself not to be so foolish and sentimental, she put the photo back on the shelf next to the one of Grandfather Hennessy and his pretty blond Austrian bride. It was taken on their wedding day and the bride was wearing a bizarre necklace of what looked to be diamonds and emeralds with a robin's egg–sized pearl in the center. It seemed a strange piece of jewelry for a young bride to wear with her simple traditional dress, but Preshy had never seen the real thing. The necklace had not turned up amongst Grandfather's possessions, and it seemed to have simply disappeared.

Of course there was a photo of Preshy's parents whose faces for her were just a blur from the past, yet she had loving memories of them and especially of the time they took her to Venice, an event everyone said she was too young to remember but that she knew she did.

There were, of course, several pictures of Aunt Grizelda: one of her sipping a gin fizz with Prince Rainier on a terrace on the Côte d'Azur; and another of her accepting the winner's trophy at some racetrack with the King of Spain at her side; and yet another in a cloud of scarlet tulle at a table of international celebrities at the annual Red Cross Gala in Monte Carlo, her long sweep of hair even redder than the dress and her wide beaming smile enhanced with a slick of scarlet lipstick. And with her, of course, was her longtime best friend, blond, rangy, ex–Follies showgirl Mimi Moskowitz, widow of a rich investment banker from a prominent family.

Grizelda adored the warm South of France climate, the fashions, the parties, the gin fizzes and the entertaining company. And so did Preshy. She was always made a great fuss over and treated like a grown-up—apart from the gin fizzes that is.

Now the two widows shared a lavish penthouse apartment in Monte Carlo, traveling together to visit the friends still left to them. Neither of them had children and they considered Preshy their daughter, so of course, over the years they'd done their best to spoil her.

"But let's face it, darling," Grizelda had said, finally defeated. "The girl's unspoilable. She cares nothing for jewels and clothes.

All she likes are those boring antiques. She's never even seriously cared about a man."

And she was, Preshy thought, smiling, probably right.

Nevertheless, thinking of what Daria had said, she decided that tonight she would put on the little black dress and the heels, and the thin little rope of diamonds Aunt Grizelda had given her for her sixteenth birthday—(so different from her grandmother's fantastical lost necklace)—as well as the canary diamond ring, a gift for her twenty-first. ("Since no man has given you a diamond ring yet, suppose I'd better," Aunt G had said when she presented it to her, and since Grizelda felt size counted, it was a whopper.) Preshy always felt elegant when she wore it and Daria said it made her look like a rich girl and added a little class to her act.

Preshy heaved a sigh. She would go to that art gallery opening after all, then she would have a late after-hours dinner with Sylvie at Verlaine. It was just another Saturday night in Paris.

THREE

SHANGHAI

LILY lived in the historic part of Shanghai known as the French Concession, in an old Colonial-style house that thanks to her efforts had survived the destructive development boom of the past few years.

In the late nineteenth and early twentieth centuries the area had been home to French diplomats, businessmen and entrepreneurs, as well as hard-partying socialites, but after the Revolution it had fallen on hard times. Now, though, it was being brought back to life with a mix of the old small traditional businesses and open-fronted shops set alongside smart restaurants and bars, with chic boutiques scattered amongst its alleys and broad tree-lined avenues.

Tucked back on a *longtang,* a narrow lane with a nightclub on one side and a noodle shop on the other, Lily's house was a gem from the past, set in its private courtyard with a red-tiled roof, tall green-painted shutters and a large verandah.

The house had been owned by the Song family for generations and was the only possession Lily's father had not been able to gamble away. It had been the single anchor in their chaotic lives, and the only thing Lily had felt no one could ever take from her. Her father had gambled himself into financial oblivion playing baccarat and *pai gow* in Macao and other gambling capitals of the world, leaving his wife to scramble for an existence. But Lily was made of different stuff. When she was very young, she had decided she would succeed, at any cost.

Her mother, who was the Hennessys' first daughter, had disobeyed them and run off to Shanghai with the gambler and playboy Henry Song. They never spoke to her again. While Lily's father played the tables, her mother attempted to make a living selling cheap copies of antiques. Somehow the family scraped by. When she was sixteen her father died and Lily left school and took over the business. Her mother died five years later. Lily was alone in the world with no one to rely on but herself.

She ran her antiques business from the house and did most of her "buying" cheaply from small villages and towns, searching out old family pieces from simple country people who had no idea of their true value. She did not consider this stealing, merely good business. More recently, though, when the Yangtze, the Great Yellow River, had been gouged out to create a dam, gangs of robbers had discovered the tombs hidden near the old villages and were secretly and illegally dismantling them, stealing the treasures of the ancestors.

Superstitious, this had made Lily nervous, but she soon shrugged it off and found herself a lucrative new source of income, buying from the gangs, or "suppliers" as she preferred to call them, then selling on to private customers like the Swiss businessman, acting on behalf of a rich collector. As a front for her illegal activities she kept up her regular business of manufacturing replicas of antiquities: the traditional Buddhas, and Mao souvenirs and the famous terra-cotta warriors of Xi'an, that she sold to tourist shops, as well as abroad.

She parked her black SUV in the courtyard and pressed the electronic buzzer that closed the gates behind her. There were security cameras overlooking the alley because she ran her business from the house and sometimes stored the valuable antiques there.

Though the house was French Colonial in style, the garden was strictly Chinese, with a pond of fat goldfish, symbols of prosperity and money, and a simple wall fountain trickling serenely onto the pink lotus blossoms, whose sweet scent lingered in the air.

It was where she enjoyed sitting in the evening, when she had a free moment that is, with a glass of wine and only her thoughts and her little canary songbird for company. There was no boyfriend; she simply did not have time for that kind of complex relationship. All Lily's time was devoted to making money.

Mary-Lou Chen came out onto the terrace, interrupting Lily's thoughts.

"Oh, there you are, Lily," she called. "Someone telephoned a few minutes ago. A man. He wouldn't leave his name." She grinned at Lily. "A new boyfriend?"

"Hah!" Lily tossed her head disdainfully. "Fat chance. I think I know who it might be, though."

"I asked for his number but he wouldn't give it to me. Said he'd call back in half an hour."

Lily grinned. "Good," she said. She knew for sure now she had the Swiss hooked.

Mary-Lou Chen was her best friend, her co-worker and partner in crime. They had known each other forever. At their all-Chinese school they had been the only biracial outsiders, with their Chinese fathers and Caucasian mothers. And both their families were poor, Lily's from the downward spiral familiar to gamblers, and Mary-Lou's from her father's bad business methods and laziness. As they grew up they both harbored the same burning ambition. To be rich. Any way they could, they were going to be rich.

Mary-Lou was a beauty, with the smooth porcelain skin of her mother and enormous slightly tilted eyes the color of speckled amber orchids. She wore her thick black hair in the traditional short Chinese bob with a low fringe over those amazing eyes.

With her high cheekbones and delicate features she had tried at first to become a movie star, but she had no talent for acting. Of course she'd had plenty of offers to star in other kinds of movies and with poverty beckoning, to tell the truth she'd been tempted. Lily had saved her from that. She'd brought her into the business, taught her the ropes and now the best friends worked together, though they did not live together.

Mary-Lou had a modern apartment on the Bund, the smartest street in Shanghai overlooking the Huangpu River and lined with palatial office buildings, smart high-rise restaurants, chic bars and deluxe condos. The small apartment was only on the third floor, the least expensive, but she had furnished it extravagantly with modern pieces imported from Italy. She shopped at the smartest boutiques for the latest European fashions and in order to afford her lifestyle, unknown to Lily, she secretly dealt in stolen jewelry, recutting and resetting the stones to disguise them, then selling them on.

Mary-Lou didn't believe in morals or scruples. When you were as poor as she had been you fought your way out any way you could. "Rich at any cost" was her motto. She owed loyalty to no one. Not even Lily.

She followed Lily into the house, her heels clattering on the polished bamboo floors.

"How many times do I have to remind you to take off your shoes?" Lily complained, irritated. "You know they bring in the dirt. There are clean flip-flops behind the door."

"Sorry." Though she had been brought up Chinese, Mary-Lou did not subscribe to the old custom of removing one's shoes when entering a house. She had become, she told herself, resentfully taking off the sandals, more Western than Lily.

The house was sparsely furnished with a hard-looking sofa, a couple of good elm-wood chairs and an antique altar table lacquered red and topped with a golden Buddha. There was a pretty wooden tray with scented joss sticks burning in a cloisonné holder, and a sheaf of bronze chrysanthemums. There was also a framed picture of Lily's mother over the altar table, but there was no picture of her father, whom she hated. Even as he lay dying Lily had been unable to forgive him for ruining her and her mother's lives, leaving them virtually destitute.

Apart from the chairs and the altar table, there were few antiques in Lily's home, no wonderful pieces, and no softness either. Her bedroom contained the only true classic; a Chinese marriage bed, also lacquered a deep red, the color of success and of happiness. It was built into the wall with a wooden canopy and shutters that closed it in completely, like a small separate room all to itself. And that's where, Mary-Lou knew, Lily slept alone. No man, she was sure, had ever penetrated past that bedroom door and closed those shutters on himself and a naked Lily, and made love until they were exhausted. The way Mary-Lou liked to do with her boyfriends.

She helped Lily stack the cartons of replica terra-cotta warriors in the cellar, then Lily sent her out on an errand. Mary-Lou guessed Lily wanted to be alone for the phone call. She got the feeling something was going on, and it did not include her. And she resented that.

FOUR

WHEN the call came Lily picked up the phone on the first ring.

"I have spoken to my client. He is very interested." The businessman's voice was firm and crisp. "Naturally, he will need to see authentication."

"Hmmm, that might be difficult, under the circumstances. As you know the piece was stolen almost eighty years ago. However, its age and authenticity can be proven, though obviously we need to use the proper—and by that I mean *very discreet*—expert. One guaranteed to keep his mouth shut."

"That could be arranged. The next thing we need to discuss is price."

"Come to me with an offer," Lily said, hanging up. She wasn't about to dicker over money with the businessman. It would take time, maybe months, but he would come up with the right sum eventually. And it would be many millions of Swiss francs. Enough to finally set her free.

She walked to the very back of the cellar. It was dark but she knew her way. She pressed the button hidden behind a beam and a panel slid back exposing an old iron safe, the kind you had to spin-dial a special combination. She knew the numbers by heart and the heavy door swung open. Amongst the sheafs of banknotes stashed inside was a flat dark red jewel case. Lily removed it. She walked into the light and opened it.

The necklace glowed back at her from its black velvet nest, the old jewels, emeralds, rubies, and diamonds in their heavy gold setting. And the great pearl, shining like a living thing in the gloom. She put out a tentative finger to touch it and felt the shock of its coldness against her flesh. Quickly, she snatched back her hand.

Lily had had this necklace for only a few weeks. On her fortieth birthday, she had been paid a visit by a stranger, an elderly man, gray-bearded and dressed like a scholar in the old days, in a long gray gown over narrow trousers. He was a picture from another era, yet somehow she felt she knew him.

"My name is Tai Lam," he told her. "I come as friend of your mother."

Surprised, she invited him in; she served him tea, treating him as an honored guest. She told him she had not known her mother had any friends. He inclined his head gravely and said indeed that was the case. Her mother had first sought him out for advice, and through that they had become friends.

"For most of her life your mother was a good woman," he said, "though always headstrong. Only one time did she stoop to thievery, and then it was out of resentment. She told me it was because she could not get her own way and obtain her parents' permission to marry Henry Song. She was very young then," he added, offering the parcel he was clutching to Lily.

"Before she died, many years ago, she asked me to give this to you when you turned forty years. She said to do with it whatever you wished. And then she told me the story of how it came into her possession.

"The necklace belonged to her own mother, a Mrs. Arthur Hennessy of Paris, a wedding gift from her husband. It was said he had bought it with a batch of antiques and jewels that had slipped into France via the melting pot of a postwar market, and though it came with a history attached, he did not deal in jewels and had no real concept of its true worth. He knew only that the stones were extraordinary and that it was a fitting present for his new wife.

"When their daughter—your mother—ran off with Henry Song, she stole the necklace. She told me she would never forgive herself for that, but she was too proud and too willful to give it back. And for all those years she hid it from her gambler husband so he would not lose that at the tables, as well as everything else.

"Finally, when she was ill and knew she might die, your mother came to me. 'Take this, keep it for my daughter, Lily,' she said. 'It's all I have to leave her. But do not give it to her until she reaches forty years because only then will she be smart enough to know what to do with it, and not allow a man steal it from her just because she thinks she is in love.'

"Your mother also left the letter for you. In it she tells the story that came with the necklace. It is the true history."

Listening to him, Lily had clasped the long dark red jewel case to her chest. Tears had stung her eyes. Her mother had given her the only thing of value she possessed in the world. The only thing she had left. She had saved it all those years, for her.

Lily knew about her French family, the Hennessys, and that she had a cousin who, her mother had said, was called Precious Rafferty. But that was all.

Later, when she was alone, she had read the story of the necklace, painstakingly pieced together from the information her grandfather had known but had discounted as some sort of fairy tale, about the pearl and the Dragon Lady Empress. She'd investigated further, and found photographs and evidence that it was the truth. And now the notorious pearl was Lily's to do with as she wished. But it must be kept a secret. If the authorities found out about it, she would end up in jail.

FIVE

MARY-LOU had several "little secrets," only one of which was dealing in stolen jewelry. Another was that she spied on Lily. And that morning when Lily sent her off on an errand, instead she followed her and hid in the cellar's shadows. She saw Lily press the button that sent the wooden panel sliding away, revealing the old iron safe.

Mary-Lou already knew all about that safe. She'd found out about it several months ago while keeping watch on Lily. Lurking in the cellar she'd crept silently closer, holding up her cell-phone camera, photographing the combination code as Lily dialed the numbers. Then she'd stolen back up the stairs, soft-footed as a sparrow.

Later, when Lily was out, she'd walked back down those steep wooden stairs, past all the crates of plaster copies of Qin Dynasty warriors and the Maos and the Buddhas. The panel slid away as she pressed the button. She dialed the combination, the safe opened and its contents were hers.

Up until now it had contained only money. *Only money,* Mary-Lou had thought. *My lifeblood.* Then she'd realized she had found Lily's stolen stash, the place where, unable to put it in a legitimate bank, Lily kept the profit from her dealings in plundered antiquities. The money was in neat bundles but Mary-Lou was almost certain Lily never counted them. Why should she, when she believed no one else knew about the hidden safe and its combination?

Mary-Lou had helped herself plentifully over the months, confident that if Lily did check, she could never accuse her of stealing, because how could she possibly know about the safe, or its combination? And anyhow she had no compunction about stealing from her friend. She needed the money so she took it.

This morning, however, always attuned to Lily's moods, she sensed something was going on, and instead of setting off on the errand Lily had dreamed up for her, she lingered on the cellar stairs, thanking fate that Lily had reminded her to remove her shoes. In her bare feet she made no sound as she crept closer. And, as she had done before, she took a photograph as this time Lily removed the flat jewelry case from the safe.

Lifting her cell-phone camera, Mary-Lou snapped quick silent pictures as Lily opened the case, but she was scarcely able to hold back a gasp of astonishment when she saw what it contained.

She had never seen jewels like that: the massive emeralds, diamonds and rubies, and the pearl the size of a robin's egg. Where, she wondered, astonished, had Lily gotten her hands on it?

She stole silently back up the stairs, her pulses throbbing with excitement, adrenaline flowing. The necklace must be worth a fortune. All you needed was the right buyer. Hah! Of course, that was the call Lily had been waiting for. She had a buyer in mind!

Mary-Lou hurried out onto the street where her little car was parked. She got in and drove quickly away so Lily wouldn't come out and find her still there and suspect her of spying. She drove aimlessly, her mind ticking over. It would be easy to steal the necklace, but first she needed to find a buyer.

THE NEXT DAY WHEN LILY was out, Mary-Lou went down to the basement and opened up the safe. She took out the necklace, letting it slide through her fingers, marveling at the weight and clarity of the jewels, and the size of the glowing creamy white pearl. Her eyes opened even wider when she read Lily's note about the provenance. It would be worth even more than she had hoped.

The fact was that the necklace could end all of her woes; it would give her the millions she needed for the good life she wanted and believed she deserved. It was worth any risk. If Lily gave her any trouble, she would deal "appropriately" with her. Mary-Lou had no fear of that. Her only problem now was to find that buyer.

SIX

A few days later, Mary-Lou was coming out of the diamond cutter's office, on the second floor of a mean little building in a bad quarter, sandwiched between a cheap "massage parlor" and one of those half-hidden stores where gamblers came to buy lottery tickets, hoping for the big win.

The building was shuttered behind double steel gates and the narrow street flickered with vivid neon signs hung, sometimes three deep, over tacky bars and teahouses that smelled of fried eels and sheeps' brains and of rice swimming in a thin pungent broth. Ragged men down on their luck or simply drunk or stoned, squatted on the sidewalks, their backs pressed up against the building, smoking and staring into space, occasionally hawking and spitting up gobs of phlegm.

Mary-Lou's perfect nose curled in disgust. She hated coming here. She knew she attracted attention with her exotic looks, that was why she always dressed down in jeans and a T-shirt, no jewelry, not even a watch. Even so, she feared for her car, small and cheap though it was. Nothing was safe on these streets and it made her nervous, especially with what she had hidden in her pocket. Two diamonds each of about four carats, stolen from a wealthy family, that had just been recut by the backstreet diamond cutter, losing some of their carat weight in the process but it meant they were now untraceable. Using Lily's money, she had made a deal with the thieves and now the diamonds were hers to sell on.

Putting on her dark glasses, she stepped into the street. She had parked her car right outside the building but now an old truck was parked in its place. She let out a howl of rage and swung round, glaring accusingly at the street bums. They glared back at her, laughing, and one hawked up his phlegm and spat it at her.

"Jesus!" She stepped back, disgusted, and felt her heel strike a foot. A man's arms snaked around her and she screamed. A crowd was gathering, staring and grinning. Furious, she swung round and let the man holding her have it with a right to the face. He caught her arm before the punch connected.

"Careful," he said. "You could hurt somebody like that."

Mary-Lou stared up at the best-looking man she had ever seen. Tall, broad-shouldered, rangy in that American way, dark-haired and with intense unsmiling blue eyes that linked sexily with her own. And she knew him. Or rather she knew who he was. Not long ago, the stories about the accidental death of his wealthy wife had dominated the media for several weeks.

"I know you," she said, still scowling.

"And I would like to know you," he said. "That is if you promise not to grind my foot with your heel and not to keep on punching."

Mary-Lou looked into his eyes for what seemed a long time. "Okay," she said finally.

He let go of her arm. "So what happened?"

"Someone stole my car."

He nodded. "I'm not surprised. They'd steal the teeth from your mouth around here. You should always bring a guard, let him stay with the car while you take care of whatever business brings you here."

He did not ask her what that business might be, nor did she ask why he was there. Direct questions about why you were in this shady area were off-limits. Everyone kept their "business" to themselves.

"My car's just down the street," he said. "How about I give you a lift, then you can contact the police, tell them the details."

"Much good it'll do," she said bitterly, making him laugh again.

"Hey," he said, "It's only a car. I assume it was insured."

"Yes," she said gloomily, "but it'll be ages and mountains of paperwork before they settle. I know how they are too."

"For such a beautiful woman, you're a true cynic," he said, motioning the guard to open the car door for her.

Mary-Lou got into the camouflage green Hummer. He walked around to the other side and got in next to her. "Where to?" he asked. She turned to look at him, a long deep look. "To the nearest good bar," she said in her throaty whisper.

SEVEN

BENNETT Yuan took her to the Bar Rouge on the Bund, not too far from where Mary-Lou lived. It was a chic modernist place with huge blowup photos of pouting red-lipsticked Asian beauties framed in matching red-lacquered wood that also acted as screens, giving privacy to the booths and tables. Dozens of ruby red Venetian chandeliers spilled a muted pink light, and the windows and terrace offered views of the Shanghai skyline.

He sat opposite, not next to her as she had expected and she pouted prettily. "I can see you better this way," he explained. "Do you know why I brought you here?" She shook her head.

"Because you are more beautiful than any of these girls on the walls." He looked her in the eyes, a long deep look that made Mary-Lou shiver right down to the pit of her belly. "You haven't yet told me your name," he said. "Or do you prefer to be anonymous?"

"It's Mary-Lou Chen. And I know your name, I've seen your picture in the newspapers."

He shrugged, dismissively. "Then I'm the one who would prefer anonymity. And what would you like to drink, Mary-Lou Chen?"

He summoned the waiter as Mary-Lou thought for a minute. "I'd like a glass of champagne," she decided, but Bennett ordered a bottle.

They sat in silence, still looking deep into each other's eyes, recognizing the possibility of what might happen between them, until the waiter reappeared with a silver ice bucket on a stand, and the champagne. He wrapped the bottle in a white cloth then uncorked it expertly with hardly even a pop, just a wisp of air floating from its neck. He poured a little for Bennett to taste and when he nodded his approval, the waiter filled the two flutes. A second waiter brought a dish of tiny biscuits and then left them alone in their screened booth under the hazy glow of the red chandelier.

Bennett Yuan picked up his glass. He lifted it to hers and said, "Here's to us, Mary-Lou Chen."

"Yes," she said, suddenly nervous. There was an intensity about him she had never encountered in a man before. He was, she thought, a man who knew what he wanted and who knew that he would always get it. And she was a little afraid of him.

"So, tell me about yourself." Bennett leaned back, one arm spread along the top of the booth.

Suddenly disconnected from her eyes, he seemed to take on a

different persona. More casual, comfortable, a man completely at ease with himself. And so handsome Mary-Lou could see no flaw. His dark hair brushed smoothly back; those intense deep blue eyes under straight dark brows; a nose almost too perfect for a man, the square jaw and a wide firm mouth that made her wonder what it would feel like to kiss him.

She shook her short swinging bob of black hair, took a sip of champagne and began to talk about her work and about Lily.

"So, who is this Lily Song?" he asked, refilling her glass.

"An old school friend. She's always dealt in antiques but mostly she makes and sells the tourist stuff. You know, the Mao memorabilia, the warriors, Buddhas."

"And is that profitable?"

She sipped the champagne and gave him a deep look. "Some of it is."

"And which part would that be?"

Mary-Lou laughed, shaking her head and sending her short black hair swinging again. "I can't tell you that," she said, peering at him from under her bangs. "Why are we talking so much about me anyway? I want to know all about you."

"There's not much to tell that I suspect you don't already know. I'm involved in the furniture components business." He shrugged again, impatiently, as though he disliked what he did for a living. "I'm based here in Shanghai, but I travel a lot. Keeps me busy." He filled up their glasses and signaled the waiter to bring a second bottle.

"Maybe that's a good thing," she said, thinking about his dead wife, Ana Yuan. "Considering what happened. . . . I mean you keeping busy so you don't have to think. . . ."

He gave her a cold look and she stopped, conscious that she was, quite literally, getting into deep waters. She drank down the champagne.

"And what are we going to do about your car?" Bennett said. She'd forgotten all about the car being stolen. He handed her his cell phone. "Here, better report it," he said.

Reporting it took longer than she'd thought, and by the time she was finished, so was the second bottle of champagne. Feeling deliciously woozy, at that moment Mary-Lou didn't give a damn whether she saw the car again or not.

"I live just down the road," she said, inviting him with her eyes.

He nodded, understanding. He paid the waiter, took her arm and walked her to the elevator. They stood apart, not talking, she with her head down staring at her red suede mules, thinking of what was to come, he gazing at the ceiling, his face expressionless.

The guard was waiting with the Hummer and they drove a few short blocks to Mary-Lou's building.

Bennett eyed the modern skyscraper appreciatively. Asking the guard to have the car valet-parked, he dismissed him. "Tell me, Mary-Lou Chen," he said, "how can a woman who sells copies of Mao and Buddha and some sort of 'antiques' afford to live in a place like this?"

She smiled at him as the elevator took them up only three

floors of the skyscraper. “That’s because I’m a clever woman. Or hadn’t you noticed?” She opened the door and they went in.

“I was too busy noticing how beautiful you are,” he said, shutting the door behind him and grabbing her close.

“You feel like soft Chinese silk,” he murmured kissing her left ear. “And you smell spicy, of ginger flowers and sandalwood.” His mouth traveled to her neck and he was kissing the throbbing pulse at the base of her throat, then moving upward to her lips. “And your mouth tastes of champagne,” he said, drinking her in until she could hardly breathe.

Pushing him away, she took his hand and led him to her bedroom, a tiny space with poppy red walls, a king-sized bed with an ebony leather headboard, a black silk spread, sweeping red silk curtains and pretty gold-shaded lamps.

“Like a high-class whore’s bedroom,” he said, laughing, and though in truth Mary-Lou was a little offended by his comment, she laughed with him.

“Wait here,” she said, pushing him backward onto the bed and walking out of the room.

She returned a few minutes later wearing a black silk robe embroidered with red dragons and with nothing underneath. She was carrying another bottle of champagne and two flutes.

“I thought we might have a little more,” she said, filling the glasses. His look as she handed one to him devoured her. He put the glass on the table and reached for the sash of her robe, pulling her toward him.

“Come here,” he said throatily. Untying the sash and throwing open the robe, he gazed at her beautiful naked body. Then he pulled her onto his lap and began to kiss her.

She wiggled her arms out of the sleeves and lay back, naked on the bed, looking into his eyes as he hovered hungrily over her. Then he picked up the bottle of champagne and tipped it up, letting the wine trickle over her breasts, down her belly, into her nakedness.

"Wonderful," he said, licking it off her cool smooth skin. "Delicious, Mary-Lou Chen."

EIGHT

IN the next few weeks, when she wasn't thinking about Bennett Yuan, Mary-Lou was thinking about the necklace. It was the answer to all her prayers—if she ever prayed that is. It would be easy enough to get her hands on it; the problem was to find a buyer rich enough to pay what she wanted. She didn't know the international superrich; they moved in a different world from hers.

She stood at the window of her apartment, smoking a cigarette and staring at the busy barge traffic on the river, thinking that she was okay as a "girlfriend" to a rich man, but that no one had ever so much as mentioned marriage. Rich men simply didn't marry girls like her. They forged alliances. Money married money, especially here in China.

Bennett Yuan was different, though. Everyone knew how his wife had died. The speculation about it had made the nightly TV reports for over a week, as well as all the newspapers. Rumor was one of the great information circuits of the city and she'd heard that when the Yuans' daughter had married Bennett, the wealthy family had insisted he change his name to theirs, so that their "dynasty" would continue through their children. She'd also seen the pictures of Bennett's wife on TV. Ana Yuan was a plain, modestly dressed young woman, and of course rumors abounded that the handsome young American had married her for her money.

Nothing wrong with that, Mary-Lou thought. She would have done the same herself, given the opportunity. But again, so rumor had it, it had turned out that the Yuans had Ana's money tied up in a family trust, and they also had Bennett tied up in such a way he could never get his hands on it.

After Ana's death, they had tried to prevent Bennett from using their prestigious name, but they had not succeeded. But they had revoked Ana's trust so that all the money and property, including the lavish marital apartment in one of Shanghai's most exclusive towers, reverted back to the family. When they were asked why they took such drastic steps, rumor said their implacable reply was "He is a foreigner. He is not 'family.' He has no Yuan children. He is of no value to us now."

Of course it was also said around town that this was true, and that Bennett had not inherited a penny. All Mary-Lou knew was that he had told her he'd loved his wife and that he was devastated by her tragic death. And that he'd never been able to find out what she was doing in Suzhou anyway.

And that was that. Bennett was on his own. And he was definitely not a rich man, even though he still acted like one. In fact Bennett was like her: a "soldier of fortune," a good-looking man who believed he was entitled to the good life, whichever way he could get it. Bennett would marry another heiress, she was sure of that. And she was just as sure he would not marry her.

She scowled with frustration as she stubbed out her cigarette. She wanted two things from life. She wanted Bennett. And she wanted to sell the necklace and get rich. Somehow the two were tied together . . . the necklace and Bennett.

The answer came to her suddenly. *Of course!* Bennett knew wealthy businesspeople, not only in China, but also abroad. He was the perfect candidate to help her find a buyer. It would mean she would have to part with fifty percent of the profit but since the necklace was stolen anyway—it would *all* be profit. Except . . . Another idea struck her and this time she smiled. She knew how to get exactly the two things she wanted. Bennett *and* the money. And this time she would not end up as the disposable girlfriend.

She laughed at how clever—how *simple*—her plan was. Bennett would find a buyer and she would steal the necklace from the safe. *But* she would not hand it over unless he married her first. Then he'd sell it and they'd both be rich. It was the perfect circle: buyer—wedding—necklace—money. They would live happily ever after.

Pleased with her plan, she called Bennett and arranged to meet him at seven that evening at the Cloud 9 bar atop the Grand Hyatt hotel, across the river in the business section called Pudong.

NINE

DRIVING through the tunnel that connected the two districts in her new red Mini Cooper, Mary-Lou thought about Bennett in a completely different way. She no longer saw him as the handsome man-about-town, the perfect lover that she couldn't get enough of. For the first time she was using her head and thinking like a businesswoman.

She was smiling as she handed over the car to the valet and entered the imposing Jin Mao Tower, the world's third tallest building. The hotel occupied the fifty-third to eighty-seventh floors and she took the high-speed elevator to the very top, emerging into the glittering art deco bar with its stunning view over all Shanghai, so high in the sky that the clouds hovered outside the very windows. Hence the bar's name, Cloud 9.

Looking around, she didn't see Bennett so she took a seat at a booth and ordered a vodka martini. "With three blue-cheese olives," she instructed the waiter, telling him she liked her martinis very cold with just a splash of vermouth. Mary-Lou always knew exactly what she wanted.

She sipped the drink, thinking about how she would approach the subject of the necklace with Bennett. She had just decided on her tactics when she saw him enter the bar. He spoke to the pretty hostess who, she noticed, irritated, smiled engagingly at him before escorting him personally to the table. She also noticed that Bennett gave the girl that deep, very personal smile back, and it irritated the hell out of her again.

"Sorry I'm late," Bennett slid into the booth opposite. He didn't kiss her, or reach for her hand, merely gave her a tired smile. "Traffic," he added.

Mary-Lou had encountered no problems with the traffic but she didn't mention that, merely waiting until he'd ordered a Jack Daniel's on the rocks and the waiter had departed, before she said anything.

"I have a secret," she said, looking him in the eye.

"I'll bet you do. I just hope it doesn't concern me." He lit a cigarette without offering her one and she frowned. Something was wrong.

"I just might not tell you," she said, ostentatiously taking out her own cigarette and waiting for him to offer to light it, which he did, grinning mockingly at her.

"So okay, don't," he said. "It's a safe way to keep a secret."

"Ah, but this one does concern you. And it's something you

would be very pleased to know." Unable to contain herself any longer, she took out her cell phone and laid it on the table between them. "Check out the photograph on there," she said softly. "I think it will surprise you."

Bennett took a slug of his Jack Daniel's, making no move to pick up the phone.

"Go on," she urged him. "I guarantee you're going to like what you see."

Sighing, Bennett picked it up and pressed the button. An out-of-focus picture of the necklace appeared on the screen. "What's this, it's all blurred," he said impatiently.

"Press again."

He did and this time the necklace appeared more clearly. He looked at it for a few moments, then clicked off the phone and handed it back to her. "So?" he asked, sitting back and sipping his bourbon.

Mary-Lou put her elbows on the table and leaned closer. Glancing around to make sure she was not overheard, she said softly, "That necklace is the real thing. Not only does it have jewels worth a fortune, it also has a provenance that discriminating international buyers will be prepared to pay a premium for."

She sat back, waiting for him to act all eager and amazed, but he did not. He simply looked coldly at her and said again, "So?"

"Let me tell you the story," she said, and feeling like Scheherazade, she recounted the history of the Dragon Lady Empress's famous pearl. "I know where this necklace is," she said finally. "I can get my hands on it right now, or tomorrow, or next week, if you wish. But first I need a buyer. And that, my darling

Bennett, is where you come in." A triumphant smile lit her lovely face as she sat back, looking at him.

He looked coldly back at her. "I'm guessing the necklace is stolen. Are you asking me to become a fence, Mary-Lou?"

"Not a fence. A partner." She was deadly serious now. "I have the goods, you get the buyer." She did not tell him the third part of the equation—marriage—and nor would she until the buyer was ready and eager to hand over his money and take possession.

Bennett lifted his shoulder in a casual shrug. "I don't need this kind of deal, I have my own business to run."

She knew all about Bennett's "business." She had made it her own business to find out about it. The Yuans had set him up exporting furniture components but with the end of his marriage that too was drying up. Bennett was a big spender. He needed money to live big, just like she did. They were two of a kind, a perfect match.

"Bennett, this necklace could make both of us very rich. You would never have to think of furniture again. I have the goods, you find the buyer, we split the take fifty-fifty."

He finished his drink in one gulp and signaled the waiter for another. "All I've seen is a picture. All I've heard is a story. How do I know it's true and that this necklace really exists?"

"I guess, Bennett," Mary-Lou said, shaking back her short, glossy black bangs and giving him that enchanting smile again, "you'll just have to trust me."

TEN

BENNETT thought Mary-Lou was beautiful. She was sexy and amusing, but for him she was like an hors d'oeuvre, tasty and to be nibbled on and enjoyed with a drink. The "main course" had to be more substantial and bring something else to the table besides just looks. He thought he'd achieved that when he married Ana Yuan—for her millions of course. Why not? But despite all his careful planning that had gone badly wrong. He'd suffered as the poor boy at the rich man Yuan's table. This time he needed to find an heiress without a family attached. And this time he'd make sure she had the money in her own pocket before he married her.

His wife had been dead more than six months and he was at a point in his life where he was just marking time, trying to decide what to do next. Mary-Lou had been an exciting temporary diversion. But it was time to move on and tonight he'd planned on telling her that. Now though, she had come up with this necklace scheme, based, as far as he could tell, on a fuzzy photograph she claimed to have taken of these "rare" jewels and the story of the "corpse" pearl. A story that appealed to him, in fact, though he doubted its veracity.

"Exactly *who* has this necklace?" He took another cube of ice from the crystal bucket and added it to his drink.

"I can't tell you that."

He glanced up, brows raised. "You mean you expect me to sell jewels for you without knowing where they come from? Come on, Mary-Lou, you won't find a criminal in town who'd go that route. How do I know you're not going to kill someone to get your hands on that necklace?"

Her amber-speckled eyes turned as cold as his iced bourbon. "I will," she said. "If I have to."

Bennett sat back and picked up his glass. He thought Mary-Lou might have the face of an angel, but she had a soul forged of pure cold steel. He liked that. They were alike in more ways than one. He took a sip of the bourbon, looking at her.

"I'm still not convinced," he said. "And anyway, I wouldn't work with you without knowing the whereabouts of the necklace and who has it now."

"I can't tell you that." She was stubborn but he knew she was softening.

He reached across the table for her hand. "Look, sweetheart," he said in the patronizing tone she knew well from other "rich" men who'd dumped her for the next pretty girl, "you're asking me to work in the dark, put myself in possible legal jeopardy without knowing the facts. Get real. Tell me what's what, or let's just say 'goodbye, it was fun while it lasted.' Right now."

It was the "let's say goodbye right now" part that got to her, just as he'd known it would. Tears swam in those beautiful eyes and she gripped his hand tightly. "Don't say that," she whispered, "please don't say that, Bennett."

He removed his hand from her grip and sat back with an indifferent shrug. "You ask too much," he said, summoning the waiter for the check.

He heard her take a deep quavering breath. Then, "It's my partner, Lily," she admitted. "She has the necklace. It's been in her family for generations. I don't know how, or why she has it now. I swear she didn't before, otherwise she surely would have sold it. I know she's looking for a buyer though, and that's why I—*we*—have to get in before it's sold."

Bennett thought about Lily, the woman Mary-Lou had implied she was prepared to kill if she had to. He wondered whether he might not be better off with Lily than with Mary-Lou. After all, Lily had the necklace legitimately, though from the provenance it seemed to him to be likely it would be confiscated by the government if it ever resurfaced. Still, it was worth exploring.

"I'd like to meet Lily," he said, paying the check and adding a generous tip. Even when he was running short of money Bennett was still a big tipper; he found it paid off, it always guaranteed him a good table and the best service, and it created a good impression.

Mary-Lou watched him, puzzled, asking herself why he would want to meet Lily. As if in answer to her question, he said, "I need to know exactly who we're dealing with, if we are to be in business together." He got up from the table and held out his hand to her. "Come on, partner," he said, "let's call Lily and take her out to dinner."

Mary-Lou's smile lit up the bar as they walked together out of Cloud 9.

ELEVEN

LILY was in her peaceful courtyard garden, feeding the goldfish. The gentle slide of water over the smooth copper surface of the wall fountain was the only sound, until the ringing phone jolted her out of her Zen state of mind. Resentful, she thought for a moment of not answering it, but then she checked and saw it was Mary-Lou. Sighing, she pressed the talk button.

"I don't want to discuss business," she said abruptly. "Can't it wait until tomorrow?"

"Oh, Lily, I don't want to talk business. It's just that I'm with someone special, someone I want you to meet. . . ."

Mary-Lou's voice was sugary-sweet and Lily guessed whomever this special "someone" was, he was standing right next to her. "Can't it wait until tomorrow?" she asked, thinking of a cool glass of wine and sitting on her terrace with the sound of the wind chimes like temple bells and the trickle of the fountain, and of the little canary in its bamboo cage, who always sang so charmingly when she came to sit near him. Then all thoughts of desecrated tombs, and of the wrath her ancestors would surely inflict on her if they knew what she was doing, would slide temporarily to the back of her mind. Sometimes she couldn't sleep at night because of those thoughts, but "rich at any cost" was her mantra, and like Mary-Lou, she lived by it.

"We want to take you to dinner. Come on, Lily, it's important."

To you it is, Lily thought, but Mary-Lou sounded excited, as though she needed her approval. And after all, she was her friend. "Oh, all right," she sighed, "just tell me where and when."

"The Italian restaurant at the Grand Hyatt, in half an hour."

"Forty-five minutes," Lily said, thinking of the traffic.

In fact it was an hour and they were already seated at a discreet table, half-hidden behind a screen, waiting for her. The restaurant had been Bennett's choice because he knew that most of its clientele would be foreign businessmen and tourists, and he was unlikely to be recognized.

Lily had chosen to wear a jade green knee-length cheongsam that showed off her pretty legs, and she carried a vintage embroidered satin bag fringed with jade and beads. She looked cool and self-assured, neither of which she was feeling. She was wishing she had not bothered to dress up and battle the traffic all the way through the tunnel under the river to Pudong just to meet Mary-Lou's latest beau, when she could have been comfortable at home, on her own terrace, alone with her thoughts.

Bennett got to his feet as she approached. She was not smiling and in her Chinese dress he thought she looked like a business-woman trying for the feminine look. He had no doubt Lily Song was a tough cookie but he'd never yet met a woman who didn't fall for his special brand of charm.

"Lily," he said, smiling deep into her eyes in that very personal way he had of greeting women. "Mary-Lou has talked about you so much I feel I already know you, but I must confess I didn't expect you to be so beautiful."

She raised a skeptical dark eyebrow, studying him as he held her hand for slightly longer than was necessary. A professional charmer, she thought, and just the sort of guy Mary-Lou would fall for.

Mary-Lou was watching them anxiously. She saw no sign of recognition on Lily's face and thought she was probably the only woman in Shanghai who did not recognize Bennett Yuan. But then Lily rarely watched TV or bothered with the news; she was too wrapped up in her own small world of business.

"This is Bennett Yuan," she said, and caught the flutter of response that crossed Lily's face. It seemed she was wrong, and even Lily had heard of the tragic death of Ana Yuan.

"Good evening, Mr. Yuan." Lily removed her hand from his. She knew the story all right, and also knew it was only just over six months since his wife died. Glancing sideways she caught Mary-Lou's eye, wondering what she was doing with the newly widowed Bennett.

"Bennett's the man who helped me when my car was stolen," Mary-Lou said. "Remember, I told you?"

"Ah, yes, I remember."

Bennett asked what Lily would like to drink and she decided on San Pellegrino water with lemon. Then the waiter arrived with the menus and began to tell them the night's specials, and the talk turned to food.

After that, though, Bennett put himself out to be amusing: he asked about her home in the French Concession, saying it was a place he had always wanted to live, and that he enjoyed its French Colonial history.

"So do I," Lily said. "Especially since my mother was French. That is, her parents were American and Austrian, but she was born and brought up in Paris and always considered herself a Frenchwoman."

Bennett had ordered a bottle of good Italian wine, a Chianti from the Frescobaldi estate. The waiter filled their glasses and she took a sip. She noticed that for some reason Mary-Lou was watching Bennett like a hunting dog, ready to spring; while he was Mr. Cool, the seasoned traveler, talking about Shanghai and Paris and New York.

"Since your mother lived in Paris, you must know the city well," he said, but Lily said she had never been there, and then she found herself telling him about how her mother had run away from her family to marry Henry Song.

"*Not* great thinking," she added caustically, "but then my mother never was a great thinker. I believe she was spoiled rotten by her father and always wanted her own way. Nothing ever changed," she added with a grim smile. "She should have stuck with the Hennessys. She told me they were very rich. There was

Grandmother's castle in Austria and fabulous old furniture and paintings, and of course the antiques store. Too bad she gave it all up."

"And is it all still there?" Bennett toyed with his grilled *branzino*. "The antiques store? And the castle?"

"I believe so. Hennessy Antiques it was called then, though now it has probably changed, on the rue Jacob. My mother had a sister, you know. She married and had a daughter too, younger than I, Mother said. Grandmother's family was rich, and all the aunts and uncles too. I imagine they left my cousin the family money, and probably Grandmother's Austrian castle as well."

She gave Bennett a knowing glance, thinking of his marriage to the rich Yuan girl, and with a little dig at Mary-Lou who was looking far too pleased with herself, said, "Her name's Precious Rafferty. Maybe you should go visit her next time you're in Paris, Bennett. I've heard you're always keen to know women with money."

Mary-Lou gave her a furious kick under the table but Bennett laughed and said what was the point of knowing people "without"? After all they could do nothing for you. "I can tell you and I are alike, Lily," he said admiringly. "On our own and determined to get on in life."

"To get rich," Lily said, lifting her glass in a toast to Mary-Lou and their old mantra. Bennett lifted his glass too, thinking that the only words she should have added were "at any cost."

He thought about the necklace that Lily supposedly had inherited, wondering if that were true or whether she had simply stolen it. Mary-Lou's story was so flimsy he had a hard time believing it, and desperate though he was to make money, the idea of dealing in stolen jewels did not appeal. His thoughts turned instead to Paris and the rich Hennessy granddaughter, the one who had inherited all the money, as well as the castle. An heiress was more his style.

Claiming she was tired, Lily left before dessert. She thanked Bennett, who again held her hand too long, something she suspected he did with all women, young or old, attractive or not. He was simply practicing his charm. Bennett said he hoped they could get together again, and then Mary-Lou insisted on walking her to the door.

"Well?" she asked, eyes glowing. "What do you think?"

"He's Ana Yuan's widower and I think he's out dating awfully early after her tragic death, if you want the truth. Which," she added, looking at her friend's furious face, "I suspect you do not."

"He can't be expected to just sit home, a man like that, he needs a woman . . ."

"I'm sure he does." Lily was suddenly serious. "But I urge you to ask yourself, do you need a man like Bennett?" And with that she stepped into the elevator and was gone.

Mary-Lou flounced back to the table where Bennett had already paid the check and was ready to leave. She'd expected them to linger over drinks and coffee, but he seemed in a hurry. He wants to get me into bed, she thought with that thrill in the pit of her stomach that she always got when she thought about sex with Bennett.

But no, Bennett dropped her off in front of her apartment with only the briefest kiss, and said he was tired and needed sleep.

"But we need to talk," she said desperately.

"Not tonight. I'll call you," he said, and he got in the car and with a wave, drove off.

She watched his Hummer weave into the busy traffic along the Bund, feeling suddenly very much alone. And she had thought the evening had gone so well, first the discussion about the necklace and her proposal that they work together; then the meeting with Lily. Until Lily made that dumb remark about Bennett going to Paris and liking rich women. Even though the last part was true.

And then the next day, Bennett didn't call. Nor the day after that. And when she tried to call him, there was no answer. A week went by and she had still not heard from him. Mary-Lou did not know what to think, or what to do. He was her only hope. And besides, she was in love with him.

TWELVE

PARIS

PRESHY was happy. Daria was visiting Paris with her professor husband, on business, and though Tom couldn't make it, she was looking forward to seeing her friend alone for dinner. Sylvie could not make it either, because of course she had her restaurant to run. She'd opened it two years before and with its emphasis on freshness it was an immediate hit.

They were meeting at seven at the Deux Magots just around the corner on the boulevard St. Germain, where they would have a drink and decide where to go for dinner. "Somewhere simple," Daria had said. And Preshy knew just the place.

So it was on with the little black dress again, the heels, and the "rich girl" diamonds. Late, as always, she ran down the steps and into the street, where she noticed a man looking in her shop window. His back was toward her and quickly, before he could notice her, she checked the blue light signaling that the alarm was on, then dashed off across the street to meet Daria. She wasn't about to open up the shop and discuss antiques with anyone tonight.

The Deux Magots was named for the two antique figurines of plump Chinese commercial agents—the *magots,* displayed inside, but mostly the customers liked to sit outdoors and indulge in the national sport of people watching. The café's popular terrace swept from the busy boulevard into the cobbled square with its simple church, the oldest in Paris, the Église St. Germain-des-Prés.

As always the café was packed, but Daria had gotten there early and had snagged one of the tiny tables and a couple of rather rickety chairs, plus she had already ordered two glasses of the house champagne, Monopole, which arrived just as Preshy did.

She dropped a kiss on Daria's cheek and said, "You're looking very Parisian tonight."

"I had my hair cut." Daria swung her head for Preshy to look and her Nordic blond hair swung with her in a smooth shiny fall.

"Fabulous. Just never cut it short, that's all."

"Oh, I don't know, I was tempted but Tom would never forgive me. He always said he fell in love with my hair before he fell in love with me." Daria leaned forward, smiling. "You want to know what else he said? This is the truth now. I've never told anyone before because I wanted you all to think he fell for me 'hook, line and sinker' as they say. Only I'm not so sure that anyone ever really falls like that."

"So what did he say that was so terrible?" Preshy took a fortifying sip of the champagne. It was crisp and clean on her tongue.

Daria had also ordered a dish of olives; they didn't go with the champagne but Daria loved them anyway.

"He said how could anybody fall in love with a spoiled preppie tomboy like me. Of course, this was after I'd beaten him at softball, whupped him at tennis and then won the swim race across the bay he'd challenged me to. Oh, and I'd stripped him down to his undershorts at poker."

Preshy was laughing. "So how'd you get him to stay?"

"I took one look at him in those undershorts, looking all sort of pale and professory and the tiniest bit vulnerable, but you know . . . sort of sexy at the same time and I wanted him so bad I'd have done anything to keep him. So I simply capitulated, gave in all the way. Here's my secret to a happy marriage. Let him win. You name it . . . backgammon, chess, poker, tennis—he wins. Except for swimming. I have to allow him to think I can do one thing well, otherwise why would he still love me?"

They laughed together, sipping their champagne and nibbling on the dark green olives from Nice. Daria's lean face, still faintly tanned from a couple of weeks on windswept Cape Cod, was animated, her eyes sparkled and she pushed her heavy hair back, sighing contentedly.

"If I weren't missing Super-Kid so much I'd say I couldn't be happier than at this moment, here with you in my favorite city." She reached for Preshy's hand. "I miss you, you know."

"I know." Preshy squeezed Daria's hand tightly. "I miss you too. And anyhow, did you speak to Super-Kid today?"

"I did. And she said I needn't hurry home, the grandparents

were taking her to Disney World. She's too busy being spoiled rotten to miss me. Tom said he knew there was a time when all parents became redundant, he just didn't realize it was at three years old. Now, where are we going to eat?"

"I thought La Coupole? It's simple, easy . . . ?"

"Sounds good to me."

La Coupole was the most Parisian of brasseries. Opened in the twenties, it was large and lofty with massive pillars wonderfully painted by starving Montparnasse artists in exchange for meals. With its colorful murals, art deco light fixtures, red banquettes, a famous bar and its rows of tables with their white cloths, crammed next to each other, it was usually jammed with a hodgepodge of actors, politicians, publishing types, models and locals and tourists. Preshy said it was fun for simple food and people watching and it was just what they fancied.

It was still early for Parisians and the place was half-empty. They were shown to one of the tables lined up against the wall and so close to each other you could eavesdrop on every word spoken by your neighbors. Daria ordered fish and Preshy the *steak frites.* They were sitting contentedly sipping red wine, enjoying their catch-up conversation about life and family and friends in Boston, when Daria nudged her.

"Just look what's coming our way," she said under her breath.

Preshy followed her gaze, and then she saw him. Tall and dark and handsome as an Armani model, he was the man of every woman's dreams. And at that instant he turned his head and looked at her. His dark blue eyes seemed to collide with hers. It was as though he was absorbing her deep into their blueness, drinking her in for a long moment and not letting her go. The connection lasted only seconds but a shiver ran down Preshy's spine as she finally dragged her eyes away.

The maître d' was showing him to a table across from them but then she heard him say, "No, this one will do." And he came and sat at the table next to her.

She sipped her wine, not looking at him, but little electric signals seemed to pass between them. He was so close she could have reached out and touched him.

"Bonsoir, mesdames," he said, acknowledging them, the way the polite French did when they were at close quarters in a restaurant, but she could tell from his accent he was American.

"Bonsoir, m'sieur," they replied. Daria nudged her meaningfully. "Smile at him," she whispered, just as their food arrived.

"Pardon me," the stranger said, "I don't mean to intrude, but I don't know what to order here, and what you're eating looks awfully good. Can you tell me what it is?"

Since it was quite obviously steak and fries, Preshy slid him an amused sideways look. She swept her long coppery blond curls flirtatiously back over her shoulder, thinking what a stroke of luck she was wearing her good little black dress.

"Hi, I'm Bennett James," the handsome stranger said. "I'm in Paris on business."

"Where are you from?" Preshy asked.

"Shanghai." He frowned. "It's a long way."

"Shanghai?" she said, surprised. "I have a cousin there. I've never met her but her name is Lily Song."

Bennett James shrugged. "Shanghai's a big city," he said, unsmiling, and Preshy felt foolish for even supposing he might know her cousin.

"And your name is?"

"Precious Rafferty." She blushed as she said it and she added quickly, "But when I was nine I cut I down to Preshy."

"I don't blame you," he said and they all laughed. Then Preshy introduced Daria, who said she definitely recommended the *steak frites* if it was comfort food he was after, so he ordered that and a bottle of red wine and they got to talking about Boston and Paris. They only talked a little bit about Shanghai though, because Bennett said he was on "vacation" tonight in the loveliest city in the world. But he did say that he ran an export business that was becoming too big for him to handle and he needed to recruit new management to help him out.

He sipped his wine and his eyes locked with Preshy's again, and again there was that electric jolt of attraction.

She felt Daria's elbow in her ribs and slid her a sideways glance. There was a grin on Daria's face as she said, "Sorry, my darling, but I'm running late. I promised Tom faithfully I'd be back at the hotel by nine."

She gathered up her bag and her pale-blue gold-buttoned blazer—Daria would be preppie to the end—and slid out from the banquette.

"You're leaving me alone with him," Preshy whispered, as Daria bent to kiss her goodbye.

"You betcha," Daria whispered back.

Bennett James got to his feet. "So nice to have met you, Daria," he said, giving her his long intense blue look and holding her hand in both his.

She nodded and said, "Enjoy the rest of your stay in Paris," then with a wave she strode away through the now crowded tables.

Preshy felt the hot flush of panic up her spine; she was alone with a man she had only just met and whom she fancied strongly. Was she just going to say goodbye politely, as Daria had done, leaving him with her number, only to hover anxiously by the phone for the next week hoping he would call? Or was she going to go with this hot flow that urged her toward him and very possibly into his bed? It was crazy; after all, she wasn't a promiscuous woman, and anyway she hardly knew him.

She felt his eyes on her and turned to meet them. In the silence it was as though he had touched her.

Finally he said, "Have you ever taken the sightseeing boat on the river Seine?"

She shook her head. "Only tourists do that."

He grinned. "Then be a tourist with me. We could see Paris by night from the river. Could anything be more beautiful?"

He reached out and took her hand. His was smooth-skinned, warm and lightly tanned. A hint of dark hair peeked from his shirt cuff with the expensive gold and enamel cuff links and a simple gold watch. Those electric signals seemed to surge to Preshy's very toes.

"I'll do it," she breathed.

"Good!" He signaled the waiter for the check, brushing away her protests and insisting on paying hers and Daria's too.

"I'm just glad I met you," he said, giving her that all-enveloping look again.

THIRTEEN

SEATED next to Bennett in the taxi on the way to the Pont de l'Alma, Preshy wondered whether he was going to try to kiss her. And if he did would she let him? After all she had met him only a couple of hours ago. What would he think of her? But to her surprise he did not attempt to kiss her. In fact he kept a discreet distance between them, filling in the silence that had fallen by asking her questions about herself and life in Paris.

"I know nothing about antiques," he said as the taxi finally squealed to a halt at the *quai*. "You'll have to teach me."

Did that mean he wanted to see her again, Preshy wondered as he hurried her toward the sleek, brightly lit *Bateau Mouche.*

As the glass-topped sightseeing boat slid smoothly down the river, Bennett led the way to a seat in the bow. The boat's floodlights lit up the magical scene as they glided under Paris's loveliest bridges, illuminating in turn the magnificent public buildings and gilded monuments; the white dome of the Sacré-Coeur; and the massive buttresses and towering gargoyle-topped finials of Notre-Dame.

Preshy had never seen Paris from this angle before. "It's breathtaking," she murmured, instinctively reaching for Bennett's hand.

His lips were close to her ear as he whispered, "I have a confession to make."

She said, surprised, "We've known each other only a few hours, what could you possibly have to confess?"

"I saw you earlier, before La Coupole. I was looking in the window of your antiques store. It was your hair that grabbed my attention." He took a strand of her long coppery hair, smoothing it between his fingers. "I couldn't see your face and you hurried away so fast, so . . . well, I just followed you." He laughed as he said it. "I promise I've never followed a woman in my life before, but there was just something about you, that long-legged lope and the hair flying all over the place . . . Anyhow I took a seat near you at Deux Magots. And then I saw your face.

"I'm surprised you didn't feel my eyes on you," he added. "I was staring so hard. I was just getting up my courage to come over and speak to you . . . actually, to try to pick you up," he confessed smiling, "when I heard you say you were going to La Coupole. So again I followed you. My luck held and I was able to get a table next to you." He shrugged. "Of course, now you'll probably think badly of me. But I'm an honest man, I had to tell you."

Nothing this romantic had ever happened to Preshy in her entire life, and she was dazzled. "I'm flattered," she said softly. "I don't think I've ever been followed by a man before."

"And I hope you never will be again," he said. Then as the boat slid silently into the darkness under a bridge he leaned in and kissed her.

Preshy's lips trembled under his. The kiss was not passionate, though. Rather it was filled with a questioning tenderness. Bennett James seemed to know not to rush things; he seemed to be holding back, taking his time with her, letting her get used to the newness of it. She was grateful he recognized that she was not the quick-into-bed let's-make-out kind of woman. She needed to be gentled along; she needed romance.

Still enchanted by the magic of Paris illuminated from the sight-seeing boat and by their kiss, they took a taxi back to the Deux Magots where they sat over a final glass of champagne, talking and watching the street performers, the acrobats and the jugglers dressed in fantastical costumes, while a solitary guitarist played out-of-tune Spanish flamenco music, making them laugh. And then later, Bennett walked her back to the rue Jacob.

They stood in the courtyard, facing each other. He took both her hands and again Preshy felt that electric connection between them. She studied his lean finely sculpted face; he was without doubt the most beautiful man she had ever seen.

"I don't know when I've enjoyed Paris so much," Bennett said. "Thank you for a wonderful evening."

"Thank *you* for picking me up."

"Could you." He hesitated. "I mean would you give me your phone number?"

Preshy scrambled in her purse for a business card. Of course she couldn't find one, nor did she have a pen so she wrote her name and number with a lip pencil on a tissue and handed it to him.

He shook his head, smiling. "What kind of businesswoman doesn't have her card handy?"

"I'm not such a hotshot businesswoman, I just happen to love antiques."

He nodded, then instead of kissing her as she'd expected, he put a finger gently to her lips. "I'll call," he said, then he turned and strode out onto the street.

As the courtyard gates clanged behind him, Preshy turned and ran up the steps, fumbling to unlock the door. Once inside she ran to the window, searching the street for any sign of him. But he was gone. Sinking into the sofa she checked her phone messages. There was just one. "Call me," Daria said, "as soon as you get in." Quickly, she dialed her number.

Daria answered right away. "I couldn't sleep thinking of you," she said without waiting. "So . . . tell me what happened."

"Oh, Daria," Preshy said in a voice that trembled, "I think I'm being swept off my feet."

FOURTEEN

AT ten the next morning the phone rang. Preshy pounced on it. "Hello?" she said, hoping it was him, yet surprised when it was.

"Preshy, it's Bennett."

"Ohhh . . . Bennett . . . hi . . . I mean . . . how are you?" Pulling her wits together, she said, "I hope you slept well," then wished she hadn't because it sounded as though she'd been thinking about him—which she had, but she didn't want him to know that.

"Not very," he said. "I was too busy thinking about you."

This time words escaped her completely.

"Listen, Preshy, I'm returning to Shanghai tomorrow. Will you have dinner with me tonight?"

"Tonight? Why, yes, I'd love to."

"Tell me where and I'll make a reservation," he said.

Preshy thought quickly. He was returning to Shanghai; she might never see him again after tonight; she could end up just a quick Paris fling . . . "No, I'll make the reservation," she said firmly. "Why don't you pick me up here at eight?"

"Eight. I'll be looking forward to it."

"Hmmm, me too. See you then."

She smiled as she put down the phone. She would take him to Verlaine. Sylvie would keep an eye on her. She wouldn't let her get into any trouble.

VERLAINE WAS ONE OF THOSE small storefront bistros in a narrow tree-lined street near the church of St. Sulpice in St. Germain. Its walls were lined with faded silvery mirrors that reflected the rosy lamplight as though through a fog, and dark green taffeta curtains swept across the windows, keeping outsiders from looking in while at the same time making the dining room feel cozy. Everything else was very simple: pale green linens, small vellum-shaded lamps, green banquettes and sturdy gilt chairs with green cushions. A great bouquet of field flowers that looked fresh-picked from some sunny meadow—daisies, sunflowers, goldenrod, lilacs and cherry blossom, depending on the time of year—greeted you as you walked in. And the fact that Sylvie used only what was seasonal and fresh in the market, combined with her true talent as a chef, was what delighted her customers and kept them coming back.

Sylvie was small and round and gamine-cute with merry brown eyes, short black hair and a temper when she was crossed. Which, in her job as chef and owner of the Bistrot Verlaine, meant a good deal of the time. Sous-chefs were the bane of her life and she had no doubt she was the bane of theirs because, as she told them frequently—and loudly—and truthfully—none of them lived up to her high standards.

Every dish turned out at Verlaine had to be perfect: perfect ingredients perfectly prepared and most certainly perfectly presented. Which did not mean towering edifices of food; nor mean-spirited small portions disguised as fashionable; nor those slurps of heavy "extra-virgin" olive oil poured over everything, completely destroying the individual carefully cooked flavors.

Anyhow, tonight she meant to outdo herself. Preshy was bringing a boyfriend—well hardly that, she'd only met him last night and the guy was leaving for Shanghai tomorrow. It certainly didn't sound too promising to Sylvie, but Daria said he was gorgeous and Preshy seemed crazy for him, and she intended to check him out carefully. Shanghai was a long way from Paris. It would be easy for a visiting businessman to have a quick affair and then forget all about it, and Sylvie wasn't about to let that happen to her friend.

They arrived at eight-thirty, windblown and a little wet from a sudden rainsquall. "Welcome, welcome," she said, advancing to greet them, smart in her chef 's whites. A flushed, smiling Preshy introduced Bennett, who shook her hand firmly. He was smiling, but not too much, Sylvie thought, not as though he wanted to impress her and try to make her his friend.

She put them at a quiet corner table, told them there was no choice and that she was in charge of dinner and she wanted no complaints. She sent over a chilled bottle of Heidsieck Rosé Sauvage Champagne and an *amuse-bouche* of a tiny curried crab cake wrapped in spinach leaves, then went back to her kitchen, where things were quite literally hotting up, since the dining room was now full.

It didn't faze Sylvie; she was used to the organized chaos of a restaurant kitchen. Her keen eye took in that everyone was in their appointed place, that her sous-chefs were chopping and stirring, cooking and plating. She ran her usual interference then went to the stove and prepared to send Bennett James the meal of his life. She'd see what he had to say to that. Then she would get the true measure of the man.

As she sent out the first course of lobster ravioli, she peeked round the door. They were sitting close together on the banquette, not opposite each other, which was where they had started out. *And* they were holding hands. Humph! This looked serious.

"She's very cute," Bennett said later, watching Sylvie moving amongst the tables, chatting to the other diners, on top of everything as always. "Not only that, she's a fabulous chef. Where did she learn to cook like this?"

"Believe it or not, she really got interested when she went to stay at Daria's family's summer place on Cape Cod. We used to hang out there together in the summer and Sylvie got a job at the local lobster house. She'd bring home the leftovers and rehash them the next day into something superb for lunch. Between that and her barbecues we all gained weight, and Sylvie's fate was sealed. A chef was what she wanted to be and she never looked back."

"Sounds like fun," Bennett said, taking her hand and lifting it to his lips. Their glance smoldered.

"You're taking my breath away," Preshy murmured, releasing her hand. "I think I need more wine."

"Will it bring back your breath?" he asked as he filled her glass with the simple chilled Brouilly Sylvie had recommended to go with the entrée.

Preshy shivered as she sipped her wine, but it wasn't because of its chill. "I confess, I don't want it back." She smiled at him. "I kind of like being 'breathless.' "

"Doesn't it impede your eating ability?"

She threw back her head and laughed. "Nothing ever stops me from eating," she said, tucking into the moist, tender Bresse chicken that tasted the way no other chicken in the entire world did.

"I'm glad to hear it," Sylvie said, passing by. "Everything all right?" she asked, in French.

"Sylvie, this food is . . ." Bennett seemed stumped for words. "It's marvelous," he said. "I've never eaten anything so good in all my life."

"Even in Shanghai? I hear the food is wonderful there, so inventive, so exotic."

"But this is different. I might have to move to Paris so I can eat at Verlaine more often."

Sylvie beamed at the compliment. "I'll welcome you anytime," she assured him, and then, while they ate a small but perfect salad, followed by a selection of impeccable cheeses, she went back to her kitchen and prepared the simplest and most old-fashioned of

French desserts called floating islands. This was a light egg custard topped with meltingly soft egg whites whipped with sugar, then shaped with a tablespoon into "islands," that she "floated" on the custard. She finished it with a dusting of crushed pralines. It looked beautiful and perfectly simple but in Sylvie's hands it became a sublime blending of delicate flavors and textures.

"Floating islands," Bennett exclaimed when she presented it. "It almost sounds Chinese. I think I might have to abduct you, Sylvie, get you to open a restaurant in Shanghai."

They laughed, and glancing at Preshy who was gazing admiringly at Bennett, Sylvie was glad to see her so happy. And besides, the man couldn't take his eyes off her. Sylvie was surprised the two of them had even had time to eat the floating islands, they were so absorbed in each other.

Later she went and sat with them as they lingered over coffee, reminiscing with Preshy about their summers with Daria on Cape Cod.

"I have to take you there sometime," Preshy said eagerly to Bennett. Then, realizing what she had said, she quickly backtracked. "Of course you're much too busy for anything like that."

"I could make time," Bennett replied, giving her that long look that Sylvie noted reduced her friend to a simmering silence.

He glanced regretfully at his watch—expensive, Sylvie observed, thankful that at least Preshy hadn't been hit on by a hard-up struggling artist, something that had happened before in her friend's search for "love." Not only was Bennett James handsome, he seemed respectable and rich.

He said they had to go and they left in a flurry of good-night kisses and promises from Bennett to return. As soon as they'd gone Sylvie was on the phone to Daria.

"Well?" Daria said.

"It's too late, she's sunk."

"Is it that bad?"

"He seems too good to be true. The only flaw is the Shanghai bit. Six thousand miles is a long way."

"Yeah, but they could always find a way around that," Daria said, then she laughed. "Listen to us, talking like a pair of old matchmakers and Preshy's only known him twenty-four hours."

"Maybe it's enough," Sylvie said, remembering how they had looked at each other.

FIFTEEN

"DID you really enjoy it?" Preshy asked as she and Bennett strolled hand in hand back through the maze of little side streets that led down to the rue Jacob.

"I thought it was wonderful." Bennett was looking at her. Raindrops misted her hair and her eyes had an underwater aquamarine quality. "But I was happy just to be with you," he added.

She squeezed his hand, smiling. "Me too," she said shyly.

Ignoring the rain, they stopped to look in the illuminated shop windows, criticizing the paintings in the many galleries and admiring the antiques and clothing boutiques. When they finally found themselves back in the courtyard, this time Preshy asked if he would like to come up. "For a nightcap," she added with a giggle because it sounded like such a ploy, which of course it was. She wasn't about to let him get away tonight.

Bennett followed her in, looking around at the pleasant place she had made home. He helped her off with her wet jacket, removed his own, then took her in his arms.

"No nightcaps," he murmured, pushing her wet curls behind her ears. "It's just us, Preshy . . . you and me . . ." She twined her arms around his neck, waiting for his kiss. "Is this what you truly want, darling Preshy?" he said quietly. "I don't want to hurry you."

She shook her head, sending raindrops flying from her still damp hair. "You're not hurrying me." Her lips were a mere breath away from his.

She closed her eyes as they kissed. Her knees had turned to jelly and she was melting into him, into the scent of him, the feel of his mouth on hers, his body against hers. She had never felt this wondrous emotion before, never known that wanting someone could be like this, where all you wanted to do was give yourself and to take and receive pleasure from your man. The real world was locked out as Bennett picked her up and carried her into the bedroom for what Preshy knew was to be the defining moment of her life.

AS DAWN BROKE SHE FELL into an exhausted slumber. She did not hear Bennett get up, shower, put on his clothes and walk into the living room. He stood for a few minutes looking out the window, a frown on his face as he thought how to play this game out.

He turned and scanned the array of family photographs on the shelves by the fireplace. He picked up one he guessed was the rich aunt who Lily had said would leave Preshy her money, resplendent in scarlet chiffon at the Monte Carlo Red Cross Gala. He studied her face for a few minutes, then his eye was taken by the wedding picture of Grandfather Hennessy and his bride in her traditional Austrian dirndl. *And a jeweled necklace with a single giant pearl.* He looked at it for a long time. So Mary-Lou was right about the necklace after all. And Lily really did have it. A glimmer of an idea entered his mind. There might be a way he could achieve both objectives—the heiress and the necklace. He put the photo in his pocket and went back into the bedroom.

Preshy heard Bennett speak her name. He was sitting on the edge of the bed, fully dressed, looking at her.

"I have to leave you," he said. "Not because I want to, believe me I don't, but I have a flight to catch."

"Of course." She sat up hurriedly, clutching the sheet over her breasts, though why she was being so modest after what had happened between them she didn't know.

He took her chin in his hand, tilting her face up to him. "You know I'll be back," he said gently.

She nodded, suddenly numb with fear that he might not be.

"Preshy," he said reassuringly. "I mean it. I'll be back for you." He leaned in and kissed her gently on the mouth, then he got up and walked to the door. He turned to look at her one last time, sitting up in bed with the sheet still clutched to her, her eyes round and sad. "Soon," he said. "I promise."

And then he was gone. Thousands of miles away, to Shanghai.

SIXTEEN

CHINA

LILY drove the black SUV slowly along the unpaved road, high over a narrow gorge on the Yangtze River. It was past midnight with that dense almost tangible darkness found only in remote country areas, far from the city's halogen glow, and it was raining hard. The headlights picked up the bitter, barren landscape, like something from an ancient Chinese brush painting, misty gray and dead white with the stark black silhouettes of trees stripped of their leaves by the perpetual raking wind.

She pushed her hair impatiently from her delicately boned face, peering into the rainy night, searching for her destination.

Next to her, Mary-Lou adjusted her rimless glasses that reflected the headlights, looking out for a landmark, anything that would tell them they were nearing their rendezvous, but her mind was only half on it. She was worried. She still had not heard from Bennett.

Both women wore knitted watch caps, jeans and black jackets, thickly padded to keep out the icy wind. And in Mary-Lou's pocket was hidden a snub-nosed black pistol. A Beretta. Of course Lily did not know about the Beretta, but if there was any trouble Mary-Lou wanted to make sure at least *she* came out alive.

The road twisted away from the river, up a steep hill, winding between thin stands of trees bending under the prevailing wind, past watery rice paddies and small fields. In the gloom Lily made out the shapes of the poor wooden houses. She quickly doused her headlights, feeling her way around a sleeping village and down the hill to the burial ground. The directions had been good and she found it without any trouble.

A pair of armed guards raised their rifles as they sighted the truck and Lily gave three short muted blasts of her horn, the signal that she was expected. Ahead, under the wall, she could see a small flatbed truck and a larger van.

She switched off the engine and the two women got out and stood, shivering, waiting for the signal to advance. A man appeared from behind the flatbed, the back of which was protected from the rain with a tarpaulin. He gestured for them to come forward, watching carefully to see there was no one else with them. His was a dangerous business with plenty of competition and he could not be too careful.

He motioned them to the flatbed, lifting the tarp to show the muddy treasures hidden beneath. The tomb he was robbing was very old and the artifacts—vases and vessels, statues and jade carvings—were prized for their antiquity. He knew their value on the hidden market and he knew what he could expect to get from Lily Song, but first there was bargaining to be done.

The Chinese are masters at the art of bargaining and Lily was no exception. Keen to get a good price, she and Mary-Lou picked out the pieces they wanted then Lily and the man went and sat in the truck to hash out the deal.

Mary-Lou remained behind, keeping a careful eye on the guards. When they finally turned their backs and took shelter from the wind behind the wall for a quick smoke, she walked silently into the cemetery. Hidden in the shadows, she watched a group of men battering down the doors to a second tomb. Glancing quickly round, she saw what she was looking for: a small pile of artifacts waiting to be collected and carried to the truck. Crouching low, she crept closer. In seconds she had picked up a small bowl. It was still covered in dust and dirt, but looking at it, she knew it was of Imperial jade. She also knew its potential value.

Her heart thumping with excitement, she slipped it in her pocket next to the gun, then ran silently back up the path to the pickup. If she were caught these men would have no mercy. She and Lily would both be shot and thrown into the river, but somehow she just knew she was safe.

Sitting in the truck, Lily handed over a wad of money to the "supplier." He counted it, shaking his head in disgust that a woman had gotten the better of him, grunting his acceptance.

Mary-Lou was waiting for her and the two took their loot, loaded it into the SUV, then got back in.

Lily could feel the supplier's baleful gaze boring into her as she started the engine; she saw the guards lift their rifles, following them in their sights as they drove past. Sweating, she half-expected to feel the bullets thudding into the vehicle, but none came. Lily Song was a good customer; she paid cash and the supplier wanted repeat business. Maybe he would kill her one day, but not tonight.

The stolen artifacts in their padded wrap cloths bounced in the rear of the SUV as the two women headed down to the river and through the night on their long journey back to Shanghai.

"We did it," Lily said jubilantly, taking out a cigarette.

"We did," Mary-Lou agreed, noting in the spark of the flame from the lighter that Lily's hand shook slightly. Hers did not. She closed her fingers over the small jade bowl hidden in her pocket and smiled. She would be rich at any cost. Lily did not know that her friend was also a thief.

SEVENTEEN

PARIS

TEN days later, true to his promise, Bennett walked unannounced into Preshy's store, laughing at her stunned expression when she swung round and saw him standing there. And within minutes it was as though he had never been away.

He gave her his cell-phone number and his e-mail address, and he returned every ten days or so after that. In two months they saw each other six times. Seven, Preshy thought, if you counted their first meeting, but it was as if they had known each other forever. Better, she believed, than many lovers who had been together for years.

They talked endlessly, when they weren't making love that is, and there was nothing Bennett didn't know about her and, she was sure, nothing she didn't know about him. She knew his beautiful body intimately, and how he made love; and she knew about his past lovers—not as many as she had expected. She knew how he felt about nature and food, exercise and travel, world events and movies and books. She also knew about his childhood.

Bennett told her he had been abandoned by his single mother when he was five years old and had spent his childhood years in New Hampshire, in a home for boys.

"I was too old to be a good candidate for adoption," he said, "so I just had to get on with it, living in an institution with other kids like me. I never knew my mother, she simply dumped me there and I never saw her again. As for my father, I don't even know who he was. Perhaps my mother didn't either, and that's why she didn't care about me."

He shook his head as though in denial, or else to shake off the bad memories, and there was a coldness in his eyes that made Preshy flinch.

"You don't make many friends in an environment like that," he told her bitterly. "All you want to do is get out. I won a scholarship to Dartmouth. It was there I learned everything there was to know about 'real life' as I called it. And that," he said, smiling ruefully at her, "is why I am who I am now. And why I'm so busy making money, trying to eliminate those years of poverty and nonentitlement. I'm always on the move so there's no time to form real friendships. Or maybe I've just been so caught up in becoming a success I've never made time for any close relationships. Until now," he added, taking her in his arms. "And you, Preshy."

. . .

SHE WAS IN LOVE WITH the romance of it all: in love with their first meeting; in love with their partings when he went away and called her to say good night sleep well, regardless of the time difference. She was in love with their reunions when he came back to Paris, back to the apartment on rue Jacob, back to her waiting arms and her bed. She shared everything with him, the stories of her life, of her family; of Grandfather Hennessy and rich Aunt Grizelda; of her parents and the little she knew about Grandfather's other granddaughter, Lily, who lived in Shanghai and whom she had never met.

She bought him gifts: a rare edition of John Donne's poems that seemed to say all there was to say about passion and love; a special bottle of wine; a silly key ring with the Eiffel Tower on it—"to remind you of Paris and me," she said, laughing. And he arrived with champagne and flowers and took her on a trip to the countryside where they stayed at a vast château made over into a hotel, and dined like royalty surrounded by servants.

How could romance not bloom, Preshy asked herself, lying in a silk-draped seventeenth-century bed in a vast gilded room with the moon outside the window bathing the gardens and parkland with a pale light. And looking at the beautiful sleeping man next to her, she thought this was surely Love with a capital *L*.

As though he felt her gaze, Bennett's eyes flew open. "Preshy," he said sleepily, "I don't think I can live without you. Will you please marry me?"

In love with the moment, the romance, the place, Preshy didn't hesitate. "Yes," she said and proceeded to cover his face with kisses.

"When?" he demanded.

"Right now," she said, laughing. Then, "Oh, but I can't. First I have to tell Aunt Grizelda."

"Don't worry about Aunt Grizelda," Bennett said. "I'll do the right thing. I'll go to Monte Carlo and ask her for your hand in marriage."

THE NEXT DAY, BACK IN Paris, he took her out to dine at the restaurant Jules Verne high atop the Eiffel Tower, where over champagne and oysters he solemnly presented her with a ring, an antique cushion-cut diamond surrounded by smaller diamonds. He put it on her finger while the other diners applauded with encouraging cries of "Bravo."

What, Preshy wondered, as she looked at her diamond engagement ring sparkling like the lights of Paris spread out before them, could be more romantic than this? But then Bennett always seemed to do everything right.

"We'll live here," he decided. "I'll commute from Shanghai, but I'll try to get home more often now. As often as I can," he added, his eyes devouring her and sending tingles through places she hadn't known could tingle. "And tomorrow," he added, "I'll ask your aunt Grizelda if she will hand you over to me. I hope she'll approve," he added, looking suddenly doubtful and making her laugh again.

"Of course she will, you can't fail," she said.

EIGHTEEN

CHINA

MARY-LOU had been showing up for work every morning, sullen and unable to concentrate, and it hadn't taken Lily long to realize what the problem was.

"So, where's Bennett?" she asked as they were driving the stolen antiquities to a client's private warehouse.

"Why? What d'you mean?"

She was so defensive that Lily laughed. "I guess that's all the answer I need. It didn't last long, did it?"

"He doesn't answer his phone, he doesn't call. . . . I suppose he's gone off to the States on business. Or Paris," she added, as an afterthought, recalling their conversation at dinner when Lily had mentioned her cousin.

"He goes to Paris often?"

"So he says. But . . ."

Lily took her eyes off the road and glanced quickly at Mary-Lou. Her mouth was pulled into a tight line and there was a frown between her eyebrows. "But . . . what?"

"Ohh, I don't know," Mary-Lou said wearily. "I thought it was the real thing this time," she said truthfully. "It was on my part anyway."

Lily patted her friend's arm sympathetically. "I'm sorry," she said. "Maybe he's just been too busy. Men are like that sometimes. I speak from experience, because as a businessperson that's the way I am myself," she added. "There's no time for diversions."

"I never thought of myself as merely a 'diversion,' " Mary-Lou said bitterly, making Lily smile.

They completed their delivery and drove quickly away, their responsibility over. Lily didn't want to know about the private plane waiting at the airport or how the buyers were going to get the stuff on board and out of the country. It was none of her business. She had the cash in her bag and that was all she cared about.

She paid Mary-Lou a hefty bonus, as she always did for taking part in a risky operation, and told her that she had another trip planned. "In a couple of weeks' time," she said. "Okay?"

Mary-Lou nodded but her mind was far from the Yangtze River. She took the rest of the day off and spent her bonus in the boutiques on the Nanking Road, but she wasn't even truly concentrating on shopping. The sale of the necklace was running through her mind in an endless stream of rubies and diamonds and the priceless pearl . . . And how to find a buyer.

She had a single contact in the jewelry world—the diamond cutter, Voortmann, who she used to reshape the stolen jewels she fenced. She called him and drove over there immediately.

Voortmann was a bald, soft-bellied, shabby Dutchman who had learned his trade in the diamond markets of Amsterdam. Long ago, he'd been convicted of theft. It wasn't a major heist but in the diamond trade once you were convicted, you were an outcast. He'd made his way via Bangkok to Shanghai, where he now kept a low profile, cutting diamonds for the lower end of the trade, and he did his job well. But everybody in Shanghai had a sideline and his was selling stolen jewels, as well as recutting them. The occasional job Mary-Lou brought him was not substantial but he never turned away business. Now she said she had a proposition to put to him.

He buzzed her in through the double steel gates, hearing her high heels clatter as she came up the wooden steps to his second-floor office. She paused at the locked door and he buzzed her in again. "Take a seat," he said, switching off the high-intensity lamp over his workbench and swiveling his chair to look at her. He thought, surprised, she seemed frightened. His hackles rose warningly, he couldn't afford trouble.

"What's wrong?" he asked abruptly.

"Nothing's wrong. It's just that I have a proposition to make you. It's very special. Unique in fact." Mary-Lou had made a copy of her necklace photograph on her home printer. She opened her purse and took it out but she did not give it to him right away.

"What I'm about to show you is confidential," she said. "It must go no further than us. This is serious business, Voortmann. Do you understand?"

He raised a skeptical eyebrow. "Some society woman in Hong Kong is missing a ten-carat diamond?"

She shook her head impatiently. "More, *much* more than that. First, listen to what I have to say."

She told him the story of the Dowager Empress's stolen jewels and the burial pearl, then sat back waiting for his reaction.

He shrugged, bored, glancing at his watch. It was time to close up shop and head for the bars. He managed to stay sober all day so his hand didn't shake—yet. He couldn't afford that in his line of work. But at seven p.m. he became a different man. "So?" he said.

She finally handed him the photograph. "This is what happened to those jewels," she said. "And that is the infamous pearl."

Voortmann studied it in silence. It was a blurred picture, obviously taken in secret and with bad light, but if the story was true then he was looking at something remarkable. "How do I know it's not a fake?"

"You trust me," she said simply.

He looked at her. She wasn't giving him the song and dance, and making excuses, and for once he thought he could. He sat back in his big chair, arms folded across his chest, looking intently at her. Her beauty had no effect on him. Alcohol and opium were his lovers and every cent he made went to fuel those addictions. "So? What do you want from me?"

"I want you to find me a buyer?"

"Hmm. I assume you have the necklace in your possession?"

"I can get my hands on it—immediately if necessary."

"It's obviously stolen. A piece such as this, the police will be on top of it. It's a dangerous game."

"No one knows about it, it's been hidden for years."

"Who has it?" He couldn't leave anything to chance.

"It belonged to a family. And when I take it, it can never be reported to the police. This piece would be confiscated, Voortmann. And the owner would be jailed. Of course this does not concern you, or me. All I want you to do is find the right buyer. And soon."

Voortmann thought about it. Like Mary-Lou, he saw riches dance in front of his eyes. This could be the deal of the century. But how to pull it off? It would mean using his old contacts in Amsterdam . . . It might just be possible. . . . "I'll see what I can do," he said finally. "But I need to see the necklace first."

She closed her purse with a snap. "No deal," she said, confident now.

Voortmann sighed. "There is only so far we can go on hearsay," he said coldly. "An important piece like this, the buyer will need to see it."

Mary-Lou slung her bag over her shoulder and got to her feet. She smiled at him for the first time. "We'll face that problem when we get to it," she said. "And remember, you need to work fast."

Voortmann buzzed her out of his grimy office. He heard her quick footsteps as she ran back down the stairs, then the buzzer signaling she wanted to get out. He opened the gates for her and heard them clang back into place. He sat back in his old leather chair, swinging gently from side to side, hands steepled in front of him, eyes closed, thinking about what might, if she were telling the truth, be the deal of a lifetime.

After a while he got up and put the photo of the necklace in his pocket. Then he locked his office, let himself out through the steel gates that had imprisoned him ever since Amsterdam, and headed for his favorite bar. Tomorrow, he would make some calls.

NINETEEN

MONTE CARLO

THE apartment in Monte Carlo that the two widows and old friends, Grizelda von Hoffenberg the aristocrat, and Mimi Moskowitz the ex-showgirl, called home was like a movie set from the 1930s, white on white with chrome and silver accents. A wall of windows overlooking the bay was lined with fragile voile curtains that billowed in the sea breeze. Shaggy white rugs were flung across pale limestone floors and oversized sofas were covered in white brocade. There were glass consoles and chrome-legged glass coffee tables; mirrored tables and cabinets. The walls and ceiling were painted a shade known as Bridal Pink, which while not exactly pink and not exactly white, contrived to give a soft glow to the room.

Of course there were flowers everywhere because Grizelda

said she couldn't live without them and besides Nice was the flower capital of the world. So there were always roses—white or palest pink of course—and swags of blossoming cherry or mimosa and lilies, as well as a favorite fluffy-topped plant that Grizelda called "cow parsley" and Mimi called "Queen Anne's lace" ("that's because I'm more refined than Grizelda," Mimi said). And of course there was Mimi's teacup-sized Yorkie, called Lalah, and Grizelda's miniature poodle, Schnuppi, who in the chilliest months of winter was to be seen in a mink jumpsuit complete with a little hood from which its topknot poked becomingly.

Today, because Preshy was bringing her new boyfriend to meet them, Grizelda and Mimi had gone all out and the penthouse was filled with enough flowers, Mimi said, to stock a florist shop. Jeanne and Maurice, the couple who had worked for them for more than twenty-five years as houseman and cook-housekeeper, and who Grizelda and Mimi considered "family," had prepared a special dinner, setting the smaller round dining table for four with an embroidered white organdie cloth, the Vietri china and Christofle silverware.

Preshy's phone call had come just last night. "I want to bring someone to meet you," she'd said in a kind of breathless excited voice they had never heard before. "His name is Bennett James, he lives in Shanghai and I've known him two months."

"Shanghai!" Grizelda had exclaimed, with visions of losing her "daughter" to a city at the other side of the world.

"Two months!" Mimi had boomed. "And this is the first time you've mentioned him?"

"Sorry, I was too busy." Preshy giggled, then added, "Anyway, you're meeting him now. And I hope you're going to like him, because I certainly do."

And now they were on their way.

"We have to make a good impression," Grizelda said to Mimi, tweaking the centerpiece of white gardenias floating in a crystal bowl.

"It looked quite all right before you put your hands on it," Mimi said crossly. It had been her job to do the flowers and she considered her work perfect.

Grizelda gave her a look. "Mimi, I do good flowers. You do good music. Each to his own."

"Then next time *you* do them," Mimi said, smoothing back her well-groomed platinum hair.

"Today, I simply did not have the time."

"Too excited, I suppose."

Grizelda sighed. "Well, it's not the first time Preshy's brought a boyfriend home, but it's the first time I've heard her sound like this."

"High on love," Mimi said with a grin.

"And no doubt on sex," Grizelda added.

"As long as it's *good* sex," Mimi said and they both laughed.

"What do you think? Do we look intimidating enough?" Grizelda twirled for Mimi, while the two dogs, sitting on the sofa, watched, alert to the excitement. She was wearing a white Saint-Laurent pantsuit with a gold necklace and an armload of clanking gold bracelets. Her red hair waved sexily over one eye and swung around her shoulders, exactly like the fifties movie actress Rita

Hayworth, who, even at an age she refused to admit to, Grizelda still liked to think she resembled. Her green eyes—greener thanks to contacts—twinkled with amusement at her own vanity.

"We look as good as the Lord and expensive plastic surgeons and cute personal trainers can make us," Mimi said crisply. "And that's better than most."

She was wearing silver gray, a simple dress that skimmed her still-pretty knees and fluttered over the ample bosom that had delighted audiences at the Follies so many years ago. Diamonds dangled from her ears and clasped the low V of her décolletage.

"I really got the feeling from Preshy this is important though," Grizelda said. "What if he's The One?"

"Then we just have to hope he passes the von Hoffenberg–Moskowitz test."

"And if he doesn't?"

"She'll probably end up with him anyway. And you'll cut her out of your will."

"She's not in my will, you know that. And so does Preshy. Of course I'll leave her my jewelry, but apart from that she can make her own way in the world."

"Hmm," Mimi said. She wasn't quite sure about not leaving her Oscar von Hoffenberg's money, after all there were no other descendants, but that was the way Grizelda wanted it.

Jeanne came in to light the dozens of gardenia-scented votive candles in crystal holders lined up along practically every surface. "Everything's ready, madame," she said, in French, of course. They always spoke French in this household.

"Bien, merci, Jeanne." Grizelda smiled at her old friend. "Tell me,

Jeanne, what do you think? Is this the special one Preshy is bringing home to meet us?"

Jeanne had met a dozen young men Preshy had brought home over the years. "Preshy's comfortable in her own skin, madame," she said. "I don't believe she's thinking of giving up her independence just yet."

"Hmm, we'll see," Mimi said.

They were expected any minute and in fact right then the concierge called to say they were on their way up.

Followed by the bouncing dogs, the women hurried into the foyer, staring expectantly as the elevator door opened. And there they were; Preshy, casual as always in jeans, a white linen shirt and an oversized handbag, her big eyes smiling, her wild gold hair tumbled from the wind. And Bennett James, knockout handsome in a blue shirt open at the neck, a dark blue blazer, immaculately pressed pants and soft suede loafers.

Grizelda thought if first impressions were anything to go by, this was a winner. And Mimi thought he was too good to be true.

Bennett smiled warmly as Preshy introduced him. He said how pleased he was to meet them, Preshy had talked about them so much. He patted the excited Lalah, who was jumping up at him, and said how beautiful Schnuppi was, and that she was obviously much shyer because she was keeping a wary distance.

They took him to the silvery white living room, wafted in on the scent of the flowers and the gardenia votives, and he exclaimed at its beauty, and at the way the voile curtains softened the light and said how charming they looked blowing in the breeze.

"Like a Matisse painting," he said, accepting a glass of champagne (the lesser Jacquart, not the expensive Cristal: Grizelda was saving that for later, *if* he passed muster).

Maurice had poured the champagne and now Jeanne came in with a tray of hors d'oeuvres. Preshy went to hug them; she introduced them to Bennett, who said he was happy to meet anybody who'd known Preshy for twenty years and maybe they had some true-life stories to tell him. They all laughed and Grizelda took a seat on the white brocade sofa. Schnuppi jumped up next to her and Lalah snuggled on Mimi's knee on the sofa opposite, with the chrome and glass coffee table in between.

Grizelda patted the sofa and said, "Come and sit here, Bennett, why don't you, and tell us all about yourself."

"There's not that much to tell." He glanced at Preshy on the tufted white ottoman, watching them. "Not really much more than, no doubt, what you've heard from Preshy already."

"In fact we've heard nothing, only that you live in Shanghai."

"I do. And unfortunately it's a long way from Paris."

Preshy's eyes met his. He knew she was enjoying watching her aunt put him through his paces, and besides, she knew what was to come.

"And what exactly do you do there, Bennett?"

Jeanne offered him the tray of hors d'oeuvres and he took a small square of *socca,* the chickpea pancake that was a specialty of the Nice area, with a smear of goat cheese, speared with a tiny black olive.

"I own James Exports. Actually I manufacture parts for the furniture business in the U.S. We make the wooden components that are then assembled in North Carolina by the major furniture companies."

"And is that profitable?" Mimi asked, looking as innocent as she could while obviously trying to find out his worth.

"Profitable enough," he replied, smiling.

"You needn't worry, I think I know everything there is to know about him," Preshy said, taking a sip of her champagne.

"Well we certainly don't," Mimi said in her booming voice that Preshy thought could shatter glass at twenty paces if she really let it rip. "I'd like to know what you think of our girl, Bennett."

He gave her a smile and that long intimate look that endeared him to women. "I think your girl is wonderful, Mimi. In fact the reason I'm here is that I very much want to make her *my* girl. I've come to ask your permission, Aunt Grizelda, Mimi, to marry Precious."

"Oh my Lord." Grizelda clasped a hand to her heart. She hadn't really expected things to move this fast. She glanced at her niece. "And what does Preshy say?"

"I've said yes, of course." Preshy could contain herself no longer. She stuck out her left hand with the diamond sparkling on the third finger. "But Bennett insisted on coming to ask your permission."

Grizelda and Mimi leapt up to examine the ring, sending the dogs yapping out of their way. Grizelda's eyes met Mimi's: the ring was just small enough for good taste and just big enough to be expensive. They were thinking the same thing. That they loved the old-fashioned touch of a man asking permission to marry their beloved girl; that he was the right age, good-looking, charming, cultured and apparently well enough off.

"As long as you love each other, I couldn't wish for anyone better to take Preshy off my hands," Aunt Grizelda said, and Bennett got up and kissed her on both cheeks. Then he kissed Mimi. And then he kissed Preshy.

Grizelda summoned Maurice and Jeanne to break out the good Cristal champagne and they raised their glasses to Preshy and Bennett's future happiness.

"I WONDER," GRIZELDA SAID THOUGHTFULLY over dinner later. "Would you prefer to have the wedding here or in Paris?"

"Neither." Preshy stroked Lalah, who was sitting on her lap, hiding under the fold of the tablecloth, hoping for handouts. "I want to be married in Venice, at the Santa Maria della Salute. You know it has special memories for me." She caught Bennett's eye and added, "And we want to be married as soon as possible."

Grizelda looked doubtful. "Of course I'll need time to prepare. Arrangements have to be made; the dress; the flowers; the invitations . . ."

"Next month," Preshy said firmly. "And we're leaving it all to you, darling Aunt G. Just tell us when and we'll show up."

"But where will you live? Not in Shanghai, I hope?" Mimi said.

"I'm keeping my business in Paris. We'll live there and Bennett will commute to Shanghai."

"That's a hefty commute," Grizelda commented, but Bennett told them he planned on spending less time in Shanghai, though he still had to travel frequently to the States.

"Don't worry though," he said. "I won't leave Preshy alone long enough to get lonely."

"It couldn't be more perfect, could it?" Preshy said contentedly, lifting up Lalah and kissing her on her sweet black nose.

TWENTY

THERE was no time to be lost and Grizelda plunged headfirst into the wedding arrangements. First she had to use all her influence, rounding up people she knew in Venice to get permission for the wedding to take place at the Basilica. Then, she had to call her friends at the Hotel Cipriani, where she had stayed many times over the years and where they knew her well, to arrange for the celebration dinner, and for the wedding cake.

She also called in a few favors and managed to rent the fourteenth-century Palazzo Rendino on the Grand Canal, owned by old friends (there were advantages to getting older after all, she thought: at least you could call in years of favors) and now the bridal party would stay at the Palazzo. She had immediately ordered her wedding outfit—a white Dior suit and an enormous

Philip Treacy hat for the ceremony, plus a long red lace Valentino dress for dinner the evening before.

She'd also had a fight with Preshy on the phone about the wedding dress because Preshy refused to wear white.

"You don't have to be a virgin these days," Grizelda said, exasperated, but Preshy just laughed.

"It's not that, Aunt G, thank goodness," she said, sounding giddy as a lovesick high school girl heading to her first prom. "It's just that I don't want to look like your typical bride in a strapless mushroom cloud of white tulle. I want to be different."

"How different?" Grizelda demanded. "For God's sakes, Preshy you have only three weeks. You'd better make up your mind fast. I'm flying to Paris tomorrow and we'll sort it out then."

Meanwhile, there were the flowers to be taken care of and right now she was driving along the precipitous Grande Corniche road, heading for the flower market in Nice. She'd been using the same man there for years and trusted him completely. Since it was a November wedding and roses were out of season, she would have him order those marvelous huge cabbage roses imported all the way from Colombia, and ask him to come personally to Venice to decorate the church and the reception, as well as do the bouquets.

Everything had to be perfect, and with only a month—now down to three weeks—she was as tight with nerves as if she were getting married herself.

Not that her wedding to Oscar von Hoffenberg had been anything like Preshy's. First of all, they'd known each other over a year and their engagement had been announced properly in the

European and American newspapers. Then his parents had orchestrated the whole event, down to the last place card and who sat next to whom—which with various members of international royalty and ambassadors, clerics and cardinals, lords and ladies, her own friends and family members as well as theirs; plus the tenants and workers at the Schloss, had been quite a feat of organization. Grizelda had just sat back and let them get on with it.

She'd chosen the dress herself, though. She still had it, wrapped in acid-free paper in a cedar chest at the back of her vast walk-in closet. It was a plain white satin affair, cut on the bias by a master of that art, and it had sleeked around her young body so sexily that the wedding guests had gasped and Oscar's eyes had popped. It had certainly helped make her wedding night an event to remember, though it had alienated Oscar's prissy family forever.

After Oscar died, of course all his money and the castle had gone to her. Nevertheless, the day after the will was read, Grizelda had packed her bags, including her wedding dress and her dog—a pale pug named Jolly—and departed for warmer and more exciting climes. With the fading memory of those long dull years with irascible Oscar, she had never returned to the Schloss.

Today the morning was blue and clear, the way it so often was in the South of France at the end of October, and without the heavy summer traffic it was a pleasure to drive the Corniche road, high above the coast with the sea stretching into infinity to meet the sky. Grizelda knew that road like the back of her hand. It was carved from the side of the mountain and she'd been driving it for years. It held no terrors for her, though she knew it did for tourists. Even though Princess Grace had not been killed on this particular stretch, many people worried that the same fate might happen to them; a second's lack of attention, a slight loss of control, was all it would take to end up in the rocky gorge to her left.

She idled along in the big silver Bentley, taking her time, thinking over the arrangements. Mimi was in charge of the music and so far she had organized a string quartet to play at the prewedding party at the Palazzo, and an organist for the church. Now she was at home, on the phone in the midst of negotiations for a dance band to play at the reception. Meanwhile Sylvie Verlaine was in charge of the menu. Grizelda was sure it would all work out satisfactorily, but she still wished Preshy had given her a month or two more notice. With a little more time she could have done it all so much better.

The road began to descend, winding around curves. It was quiet. There was no one in front of her and only a couple of cars had passed on the other side. Switching on the radio, she was searching for a station that played "oldies but goodies" when, glancing in her rearview mirror, she noticed a white truck behind her. She thought that it was traveling too fast, and frowning, she honked her horn. The driver took no notice. She flashed her lights in warning and put her foot to the metal, taking the curves faster than she liked in an attempt to get out of his way. But still he did not slow down. Now he was right behind her.

She slammed her hand on the horn and left it there. He was almost upon her, close enough that had the truck's windows not been so dark she would have been able to see the driver's face.

Sweat filmed the back of her neck as fear hit her. *He was trying to run her off the road . . .*

She felt the thud as the truck grazed her bumper . . . *he was crazy . . . oh Christ, what was happening . . . she couldn't drive at this speed . . . she would die . . . but she couldn't die yet . . . she couldn't miss Preshy's wedding. . . . She had to use her head. . . .* Think, *she told herself,* think! *She knew the road well. . . . There was an emergency lay-by carved from the rock on the other side just around the bend . . .*

Praying there was nothing coming the other way, she swung the Bentley across the road, simultaneously slamming on the brakes. The car slid sideways, it swung round once, twice, three times before hitting the rock face, hard. The air bags exploded and she was slammed back in her seat, shaking and screaming her head off. But she was alive. And the madman in the white truck had flown past her and was gone.

Still shaking, she sat with the air bag in her face, telling herself not to panic. The car ticked and groaned; steam surged from under the hood and a thin trail of smoke escaped from the back. She knew she had to get out; it might burst into flames any minute.

To her surprise the door opened easily and then she was standing out on the road, cursing the mad bastard who had done this to her—and to her beautiful silver-gray Bentley.

Staring forlornly at the wreckage of her car, she asked herself, bewildered, what the hell that was all about.

Later, when she had been checked out at the hospital and Mimi had arrived in tears to fetch her, they talked about it.

Mimi said, "*Chérie,* somebody wanted to kill you. They wanted you dead."

Grizelda glared at her. "Don't be ridiculous, Mimi. Why would anyone want me dead? Except maybe my husband and he's long gone and ghosts don't come back for vengeance. At least I don't think so," she added doubtfully. "No, it was just the act of a madman, and I don't want you to bother Preshy with it. She'd only worry about nothing." Then, remembering, "And dammit, I still didn't get to see the flower man. Now I'll have to go tomorrow."

"Well this time I'm coming with you," Mimi said grimly. She didn't think the incident was "nothing" and she wasn't at all happy about madmen driving women off the road. In fact it made Mimi very uneasy.

TWENTY-ONE

SHANGHAI

BENNETT flew from Paris to Singapore, then took a connecting flight to Shanghai. It arrived at Pudong Airport twenty minutes late. He hurried through immigration and customs, then into the arrivals hall, where a limo driver was waiting for him. While the man went to fetch the car, Bennett called Mary-Lou.

"I'm back," he said, when she answered.

There was a long silence, then, "I didn't even know you'd gone," she retorted, making him smile.

"You mean you didn't miss me?"

"Not one bit."

"Then you don't want to see me tonight?"

"Only if you beg me."

Bennett laughed. "I'm begging," he said.

"All right. Where?"

"Your place, at eight." He had a lot to talk over with her and he needed to do it in private.

SHE WAS AT THE DOOR to greet him when he rang her bell at exactly eight. No words passed between them. She was in his arms, kissing him. He was holding a bottle of champagne in one hand, kissing her as though he intended to eat her up. He hooked a foot behind him and slammed the door shut. She threw back her head, looking at him.

"That's quite a welcome," he said, smiling down at her. "And did I tell you how beautiful you look tonight?"

"You did not, but you may tell me now," she said, taking the champagne from him and leading him to the small bar where an ice bucket awaited. She swished the bottle around in the ice and took two flutes from the shelf, waiting for him to open it. He filled the glasses, picked them up and gave her one.

"To us," he said, smiling right into her eyes, the way he always used to, and sending nervous little tremors down her spine. Still, she was careful not to mention the thing uppermost on her mind, and instead she sipped the champagne and asked how his trip was.

"Paris was okay," he said, walking to the window and staring out at the sludge-colored river and the surging traffic below.

Mary-Lou paced nervously behind him. Because she was concerned about good *feng shui,* she had hung a large crystal in front of the window, to repel the bad *chi* from the evil Dragon River Gods. She never questioned whether she really believed this or not, she just went along with it on the basis that it couldn't hurt and who knew, it might be true. Her ancestors had believed in it for centuries, hadn't they? Much good it had done her parents though; they'd had enough bad *chi* to send them to an early grave, crystals or no crystals.

But watching Bennett staring out of her window, she surely hoped it was working now. She still hadn't heard from Voortmann and she needed all the luck she could get.

Standing behind him, she said, "Shall we eat now? Or shall we go to bed?"

Bennett turned to look at her. "Guess," he said.

MUCH LATER, WHILE BENNETT SHOWERED, Mary-Lou opened the take-out cartons she'd had the forethought to buy from the local restaurant. She put them on the coffee table with a bottle of Tsingtao beer and a glass chilled almost to an icicle in the freezer. Bennett liked his beer cold.

His clothes were flung across the sofa and she gathered them up, stooping to pick up the wallet that had fallen from his pants pocket. Something bulky was stuffed inside. It was a tissue. Smoothing it out, she read the phone number written in lipstick. And the name. Preshy Rafferty.

"Oh my God," she whispered, clutching the wallet to her chest. *"Oh my God, you bastard. . . ."*

When Bennett came out of the bathroom, she said nothing about the tissue, now carefully tucked away in her own purse. She poured his beer and served his food and they knelt on cushions at the low coffee table to eat.

Bennett wanted to talk business but he was aware of Mary-Lou's silence. Of course she was angry because he'd simply left her without saying anything, and the truth was he *had* never intended to see her again. But now, as the old adage went, he wanted to have his cake and eat it too. He needed her.

"Do you love me, Bennett?" she asked after a while.

His eyes flicked coldly toward her. Love was not an issue between them. He picked up a spear of asparagus with his chopsticks. "We are alike, you and I, Mary-Lou," he said. "We both have hearts of steel." He stared at her, still able to admire her beauty. "I doubt you've ever loved anyone in your entire life."

"And did you love Ana?"

His glance turned even colder. He ignored what she had said. "You and I have a business deal," he said instead. "I came here to tell you I've found a buyer in Paris who's interested. He's willing to pay a deposit pending delivery, but naturally he wants a guarantee that what he's promised is what he'll get. I need to see that necklace."

"I can't do that."

"Then there's no deal."

She stared angrily at him, eating his dinner so calmly while she was in a turmoil. "Who is Preshy Rafferty?"

He put down the chopsticks. "Why do you ask?"

"Her number was in your wallet. Written in lipstick."

He got to his feet and shrugged on his jacket. “Thanks for dinner, Mary-Lou,” he said, walking to the door.

“Wait,” she called.

But Bennett did not wait. He didn’t have to. He knew he would get the necklace. She’d be back to him, and soon.

TWENTY-TWO

VOORTMANN was having trouble with his contact in Amsterdam. "How big are the stones?" he'd asked. "What's their rating? The diamonds are old, they'll have an old-fashioned cut. . . ."

No matter how Voortmann tried, he could not get the man—an expert gemologist who knew his trade but little else—to understand the special circumstances of the Empress's jewels, and especially the giant pearl. He'd need to look elsewhere for a buyer, and where better than right here in Shanghai?

At seven that evening he was, as usual, in the Surging Hot Waters Bar, a massive low-end dive of a place patronized by three levels of drinkers: men out for a night's social drinking and entertainment enhanced by the hot "bar girls"; men escaping from their families and drowning their marital woes; and the alcoholics like himself. The first two groups were a shifting population, different every night, but he knew everyone in the third group. Like him, they were always there. And at least two of them came from rich Shanghainese families.

Voortmann went every night to the bar for over a week, waiting for them to show up. The latest pop music pounded at an ear-splitting level from enormous speakers but he was so used to it he barely noticed. He drank his Scotch straight, not gulping it, just sipping; never getting loud; never falling down. He was, he told himself proudly, a refined drunk. And just the kind of man the rich Shanghainese would talk to. He'd done business with them before, in a small way, fencing jewels stolen from their wives, when their families had cut off the money until they reformed and stopped drinking and whoring.

A couple of hours later, he spotted them at a table in a dark corner, a bottle of Scotch in front of them.

He pushed his way through the crowd. "Good evening," he said.

They nodded good evening back and he waited for them to invite him to sit at their table. When they did not, he said, "Gentlemen, you have done business with me before. Now I have something that will be of interest to you." Not waiting for their invitation this time, he pulled up a chair, signaled the barkeep for another drink and sat down.

He took the photograph from his pocket and laid it on the table between them. "Feast your eyes on this, gentlemen," he said, smiling. "I guarantee it will put money in all our pockets."

The two men peered through the gloom at the photo. One picked it up, studying it. "Did you steal this?" he asked.

Voortmann shook his head.

"I know where it is," he said. "I could have it to you tomorrow. At a price."

"Such as?"

This time Voortmann downed his Scotch instead of sipping it, and this time the Shanghainese filled up his empty glass. "First I have a story to tell you, my friends," he said softly.

When he had finished the two Shanghainese glanced at each other. "We could go to jail for this," one said.

"How much?" said the other.

"Thirty million." Voortmann came up with a number. "But for you, I will make it ten, so you can sell it on and make a good profit."

The Shanghainese knew that the necklace was priceless, but they were not collectors, and they didn't need to risk being imprisoned for buying it.

They filled his glass to the brim, watching as he drank it down. Sweat beaded his upper lip.

"Tell us," one said, "who has this priceless object?"

But Voortmann still had enough smarts about him to know not to tell. He shook his head. "Just let me know if you want it or not, my friends," he said, getting up and heading back to the bar.

But the Shanghainese were no friends of his.

TWENTY-THREE

MARY-LOU couldn't resist. She called Preshy Rafferty's number and got an answering machine.

"Bonjour, Rafferty Antiques, Preshy Rafferty speaking," the voice said in French. *"If you wish to leave a message, please do so at the tone."*

Anger churned like molten lead in Mary-Lou's stomach. She felt sick. Was Bennett romancing Lily's cousin in the hope of marrying another heiress? She wouldn't put it past him.

She paced the small apartment, brushing impatiently past the dangling crystal that was supposed to ward off the evil Dragon River God spirits, sending it jangling, like her nerves. She'd lost him, she knew it. And with him the buyer. And Voortmann was turning out a loser, she hadn't heard from him in a week.

But Bennett said he had a buyer willing to pay a deposit. She had no choice but to work with him. She *had* to get the necklace. There was no time to be lost.

She remembered that Lily went for breakfast at eight every morning to the Happybird Tea House and that she would be likely to be away for at least an hour. Time enough to get the necklace from the safe and be gone.

THE NEXT MORNING MARY-LOU ARRIVED EARLY, waiting until she saw Lily's car emerge from the courtyard and disappear down the alley. Once it was out of sight, she opened the gate with her own electronic key and drove in. She parked, then temporarily disengaged the security camera that tracked her movements. By the time Lily got back from her breakfast, the camera would be working again, but Mary-Lou would not be on it.

The little canary bird in its cage gave her a hopeful chirrup as she crossed the verandah but she ignored it, and unlocked the door and entered the house. Slipping automatically out of her shoes she walked barefoot to the cellar door, and leaving it ajar, climbed down the rickety steps. Hurrying past the piled boxes to the back, she pressed the button, the panel slid away and the safe was revealed. It took only a minute to open it. The heavy iron door swung back. And there was the red leather jewel case.

She ran her palm across the smooth expensive leather. Even age had not destroyed it and she guessed it had been kept somewhere clean and dry all these years. She clicked the case open. Her eyes widened and a shiver ran down her spine as she touched the pearl, thinking of it in the dead Empress Cixi's mouth. What a waste, she thought contemptuously, clicking the box shut. The other stolen pearl that Soong Mai-ling had worn on her party shoes was put to much better use than in a dead woman's mouth.

She was about to close the safe when she heard a noise. Lifting her head, she listened.

"Mary-Lou? Is that you down there?" Lily's voice echoed down the cellar steps.

Heart throbbing, Mary-Lou flung the jewel case back into the safe, slammed the door and locked it. She leapt backward and pressed the panel, hearing it whirr shut just as Lily appeared at the top of the steps. She stood, hands behind her back, facing her.

"Mary-Lou, what on earth are you doing here this early?" Lily said, astonished. "You gave me quite a fright. I thought I had burglars."

"No, no burglars, only me. I came to work early to take care of packing the rest of the Buddha replicas. I know we have to deliver them today."

Lily came down the steps. She was holding a paper cup of coffee and looked disturbed. "That's very unusual for you. What's wrong? Couldn't you sleep?"

Mary-Lou allowed a few tears to trickle down her cheeks. "No, I couldn't. And it's all Bennett's fault. He came back last night, just showed up on my doorstep as though nothing had happened. And do you know where he'd been, Lily? To Paris."

Lily took a sip of her coffee. "So why does that upset you?"

"Because he was with your cousin, Precious Rafferty."

"What!" Lily was so shocked she spilled her coffee.

"That's right. Remember, you told him about her, said she was a rich girl? Well, that's exactly what Bennett's looking for. Another rich girl to marry. Just like Ana Yuan. Maybe the rumors were right and he really did marry his wife for her money. Maybe he killed her for it. Maybe he's thinking of doing the same to your cousin. Who knows . . . with Bennett anything's possible."

"Come on, you can't be serious," Lily said shocked. "You're just upset, that's all."

But Mary-Lou looked blankly back at her. She had lost Bennett and now she'd lost the necklace. Right now she would have killed him if she could have gotten away with it.

"He came over to my place," she said. "We made love. Then I found the phone number written in lipstick on a tissue in his wallet. I have it upstairs, I'll show it to you." She wanted to get Lily out of the cellar in case she noticed that she had not packed a single one of the waiting Buddhas.

Lily led the way back upstairs and Mary-Lou followed her. She had left her purse on the chair by the open cellar door and now she took out the tissue with the number and handed it to Lily.

"Keep it," she said disdainfully. She already had the number and address written in her phone book. "Maybe you'll want to call your cousin someday. And I certainly don't want it."

Lily put the tissue in her pocket. She looked worriedly at her friend. "Are you sure you're all right? Listen, I know what. I was just going for breakfast but I forgot my purse and had to come back. Why don't we go and get a bite and you can pour out your heart to me."

The heart that's made of steel, Mary-Lou thought bitterly, as she closed the cellar door and followed Lily out to her car. *Oh my God, she'd forgotten about the camera.* It was too late now, Lily was waiting for her, she would have to fix it later.

LATER THAT EVENING, MARY-LOU CALLED Bennett. To her surprise, he answered.

"I tried to get the necklace today," she said.

"And you failed. You are letting me down, Mary-Lou. 'Tried' simply isn't good enough, I want the necklace by tomorrow evening. Or . . ."

"Or . . . what?"

"Or it's too late and you and I have lost a multimillion-dollar deal. Better pull up your socks, Mary-Lou."

He rang off and she slumped back in her chair. Real tears coursed down her cheeks this time. Voortmann had given her his cell-phone number and sitting back up, she punched it in.

He answered after a dozen rings. "Voortmann."

His voice was gruff and there was a lot of background noise: loud music, a woman's shrill laughter, the roar of conversation and clink of glasses. It didn't take a genius to figure out he was in a bar and from the tone of his voice, already drunk.

"It's Mary-Lou," she said impatiently. "What news do you have for me, Voortmann?"

"Hah, Mary-Lou. . . . You'll be pleased to know I'm on track, I have a couple of customers interested, wealthy men, Shanghainese. . . ."

"Shanghainese?" she repeated, horrified. This was much too close to home. Rich or not, they were unlikely to be interested because it was too dangerous a game for them. She needed an American, or a Swiss, a true collector, a man with real money, not a rich Chinese businessman.

"I showed them the photo," Voortmann boasted, his words tripping over each other without pause. "Don't worry, they'll get back to me soon."

Mary-Lou cut him off. The man was a drunk. He'd shown the picture around to his cohorts in the bar and they would tell their friends. It didn't take long for rumors to start in this town and she knew she was in trouble.

Tomorrow, she had to get the necklace out of the safe.

TWENTY-FOUR

LILY was in her office filling out some forms for the tax man, when her doorbell rang. She switched on the security camera to see who was there and found herself looking at a blank screen. Disturbed, she pressed the gate intercom and asked who it was.

"Police" was the reply.

She shrank back in the chair, pulses racing, mouth suddenly dry. What had they found? What did they know? Had the antiques smugglers been caught at the airport and spilled the beans? A million questions ran through her mind. Sweeping the papers from her desk into a drawer, she slammed it shut and pressed the button to allow them to enter.

There was only one, a young officer, hard-faced and solemn.

"Madame Song, I have complaints about parking on the street. They say it is your car that blocks the way."

"Ohh," Lily said, relieved. Of course it must be Mary-Lou's car, and since she had no wish to incur a fine or the wrath of her neighbors, she promised to do something about it. Still, she was glad when he left after delivering his warning. And there was no doubt seeing the cop had given her a shock. In her line of business she needed to stay as far away from the law as possible.

The necklace was still uppermost in her mind and she got on the phone and called her Swiss contact. He told her his client wasn't sure, that it might take time, and that anyhow he feared the price might be exorbitant, even for a rich collector.

"We can come to some arrangement on the price." Lily backed down, but still he demurred.

"I'll get back to you" was all he said.

As if to reassure herself that the necklace was worth the fortune she believed it was, she walked down the cellar stairs in her house flip-flops and dialed the combination numbers to open the safe. When the door swung back she stared, stunned, at its contents.

The jewel case was flung to the very back and the packets of banknotes were tumbled untidily to one side. She was a neat woman, everything had its place—and this was not it. She knew she had left it in perfect order with the jewel case in front.

She took it out and, fearful the necklace had disappeared, opened it. Relief made her hands shake. It was still there.

She sank onto a packing crate, clutching it to her heart. Someone had been there. But who? She got to her feet again and went and counted the bundles of money. A substantial amount was missing. She remembered the security camera that was no longer working, and Mary-Lou down here alone so early in the morning when she had known Lily would be taking breakfast a couple of miles away.

But then how did Mary-Lou know about the safe and the combination? Only she knew that and it was written in her brain, not on a piece of paper for anyone to read.

She rearranged the bundles of money and taking the jewel case, locked the safe. She walked outside to inspect the camera and found it had been dismantled. She fixed it and ran the tape back. There was only one person on it and that was Mary-Lou, at eight-o-five on the morning she had found her here, in the cellar, supposedly packing up Buddhas.

She had to find another hiding place for the necklace. Of course she could put it in a bank vault, but that might prove dangerous if things went wrong and there was an investigation. She thought about hiding it under her mattress, but that was the obvious place anyone might look. She heard her little canary chirping out on the verandah and the answer came to her. Of course, she would hide it under the sandpaper base in the bottom of his cage. No one would ever think of looking there.

The bird came and sat on her hand while she accomplished her task, singing with delight at her attention. He was a sweet little creature, she thought smiling. Little did he know he was sitting on top of a fortune.

She decided to set a trap for Mary-Lou, try to catch her in the act. She called her, said she had to go out for the day. She had a meeting with a dealer and expected to be away for several hours.

Would Mary-Lou please come over and hold the fort while she was gone? As she had expected, Mary-Lou said yes.

Then she hurried back upstairs, put on her shoes, smiled at the songbird and drove out of the courtyard. The gates clanged shut behind her.

TWENTY-FIVE

THE first thing Mary-Lou did after Lily called was telephone Bennett. To her surprise he answered on the first ring.

"Well?" he said coldly, and she sighed.

"I'll have it for you tonight," she said.

"Where and what time?"

Mary-Lou hesitated. There was something icy about Bennett that had her scared. Like now for instance, when he'd answered the phone in a tone of such total indifference she felt she didn't really matter. She didn't want to risk being alone with him while she handed over the necklace. She didn't trust him.

"At the Cloud 9 bar, eight o'clock," she said. And this time she was the one who rang off.

She drove over to Lily's house and checked the security camera in the courtyard, but it had been fixed. Once inside she went directly to the cellar. She opened the safe, then stepped back in horror. The jewel case was not there!

She shuffled through the bundles of money, for once uninterested, but the red leather case was gone.

Oh—My—God. Lily had sold it. Or else she'd hidden it someplace new. Hope spurred her on and she ran back upstairs, found the key to Lily's little "home safe" hidden under a pile of sweaters, then opened it. The necklace wasn't there. She rummaged through every drawer and every cupboard. She even looked under the mattress. Nothing.

Still in Lily's bedroom, she stared with empty eyes at her pale reflection in the mirror. She would have to stall Bennett again, keep him guessing until she found out the whereabouts of the necklace. It was her only chance.

Shaking with nerves, she knew she had to get out. Grabbing her bag, she walked out onto the verandah. The canary fluttered on its perch then burst into song. Its shrill warbling seemed to dart like needles into her head and she wanted to kill it. She stood looking at it in its pretty little cage. Her hands shook with fury, but of course it wasn't the bird's fault.

She needed a drink, and praying that the false courage it might give her would get her through the day, she drove to a crowded bar in the Old City patronized mostly by antiques dealers.

She found a free stool, ordered a vodka martini with three olives and, still shaky, sat looking morosely at her unhappy reflection in the mirrored wall in back of the counter.

"Mary-Lou, how are you?"

She turned to look at the man who'd slipped onto the barstool next to her. He was an antiques dealer she knew slightly.

"I'll have the same," he said to the bartender. "So how's business?" he asked, smiling.

Everyone knew everyone else's business and just how well they were doing, except for the secret trading of course. "Much as usual." She took a gulp of the martini.

"There's a rumor about a special piece going around," he said. "Have you heard it? About some jewels. A necklace. Said to have belonged to the Dowager Empress. Now wouldn't I like to get my hands on that!" He laughed loudly. "And so no doubt would the cops."

Mary-Lou's blood ran as cold as the martini. "I hadn't heard," she said. "And where does this rumor come from anyway?"

The man shrugged. "Ohh, you know how rumors are here, but this is said to come from a rich businessman who's been approached to purchase it." He shrugged dismissively again. "Of course no one claims to have actually seen this phenomenon yet, it's all just hearsay. Still, you never know." He lifted his glass. "Cheers," he said, watching amazed as Mary-Lou drank down the rest of her martini in one gulp.

She slid off the barstool. "I'm supposed to be working," she said, heading for the door.

"See you around," he called after her.

Trembling with anger, Mary-Lou headed for Voortmann's office. "The fool," she muttered, sitting in her car, stalled once again at a traffic light. "The fucking crazy drunken fool, I'll kill him."

She found a parking spot down the street, marched angrily to the steel gates and pressed the buzzer. There was no answer and she pressed it again, this time leaving her finger on it. A minute passed. Still Voortmann did not answer. Stepping back she glared up at his windows. There was no light. Where was the idiot?

She marched to her car and drove straight back to Lily's. She had at least to pretend to be working. And she had to gear herself up for her meeting with Bennett that night. And decide exactly what she was going to tell him.

MARY-LOU HAD NOT BEEN ABLE to find Voortmann because he had been visited by two cops that morning.

He'd heard their sirens, looked out of his window, watched the loiterers and petty criminals scattering like prey before a hunter, disappearing into the maze of filthy back alleys. He'd seen the two cops marching toward his door and shrunk back terrified at the sound of the buzzer and their harsh shouts demanding he open up.

Quicker than he'd moved in years, Voortmann had swept the diamond necklace he was working on from his workbench, scooped up a few other stones and shoved them all into the small metal safe hidden beneath the floorboard under his leather swivel chair. He'd burned the photo of the necklace in an ashtray then scattered the tiny fragments across the floor so no evidence could be put together from the blackened pieces.

Heart in his dry mouth, he'd buzzed them in and sat, waiting for the ax to fall. And it had. He was arrested peremptorily on charges of dealing in stolen goods. He was also wanted for questioning in the sale of valuable antiques.

Voortmann was in jail without a lawyer, and knew he would be there for a long time. His whole body was shaking. He wished he had a drink.

TWENTY-SIX

LILY heard the rumor that morning, at a café on the Wuzhong Road, near the Dongtai Antiques Market, whispered over cups of hot green tea and *xiao long bao,* her favorite steamed pork dumplings. Her face flamed with anger and she left abruptly without even tasting the dumplings. She needed to talk to Mary-Lou. And right now.

Bennett heard it on the treadmill at the splendidly equipped gym at the J.W. Marriott Hotel on the Nanjing Road, where he worked out every morning. His half hour was coming to an end as he turned down the treadmill's pace and overheard the low-key conversation behind him. He turned to look and saw that he knew one of speakers. He was the son of a rich businessman who'd made a fortune in the electronics export business. The man was a notorious lowlife, but that meant he had an ear to the underground dealings of the city, and Bennett had no doubt he knew what he was talking about.

Realizing what must have happened, he cursed Mary-Lou, got off the treadmill, took a shower, dressed, and went in search of his car. He was so angry he could have killed her, but before he did, he needed to see if she'd gotten the necklace.

MARY-LOU WAS BACK AT THE house when Lily returned, busily sorting orders for the replica figurines. She had decided to put a good face on things, pretend nothing was wrong, and now she glanced up, smiling as Lily walked in.

"Business looks good this month," she said, flourishing a small sheaf of order forms.

"Stand up," Lily said. "I have something to say to you."

Mary-Lou stood, looking uncertainly at her. "What's wrong?"

"You are a liar and a cheat. You've stolen from me over this past year with no regard for our friendship, nor for the helping hand I offered you when you were down on your luck. I trusted you, Mary-Lou Chen, and you have betrayed that trust. And now half of Shanghai knows about the necklace."

"What necklace?" Mary-Lou interrupted, still trying to maintain her innocence.

"The one you saw in my secret safe. The one you attempted to sell on the low end of the market to the most dangerous of buyers. A Chinese." She put up a hand, palm out, to stop Mary-Lou as she began to protest. "Don't try to find excuses, I know they are all lies. I don't even want to know how you did it. I just want you out of my house. Now."

Mary-Lou saw there was no point in arguing. She had been judged guilty. There was no hope now of her ever getting the necklace. She picked up her jacket and her bag and walked past Lily to the door.

"I won't wish you luck with your sale, Lily," she said bitterly in passing. "In fact I'll do everything I can to sabotage you. Including going to the authorities."

"Do that," Lily retorted. "They'll find nothing. Only a safe with my meager savings, earned from selling replicas to the tourist trade. Don't think I'm a fool, Mary-Lou, because you're wrong. Neither you nor the authorities can ever touch me."

Maybe not, but Bennett Yuan can, Mary-Lou thought as she stormed out of the house for the last time.

EVEN THOUGH SHE WAS ON time, Bennett was already waiting for her at the Cloud 9 bar at eight that evening. She had taken particular care with her appearance, and was wearing a new short cream silk dress and pale suede mules with very high heels. Her eyes were emphasized with bronze shadow and her full lips were glazed their usual shiny red. She wore dangling gold earrings and a gold snake bracelet twined around her slender upper arm. She looked beautiful and she knew it.

"Sit down, Mary-Lou," Bennett said without preamble. "I assume you have the necklace in that purse you're holding?"

"Not exactly. . . ."

"Yes? Or no?"

"No," she admitted. "But tomorrow. . . ."

He threw her a disgusted look and she turned away. Since he hadn't asked what she wanted to drink, she called the waiter to bring her a martini. She was so flustered she forgot this time to ask for the three blue cheese olives and for it to be extra cold.

"You may not have the necklace," Bennett continued, relentless as a hunter with his prey. "But half of Shanghai knows about it. How do you explain that?"

Oh God, like Lily, he'd heard the rumors. She should never have gone to Voortmann, she'd only done it out of desperation.

"You didn't seem interested and I needed to find a buyer quick, so I went to Voortmann. . . ."

"The Dutch diamond cutter? That cheap asshole? My God, he couldn't sell anything worth more than a couple of thousand dollars. Were you out of your mind?"

She hung her head, while the waiter placed the martini in front of her. When he'd gone, she grabbed it and took a long drink.

Bennett leaned across the table. His face was close to hers as he said softly, "To tell you the truth, I wouldn't have believed the story of the necklace if I hadn't found evidence of it myself. Of course Lily Song has it, doesn't she? And now I'm asking myself why go to the salesman when I can go to the source? Lily owns it, my dear, and you do not."

She watched, dumbstruck, as he got to his feet. He didn't even say goodbye as he left.

She had lost her job and lost the necklace. And now she had lost Bennett. The world as she knew it had come to an end.

TWENTY-SEVEN

BENNETT knew that the rumor was rampant throughout the city, fueled by speculation as to how much the necklace might be worth and who had it. He also knew that stolen jewels of that kind of museum quality would be impossible to sell at any of the world auction houses. Only a private collector, someone obsessed with the idea of the fabulous sinister jewel, would be prepared to pay millions and then keep it hidden, taking it out when he was alone, to gloat over it, to handle it, remembering where it had come from. Just the way certain collectors of stolen paintings were reported to do, keeping them locked behind secret sliding panels with electronic buttons only they knew about, that, when pressed, slid away to reveal the treasures meant for their perverse solitary enjoyment.

No one knew better than Bennett that men were strange and this special kind of collector was a rare breed. But not that rare. He had a few ideas.

But for now the bottom had dropped out of the market. It was too dangerous to try to sell. No buyer would even bite. He knew Lily would have to play it safe and hold on to her secret. There was no way she would even attempt to unload the necklace now.

Meanwhile, he was pursuing the easier of the two options that would eventually make him a rich man. He was off to Venice to get married.

MARY-LOU TRIED INTERMINABLY TO CONTACT Bennett in an attempt to salvage their relationship. Finally, in desperation she went to find him at the Marriott gym but was told that Mr. Yuan was away. He'd gone to Europe, the hostess there told her. "To get married," she added smiling.

Mary-Lou thought she would faint. Her heart fluttered and jumped and the girl brought her a glass of water and made her sit down for a while. In fact she had no memory of leaving the hotel, nor of driving home, but she went up to her apartment and locked the door. She stood, trembling by the big window with the crystal for good *chi,* screaming silently, torn apart by Bennett's treachery. She had no one. Nothing. And nothing left to lose.

. . .

BENNETT WAS RIGHT ABOUT LILY. She couldn't attempt to sell the necklace until the rumors had died down. The Swiss had backed out and she would have to wait before she contacted her second candidate.

She sat in her pretty courtyard with its rippling fountain and the goldfish darting, with the perfume of the pink lotus blossoms in the air and her little songbird trilling a melody, and for the first time she wished her mother had never given Tai Lam the necklace. Then she would not have this problem. She had her lucrative sideline with the stolen antiquities, she would have just stuck to that. Sometimes the lure of great wealth moved you to do drastic things. It almost wasn't worth it.

TWENTY-EIGHT

VENICE

THE month had passed quickly and Grizelda had everything perfectly organized: the Basilica; the flowers; the wedding reception at the Cipriani. She had even flown to Paris to supervise the dress and an elegant compromise had finally been reached. Preshy was to wear long mist-colored chiffon and, because it was cold in Venice in November, a sweeping gold brocade hooded cape, lined with bronze velvet and trimmed with fur.

Daria and her family and Sylvie would stay with them at the fourteenth-century Palazzo Rendino, but in keeping with tradition, Bennett was not sleeping under the same roof as his bride the night before their wedding. He'd chosen instead to stay on the Lido across the lagoon from Venice, at the Hotel des Bains, an extravagant fin de siècle monument to luxury, because, he said, he wanted to be able to speed across the lagoon to his wedding like a buccaneer of old.

The night before the ceremony, Grizelda and Mimi threw a party for all of the guests, fifty of them, in the faded gilt luxury of the Palazzo. Grizelda was glamorous in red lace Valentino, and Mimi in apple green chiffon Versace, bustling around, making sure everyone was having a good time. Daria held hands with her bearded professor husband, Tom, who held Lauren the Super-Kid and future flower girl, who was overexcited and a bit cranky.

"Less than 'Super' tonight I'm afraid," Daria said ruefully but Tom said she'd be better when she had some spaghetti in her, it was her favorite food.

Daria of course looked like a blond preppie angel in a tailored cream suit, and looking at Tom, Preshy couldn't help but smile, remembering her description of the time Daria had beaten him down to his undershorts at poker and fallen in love with him, all "pale and professory-looking."

Sylvie wore black. "It makes me look thinner," she said with a regretful sigh, but she was pleased just to be an honored guest and not to be doing the cooking this time around. And the others, mostly friends of Aunt Grizelda's and Mimi's, wore everything that was elegant and in fashion and very probably too young for them. And of course, the bride-to-be was as chic as her aunt could make her, in a dark blue wrap dress that, with her long curly hair flowing free, Bennett said, made her look like a Pre-Raphaelite angel.

Fires burned in the great hearths at either end of the paneled and gilded salon, and candlelight reflected off the lusters in the old Murano chandeliers, illuminating the faded ceiling frescoes and softening the lofty room into an intimate space. A string quartet played Vivaldi, Venice's own composer, and white-jacketed waiters circulated bearing large silver trays of champagne and hors d'oeuvres, while Lalah and Schnuppi yapped and snapped and ran excitedly through everybody's legs.

Outside of the tall windows the canal glimmered in the deepening dusk. "How beautiful it is," Bennett said, standing by the window, looking out at it. "So dark and still."

Preshy squeezed his hand. "Now you understand why I love Venice so much."

He nodded. "Yes," he said thoughtfully. "Now I know."

Soon Grizelda was marshaling the guests down to the watergate entrance to the Palazzo where gondolas waited to ferry them to the restaurant chosen for the prewedding dinner.

Their little flotilla glided down the canal to a trattoria on the Fondamenta Nuevo, with a view over the misty lagoon to the Isola di San Michele, and what may be the most beautiful cemetery in the world. And dinner turned out to be a merry raucous event of silly toasts and singing and too much wine and, amongst other goodies, a terrific seafood risotto that Sylvie said was the best she had ever tasted.

Preshy was enjoying it all, laughing with her friends, when she noticed Bennett involved in a serious conversation with Aunt Grizelda. "Aunt G's reminding him of his responsibilities as her 'son-in-law,'" she said, nudging Daria and laughing. "I'm surprised she hasn't had a little talk with me about the birds and the bees."

Much later, full of good food and wine, she and Bennett decided to walk back alone to the Palazzo Rendino. Arms around each other's waists, they strolled through the narrow cobblestoned *calli* and over the many little bridges, while Preshy talked about her plans for their future life together.

At the street door of the Palazzo, she turned to her future husband. He held her close and she twined her arms around his neck, smiling up into his handsome face. "Tomorrow, my love," she whispered as she kissed him good night.

"Tomorrow," Bennett promised, with a final lingering kiss. "I can't wait."

Preshy watched him walk away, a tall, elegant, handsome man in a dark suit. He turned at the corner and lifted his hand in farewell. He was every woman's dream and, for her, that dream was about to become a reality.

TWENTY-NINE

HER wedding day dawned clear and ice blue. The tranquil lagoon shimmered under a pale sun, ruffled here and there by the froth of a *motoscafo*'s wake. Preshy stood for a moment, alone in her wedding finery, on the Palazzo's embarcadero. She thought she had never seen Venice look more beautiful. Her gondola awaited, moored to the striped pole, its festive canopy swagged with garlands of greenery, intertwined with tiny white blossoms. The ribbons on the gondolier's straw boater floated on the breeze as he came to help her on board and his hand was as cold as the north wind.

She smiled her thanks, settling on the white cushions, arranging her long mist-colored chiffon dress and adjusting the cape's fur-trimmed hood over her upswept hair. She clutched the small trail of honey-colored orchids tighter. She was nervous but happy.

People turned to stare as the gondolier poled along the Grand Canal. At the *vaporetto* stop, the crowd waiting for the water bus waved and yelled good luck and Preshy waved back, smiling. She felt like Cleopatra entering Rome.

Since her uncle Oscar had long since ascended over the mountains to the place he'd assumed heaven was, there was no close male relative to give her away and, despite Aunt Grizelda's protests, she had chosen to ride to her wedding and walk down the aisle alone.

"I'm not a child," she had told Aunt G an hour earlier as they sipped a fortifying glass of fizzy Prosecco in the Palazzo's *piano nobile,* the first-floor drawing room where the party had been held the previous night. This was before Grizelda and Mimi left for the church in their own gondola, complete with the yapping beribboned dogs and a flurry of old friends, all fluffed out in enormous hats and gauzy scarves and furry muffs, glinting with old jewels and shrieking with laughter at shared old jokes.

"I'm thirty-eight years old and I can surely make it to the church for my own wedding," she'd said.

And Aunt Grizelda had sighed, recognizing defeat, something she was not too familiar with. But she had finally given in and now she was waiting in the front-row aisle seat at the gorgeous Basilica di Santa Maria della Salute, along with Bennett and their guests. However, there were no personal guests for Bennett James because he had no family and no close friends. That was why Daria's Tom had agreed to be his best man.

As the gondola slid alongside the Basilica, Preshy stared up at its great glimmering dome. It was her favorite church in all of Venice, a city with surely more churches than any other. There seemed to be one around every corner, each more beautiful than the last. But for her the Salute was special.

She had first been brought there by her parents when she was four years old. She'd been told many times that there was no way she could possibly remember that visit, but she knew she did. She remembered the soaring height of it, a giant's church to a small child. She remembered the rich colors and the glitter of gold and the paintings and the mosaics. And she remembered her mother holding one hand and her father the other as they walked down that aisle to inspect the great altar. It was the only true memory she had of them, and it was because of that memory that she was there today, for her wedding.

Her gold brocade cape billowed behind her as she stepped from the gondola, her face half-hidden behind her soft fur-trimmed hood. A mystery bride, she thought, smiling and feeling like a heroine in a romance novel.

The church was cold and the scent of two thousand roses flown in from Colombia filled the air. Aunt Grizelda hurried to meet her, a flamboyant ageless redhead in a pearly white suit and a vermilion cartwheel of a hat that clashed marvelously with her red hair. She was wearing a diamond brooch Queen Elizabeth might have envied, but Preshy saw there was a frown on her face instead of a smile.

"Come here, darling." Grizelda grabbed her hand and pulled her to one side.

Preshy glanced, astonished, at her. The organist was playing Vivaldi and she knew he was simply marking time until he could segue into the Haydn she had chosen for her walk down the aisle.

"He's not here," Aunt Grizelda said.

"Who's not here?" she asked, bewildered.

"Bennett. My dear, he's not here."

"Oh . . ." She stared, surprised at her aunt. "Well, of course it must be the traffic. He's held up in traffic, that's all."

"We're on the Grand Canal not Madison Avenue." Grizelda gripped her hand even tighter. "And anyway, Bennett's not at the hotel either. I called, Preshy. They said he checked out last night."

Preshy stared, bug-eyed, at her aunt. She clutched her honey-colored orchids in a death grip. Grizelda unhooked her fingers and threw the orchids to the floor. She took both Preshy's hands in her own. They were cold.

Tears stood in Aunt Grizelda's eyes. "There will be no wedding," she said. "Bennett's gone."

Preshy felt as though she were floating somewhere in space. She was aware of Mimi, pale as a lily, and of the shocked faces of Maurice and Jeanne; of the flutter of old friends, glamorous in their big hats, quiet now, watching. Her bridesmaids, Sylvie and Daria hovered, lovely in pale apricot with big anxious eyes. Tom was holding the silent Super-Kid's hand and even the beribboned dogs had quit their yapping.

She looked at them and then at her aunt, still clinging to her icy hands. "There must be some mistake," she whispered. "Surely he'll call, tell us what's happened. . . . We can wait. . . ."

No one said anything.

"We can check the hotel again," she said desperately. "They've made a mistake."

"Oh, my dear . . ." Tears spilled down her aunt's cheeks.

Preshy had never seen her cry before. "Don't," she said, suddenly calm. "Don't cry, Aunt Grizelda. Your mascara will run."

"Oh, *merde* to my mascara," her aunt yelled, suddenly furious. "How *dare* he do this to you? *I'll kill him, I'll castrate him, I'll wring his neck with my bare hands. . . .* "

Daria and Sylvie came quickly and put their arms around her, murmuring that they were sorry, that it was unforgivable, that they loved her; that it would be all right soon.

Preshy said nothing. She was the eye in the center of the storm of anger and sorrow whirling around her; the shamed bride left at the altar. And such a beautiful altar where once upon a time her mother and father had escorted her down the aisle.

She looked around her, thinking of what to do. The guests had converged from all over the world for her small intimate wedding. A reception was to be held at the wonderful Hotel Cipriani across the canal on the island of Giudecca. There was champagne and a wedding cake and more roses flown in from Colombia, and later there was to be a celebratory dinner and dancing.

She got to her feet, icily calm. "It's all right, everyone," she said. "Remember the old saying, 'The show must go on'? The water taxis are waiting to take us to the party, so let's go."

And followed by Daria and Sylvie, she led the way out of the great church and to what, when she thought about it afterward, felt more like a wake than a wedding.

PART TWO

RAFFERTY

THIRTY

PARIS

IT was the thought of winter with its long dark days closing in on her, all alone in her now empty-feeling apartment that got Preshy on a plane to Boston, and to Daria.

She had been home for a couple of weeks, fending off smiling inquiries by neighbors and friends as to how married life was with the curt answer that she wouldn't know, since she was not married and didn't plan to be, and people were either too polite, or perhaps just too kind to ask why, and what went wrong.

At Logan Airport, when she emerged from the tunnel into arrivals, Daria took one look at her, a sorrowful, stringy-haired waif with only one small carry-on bag, and they both burst into tears.

In the car on their way to Cambridge where Daria lived, she handed Preshy a box of Kleenex, glancing at her out of the corner of her eye. "You can't go on like this, you know. You're not the first woman to be dumped, even though yours was at the altar."

"Don't remind me." Preshy gave a little sob and stared blankly out at the rain. "He's never contacted me, you know. Not even a phone call, or an e-mail, to explain. And I'm too proud to try to contact him. Not Aunt G, though, she's had detectives searching for him." She giggled through her tears. "Maybe I'd better hope she doesn't catch him or she'll kill him."

"*Castrate* is a word I also seem to remember her using."

"Anyway, they came up empty-handed. There is no Bennett James living in Shanghai. There's no grand apartment; no James Export Company. And nobody ever heard of him at Dartmouth. Bennett James really doesn't exist. Exactly who he is and why he did what he did, is still a mystery to me, though Aunt G says he was after my money."

"What money?" Daria slammed on the brakes, squealing to a stop at the red light. She turned to smile at the cop in the squad car who'd pulled up next to her. He glared at her. "I didn't do anything wrong," she mouthed at him and he raised his eyebrows and shook his head, wagging a finger at her.

"Oh shit," she said, moving more cautiously as the light turned green, "I'm so caught up in that bastard Bennett I'm not thinking what I'm doing."

Preshy seemed not to hear; she just went on. "That's exactly what I said to Aunt G. *What money?* I don't *have* money. All I have is my shop from which I make a fair enough living but nothing extravagant. But Aunt G said well I looked rich, with my diamonds and my Paris apartment. She said Bennett *thought* I was rich, especially when he found out she was my aunt and I was her only living relative. 'Add it up, girl,' she said to me. 'Ask yourself, as I'm sure Bennett did, exactly *who* is your dear Aunt G leaving her fortune to?' "

Preshy turned to look at Daria, who was concentrating on her driving. "I told her I hadn't ever thought about that. I mean her dying and . . . well you know. Aunt G said it was a good thing I hadn't, because she had no plan for an imminent departure. But then she said she had a confession to make."

Daria took her eyes off the road for a second to look at her. "A confession? What on earth had she done?" She swung the car into the brick driveway—if eight or so feet in front of the small Federal-style house could be given the grandiose title of "driveway." She put the car into park and turned to face Preshy again, waiting for her answer.

"Remember the night before the wedding, when we all had dinner at the lovely little trattoria on the Fondamenta Nuevo?" Daria nodded. "Remember, we were all having such a good time, making silly toasts and laughing at each other's jokes . . ." Daria nodded again. "All except Bennett," Preshy said. "I noticed him deep in conversation with Aunt G, and this is what she told me that conversation was about.

"She said she was telling Bennett how some madman almost sideswiped her off the Grande Corniche a few weeks previously. She told him she thought she was going to die and her first thought was that she was damned if she was going to miss my wedding. Bennett laughed, and then he said, 'Maybe it was Preshy, trying to get you out of the way so she could get her hands on your money.'

"Aunt G said she was a bit surprised but she put him straight right away. 'Oh, no,' she told him. 'Preshy knows she won't inherit. She's a strong girl, and she's clever. I want her to make her own way in the world. Everything I have will go to my favorite charities: to the Princess Grace Foundation, and children's cancer care, and to take care of retired racehorses. Mimi's doing the same thing,' she said she told him. 'Only with her it's retired racing greyhounds.'

"Bennett became very quiet after that, and I remember now, he did fall kind of silent on the walk back to the Palazzo as well. It was I who was doing all the talking, making all the plans."

"The bastard." Daria reached out so they could hug across the center console. "You're like that heroine in the Henry James novel. What was it called? *Washington Square?*"

Preshy managed a grin as she mopped her eyes prior to going inside and meeting her goddaughter. "Well, I'm in the right town for it," she said, sniffing.

Lauren the Super-Kid, hurled herself at Preshy as soon as she stepped through the door. Preshy grabbed her, swinging her up high, groaning at how heavy she was getting. "You're growing up on me, Super-Kid," she complained, "and you promised you wouldn't."

"I'll try, Aunt Presh, really I will," Super-Kid said between giggles.

Tom was waiting for them, shabby as ever in that professorial style, in an old sweater and cords. Not only was Tom an esteemed physics professor, he was also a good cook and he had dinner ready and the table set with a mishmash of old dishes and paper napkins.

The great room that was the entire ground floor of the house with its inner walls removed to make a combined kitchen, dining and living area, was in its usual chaotic state, with coats flung where they had been taken off, kid's wellies and toys scattered all around and a fine layer of dust over all. A fire burned in the grate with its carved white-painted surround, and Neil Young played on the stereo while Anderson Cooper mouthed silently on the turned-down TV.

Tom was opening a bottle of inexpensive Côtes du Rhône with an old-fashioned corkscrew, the bottle clamped between his knees. He pulled the cork out finally with a smart pop and grinned at Preshy.

"Welcome to the lovelorn," he said, pouring her a glass and handing it to her. "Here, baby, drown your sorrows in this."

"Oh, Tom . . ." She gazed at him, all wide teary eyes, and he shook his head.

"Gotta get over it, baby. Bennett's not coming back and if he tried it would be over my dead body. Or his," he added darkly, pouring wine for his wife and handing Super-Kid her orange juice.

"Here's the deal," Daria said, as Preshy moved a PlayStation and a couple of sweaters and plumped down on the sagging slipcovered sofa. "We've decided to allow you exactly thirty 'Pity Days.' That means thirty days when you can cry and moan and complain and feel sorry for yourself. After that—it's all over. Get it?" She moved the PlayStation further over and sat down next to her friend. "Get it, Presh? Thirty days to wallow in self-pity, then you've got to get on with things. Now, as they say, Deal? Or No Deal?"

Preshy glanced doubtfully at her. "Okay. I'll try."

"Trying is not enough. You *will* do this, Presh. You'll survive. No one's died, no one got hurt—only your pride and your feelings. You have a life, you *will* move on. Promise me that—and we promise to listen and be sympathetic for exactly thirty Pity Days. Okay?"

Preshy took a deep breath. She wasn't sure she could live up to it but she promised anyway.

Tom raised his glass. "Bravo," he said. "I'll drink to that." Then he took the pot of boeuf bourguignon off the stove, plonked it down on the trivet in the center of the table, sliced up a crusty loaf, took out the salad and said, "Come and get it, kids."

Preshy thought it was the most comforting food she had ever eaten, right there with her true friends, surrounded by their love and free to weep into her wine on the first of her Pity Days.

DARIA AND SUPER-KID CERTAINLY KEPT her busy on another more innocent level, taking her to the Montessori school and for walks by the Charles River, shopping in the Harvard Coop for sweatshirts and baseball caps, browsing in the book and CD stores. But when even that and the Pity Days got on top of her, she escaped alone to the tumbledown family cottage on Cape Cod with its youthful happy memories.

She walked the winter beach alone, staring at the crashing waves. And later, huddled on the deck, swathed in sweaters and blankets to stave off the cold, she asked herself over and over how the man she believed loved her could do such a terrible thing.

But then she began to ask herself a few other questions. Like, did she really still love Bennett? Had she ever loved him? Or had she simply been "swept off her feet" by his looks, his charm and the sheer romance of their long-distance affair? Swept away by the telephoned "good night sleep wells," from wherever he was in the world; by the flowers; the champagne; the country weekends; the engagement ring? Thinking about these things, she realized that Bennett had swept her along to their wedding so quickly she'd never seriously even thought of their lives together as a married couple. And thinking back, she did not really know that much about Bennett, only the things he'd told her—all of which she had believed.

For instance, the story of his childhood in the orphanage, and the reason for his lack of friends; and about the successful business he ran and that she'd understood made him a lot of money. She still didn't even know his home address; all she'd ever had was his e-mail and his cell phone because he'd told her he was on the move all the time.

Thinking back, she knew she had been a fool. Much as she didn't want to believe it, Bennett James, or whoever he really was, had never loved her and he'd only been marrying her for her supposed money. She didn't know which hurt more. And unlike the woman in the novel *Washington Square,* she couldn't lock him out of her home, because he'd simply disappeared into thin air. Or wherever men like him disappeared to. More like Marbella, she thought bitterly. Wasn't Spain where all good con men went to spend their ill-gotten gains?

Feeling a little better, she returned to Boston and told Daria she had come to terms with everything. She'd taken the punch and was back on her feet again, and the hell with Bennett James.

"You've still got some Pity Days left," Daria reminded her, and as if on cue, she burst into tears, and sat weeping on the sofa.

"You've got to get a life, Presh," Daria said, sadly. "It's time to move on."

THIRTY-ONE

PARIS

A week later Preshy was back home. It was a bright December morning but the shutters were closed and she was lying on the sofa. There was no sound in the room. No phones ringing, no music playing, even the traffic on the rue Jacob was inaudible behind the closed shutters. Normally, she would have been taking her coffee and baguette at the café, but she couldn't even face that. She was deep into day twenty of the thirty Pity Days Daria had allotted her. And deep into the same old questions. Was Bennett really that wicked? Had he really intended to marry her for her supposed inheritance? How could he do that? He was so nice, so loving, so charming.

Last night Aunt Grizelda had called, begging her to come and stay. "We could go skiing," she promised, making Preshy laugh because the idea of Aunt G skiing at her age (though she still didn't know exactly what that was) was scary, and anyhow she knew it was an excuse and that her aunt simply wanted to keep an eye on her. "I want to make sure you don't do anything 'foolish,' " was what Aunt G had said.

"No man is worth doing anything 'foolish' for," Preshy had promised her, but it still didn't change the facts. It was stalemate with nowhere to go. Except, as Daria and Sylvie both told her, *Forward.*

Sighing, she slid off the sofa and went and looked at herself in the ornate gilt-framed Louis XVI mirror over the mantelpiece. She did not like what she saw. Her unmade-up face was pale and splotchy, her eyes red-rimmed, her untrimmed hair a tangled mess. She dragged her fingers through it, skewering it away from her face, wondering why she had to have curls when the rest of the world had straight. Life just wasn't fair, she thought, as a tear stole down her faded cheek. She stared at the horror reflected in the mirror.

"You idiot," she told her image sternly. "*Wallowing* in self-pity. Do you think Bennett is doing this? Oh no. No, he's certainly *not.*" She let her hair fall back around her face. "Well, I can't do anything about Bennett," she said out loud. "But I can do something about my hair."

An hour later she was sitting in the chair at a salon on the boulevard St. Germain. "Cut it all off," she told the stylist.

He picked up a curly lock, running it admiringly through his fingers. "Are you sure?" he asked. "We could maybe just cut it to shoulder length, start there, see how you like it. Short is a drastic change."

"That's exactly what I want," Preshy said firmly. "A drastic change. I want to look like Audrey Hepburn."

Two hours later she didn't look exactly like Audrey Hepburn, but it was certainly a drastic change. Her mane of curls was gone and in its place was a sleek copper-blond cap, short in the nape with deep bangs dangling in her eyes. She ran her hands through it, shook her head, fluffed it with her fingers. Somehow with the new haircut, she felt freed from the past, freed from the weak romantic woman she had once been. *This* was the new Preshy Rafferty.

As if to emphasize the point, she took the Métro to the boulevard Haussmann and Galeries Lafayette where she headed for the lingerie department. An hour there netted a treasure trove of pretty underthings that, even though she was the only one who was ever going to get to see them on, somehow made her feel better. Next, she tackled the cosmetics and perfume section. Sitting in a chair at the Chanel counter, she had her face made over by a dazzlingly chic young woman who looked at her coppery hair and insisted she buy a pink lipstick and a pink blusher. "It will make your skin glow," she assured her. And longing for "a glow," Preshy bought them.

Hovering over the perfumes she thought how long she'd been wearing her scent. Probably ten or twelve years. She'd always thought of it as *her* "signature" the way many women do, though of course it was worn by millions of others. Now she was about to change that too. Hermès was her choice. 24 Faubourg, it was called, which was the Hermès address on the Faubourg St. Honoré. "It was Princess Diana's favorite perfume," the saleswoman told her, making Preshy wonder for a moment if she had made the right choice. After all, Princess Di hadn't had too much luck with men, had she?

She thought about buying an expensive pair of shoes but decided it was the cliché "woman-scorned" purchase, and she definitely didn't want to be a cliché, so instead she took a taxi over to Verlaine where she found Sylvie busy assembling her menu for the evening.

Sylvie looked up as Preshy pushed through the door and gave her a little twirl.

"Well?" Preshy asked.

"You look completely different. I don't know whether it's the hair or the pink lipstick, but I think I like it."

"Think?" Preshy's face fell and she shoved her hands worriedly through the short cap of hair. "This is the new me and you're not knocked out by it?"

Sylvie laughed. "Of course I am. It's just that I hardly recognized you. After all, I've never seen you without that great cloud of hair. I can see your face now though and it looks pretty good."

Preshy preened under her praise. "I took one look at myself in the mirror this morning and said, 'This is it.' I'm moving on."

"I like that. Anyhow you're almost at the end of your Pity Days, it's time you got yourself together. Come on, let's go get a cup of coffee and a sandwich. I'll leave the boys in charge. They can't do too much damage in half an hour. At least I don't think so."

. . .

IT WAS GOOD SPENDING TIME with Sylvie, but later that night, alone again in her apartment, Preshy was back thinking about Bennett again, remembering the *Bateau Mouche* and the intimate dinners together at little neighborhood restaurants; remembering the way she would catch him looking admiringly at her; and the welcome whenever he came "home" to the rue Jacob. *Oh God,* she thought, hating the silence, *what am I going to do?*

She was browsing the Internet when she came across a picture of a bunch of big-eyed, big-eared, skinny little kittens. She melted just a little, looking at their innocence. On an impulse she called the breeder, who said there were no kittens left but that she had a slightly older cat, nine months, who had been returned because the buyer was allergic to her.

"I'll take her," Preshy said immediately.

"Maybe you want to meet her first, see if you're compatible," the breeder said doubtfully, concerned that her cat was going to a good home.

"Oh, we are. I know we are," Preshy replied. After all, hadn't they *both* been rejected? Both been "returned to sender" so to speak. And so the seal point Siamese with the fancy kennel name of Mirande de la Reine d'Or became hers.

Preshy drove to pick her up the next day, a cream and chocolate beauty with eyes more glitteringly blue than any sapphires. She brought her home, safe, or so she thought, in a cardboard traveling box on the backseat. But she hadn't reckoned with the ingenuity of a Siamese determined to get out and, Houdini-like, soon the cat was sitting on her lap. "Maow," the cat said, gazing earnestly into Preshy's face at the red light.

"And Maow to you too," she retorted, grinning. And so Maow the cat became.

And of course, Maow immediately knew all Preshy's secrets. She confessed her troubles into her delicate chocolate ear and the cat gazed knowingly back, rumbling with faint purrs of sympathy.

The next day she bought a special and rather chic, and supposedly Houdini-proof, travel carrier and took the cat to visit the aunts in Monte Carlo.

Lalah and Schnuppi galloped, barking, toward her as she stood in the foyer clutching the carrier to her chest, while from behind the safety of the mesh door, Maow yowled and stared them down.

The Aunts watched, bemused, as their dogs, tails tucked under, ran and hid behind them.

"Of course the cat's obviously a substitute for a man," Aunt Grizelda said suspiciously.

"And what's so wrong about that?" Preshy demanded. "At least I know where I am with her."

And faced with that unblinking blue Siamese stare, the dogs went and sat quietly on the floor while Maow emerged and curled triumphantly on the sofa, in pride of place between the Aunts.

It was, Preshy thought, patting her new short hair that Grizelda said made her look like a shorn duck and smiling at the people she loved, a good new start.

THIRTY-TWO

SHANGHAI

If Lily had thought to make a list of people she never expected to hear from again, Bennett would have headed it, with Mary-Lou in second place. So she was surprised when she heard from each of them in turn.

Bennett did not call; he came round to see her, ringing her doorbell at seven o'clock one evening about a month after she had fired Mary-Lou. When Lily checked the security camera at the gates she was astonished to see him standing there, holding a large bouquet of Casablanca lilies. Pressing the intercom she said curtly, "What is it you want?"

He said, "I'd like to speak to you, Lily. If you can take the time, that is."

At least he was courteous, and besides she was curious to see what he wanted, so she opened the gate and let him in. She stood on the verandah as he walked toward her, the flowers held in front of him. Like a peace offering, she thought, wondering if he had come to plead Mary-Lou's case.

He said, smiling, "I meant to be in touch with you earlier but I've been in Europe. I thought when we met that night, we had so much to talk about and not enough time to say it all."

She wondered what on earth he believed they had in common, but then Bennett was a practiced charmer.

"Won't you please invite me in?" he said, giving her that gentle heart-melting smile that, despite herself, she reacted to.

He walked up to the verandah steps, stopping to admire the canary. Her heart beat so loudly as he stared into the cage with the hidden necklace, she was surprised he didn't hear it.

"A songbird with no song," he said as they went into the house. "How unusual."

The scent of the lilies he was holding wafted toward her, potent as French perfume. "Lilies for a Lily," he said. "But I'm sure I'm not the first man to say that to you."

She took the flowers and with a brief unsmiling thank-you, dropped them onto a small side table, then waved him to a chair.

"I suppose you've come to plead for Mary-Lou," she said, sitting on the sofa, watching him carefully.

His brows rose in surprise. "Why should I do that? What happened to her?"

She thought he was a good actor. "You mean you don't know?"

"I don't know what you're talking about. I told you, I've been away, and anyway things are finished between us." He shrugged dismissively. "It was fun while it lasted but it was time to move on."

"Then that makes us equals. Mary-Lou no longer works for me. So, may I ask exactly why you are paying me this visit?"

"I was impressed when I met you. Ah, this is no flighty party girl, I thought. This is a woman of substance. A woman I could do business with."

"And what business would that be?"

"I have a proposition to put to you," he said, choosing his words carefully. "You have an exceptional piece of property. Rumors are rife in this city, but so far only you and I and Mary-Lou know where the truth lies."

"I've heard the rumors. But they have nothing to do with me."

"That's not what Mary-Lou said. And I have good reason to believe her."

Lily's cheeks flared with heat. Mary-Lou had betrayed her one more time. She said, "I think you should know that I fired Mary-Lou because she was stealing from me. A disgruntled ex-employee will say anything to exact revenge. I'm sure, as a businessman, you are aware of that."

"I'm also aware that she was telling the truth, and that she tried to sell the necklace through Voortmann, the third-rate diamond cutter, who then tried to sell it to a rich Shanghainese no-good, who in turn opened his mouth and blabbed the story to the world. And if he had not, I would not be here, because by now I'm sure you would have already sold it."

He shook his head, looking regretful. "Too bad your deal with the Swiss agent fell through." He put up a hand to stop her protests.

"Don't ask me how I know. It's unfortunate that the rumor came between you and your deal, but now that leaves the way open for me to offer you a new one. And this time, Lily, the deal is foolproof."

Lily's stomach was churning with nerves. She went to the kitchen and came back with a bottle of San Pellegrino and two glasses. She filled them both, took one and sat back in the elmwood chair, watching him.

"Shall we drink a toast to our collaboration?" Bennett lifted his glass, sure of himself now.

"Tell me exactly what you are talking about," she said, sipping the water.

"It's very simple. You have the corpse necklace. I have a buyer. My buyer is prepared to pay a substantial deposit pending delivery, but he needs to know that what he's contracting for is exactly what he gets. And therefore I need to see the necklace. I also need the written documentation of its authenticity." He took a drink but his eyes never left her face. "And of course, we need to come to a decision on the price. My guess would be about thirty million."

That was far more than Lily had anticipated and she guessed he was exaggerating in order to impress her. He was pulling the old con-man game of telling her what he thought she'd want to hear, dangling the millions in front of her like the carrot before the donkey, so she would leap for it, mouth open. Did he really think she would hand over the necklace and say, "Okay, let's take it"?

"Fifty-fifty." Bennett leaned forward eagerly. "You'll never have to sell fake antiques again. What do you say, Lily? Are we partners?"

"You'll have to look elsewhere for your partner, Bennett, because I don't have this corpse necklace. And I don't know who does. Rumor is all it is." She got to her feet, dismissing him. "Just a rumor."

Bennett also got up. He went and stood close to her. Fear shot up her spine as his suddenly cold eyes bored into her.

"Oh, but you do have it, Lily," he said softly. *"And I intend to get it. Any way I can. Why don't we just do this the nice way, make a deal, become partners? Or do you prefer the other, less pleasant way? Because you know what, Lily? No matter what it takes, I intend to have that necklace."*

He stepped back and the charming smile flashed again. "There! Now we've discussed it. I'll leave you in peace, give you time to think it over. Let's say until this time tomorrow night?"

His threat dangled in the air between them and Lily remembered Mary-Lou saying maybe Bennett had killed his rich wife for her money. Shivering, she now believed he was capable of it.

"Until tomorrow night at seven," Bennett said. "And then we'll see what to do."

Her heart leapt into her mouth again as he stopped to look at the little bird on his way out. Panicked that he might catch a glimpse of the red leather case, she quickly pressed the buzzer to open the courtyard gates. And then, without turning to look at her, he was gone. But she knew he would be back. And that he meant business. And she was afraid.

THIRTY-THREE

MARY-LOU had purposely befriended the young woman receptionist at the health club Bennett frequented. They met for drinks, had the occasional lunch together, did a little shopping; though that was becoming rarer now that she was out of work.

That same evening Bennett called on Lily, they were in a crowded bar called Sasha's, just off the Hengshan Road, in the mansion once owned by the famous Soong family, at one time the most powerful in all of China. By a strange coincidence, one of Charlie Soong's beautiful daughters was Mai-ling, who'd married Chiang Kai-shek, and whose party shoes were said to have been adorned by a pearl stolen from the Dowager Empress Cixi's crown.

But now the Soongs' old home housed a smoky bar, crowded with noisy young people who had no thought for its history. In fact Mary-Lou doubted her new friend was even aware of it. Over martinis the girl told her that Bennett was back in town and that the "wedding" had fallen through.

"He changed his mind," she said, smiling over the rim of her glass at Mary-Lou, whom she greatly admired for her beauty, her expensive jewelry, and her chic style. "I'll bet he just couldn't forget about you," she added. "And now I'll bet he's yours for the taking."

Shock, then relief, left Mary-Lou limp. But remembering the last time they had met, she knew Bennett was finished with her. And that she had vowed she wanted revenge, no matter how, where, or when.

Leaving her new friend at the bar, she drove over to Lily's. Outside the gates, she telephoned her. When Lily answered she said, "I need to speak to you. Please let me in."

Lily put down the phone.

Mary-Lou called again. "You must see me," she persisted. "It's about Bennett."

Lily hesitated, but then she thought about Bennett's threat and she pressed the buzzer that opened the gates. She stood at the top of the stairs on the verandah, arms folded, as Mary-Lou walked past the fountain and the serene goldfish pond with the scent of the lotus blossoms. Lily thought how beautiful she was. And how treacherous.

Mary-Lou stood at the bottom of the three steps leading to the verandah, looking up at her. Recognizing her, the canary bird gave a little trill and Lily quickly covered his cage with a cloth. "I need to speak to you," Mary-Lou said.

"So, speak."

"Bennett's back in town. He went to Europe to get married. Remember you told him about your cousin, Precious Rafferty in Paris? The one who inherited all the family money? Well, it was her he was marrying. But something went wrong and it fell through. Maybe she didn't inherit enough, and to Bennett a woman without a lot of money isn't a woman worth marrying. Or killing. Not after what happened with the Yuans."

Bennett marrying Precious? Lily smelled danger, not only for herself but also for her cousin. She suddenly knew, without a shadow of a doubt, that Bennett would kill her to get the necklace. She had to get out before seven tomorrow night when he planned to come back for her.

She said, "I don't want to hear any more, Mary-Lou. Please go away." And she opened the gates again, waiting for her former friend to leave.

Mary-Lou stared numbly at her. She'd thought Lily would be shocked, that she would join her in seeking vengeance on Bennett.

"He knows about the necklace," she said quickly. "He wanted me to get it from you, that's why I broke into your safe. . . ."

"I know," Lily said wearily. "And you know what, Mary-Lou? I don't care anymore."

Mary-Lou's shoulders sagged as the hope that somehow she could make an ally of Lily left her. She walked back through the courtyard, then turned to look at her.

"He'll kill you for it," she said as the gates clanged shut behind her.

. . .

LILY PACED THE BAMBOO FLOORBOARDS, filled with fear. She had to take the necklace and leave Shanghai, and she had to warn her cousin. Then something occurred to her. Precious was in the antiques trade. *She* might know collectors who'd be interested in the necklace. She was the only one who could help her now.

She looked up Rafferty Antiques in Paris, found the e-mail address and sent her cousin an urgent message.

"I need your help," she said. *"It is imperative I speak to you."* She calculated the time difference and the flying time and how to prevent Bennett from finding her, and wrote: *"Please book me into the Ritz Hotel for one week under your own name. I will be arriving Saturday on Cathay Pacific. This is urgent and it involves you. Please do not let me down."* She signed it, *"Your cousin, Lily Song."*

Next, she called Cathay Pacific and booked the earliest flight to Paris, via Hong Kong, leaving the following morning.

She walked back out onto the verandah and looked at her little canary bird, sleeping in his ornate bamboo cage. She removed the red leather case from under the sandpaper base, put it in a zip-lock bag and hid it temporarily in the crisper section of the refrigerator. Then she carried the canary to her next-door neighbor at the nightclub, told him she had to leave urgently for Paris, and asked if he would take care of the bird while she was gone.

That done, she went to the cellar, selected one of the fake

warrior statues and packed it. She called a courier to pick it up immediately and ship it on to Cousin Precious.

She went back to the house and hastily packed her bags, then arranged for a limo to pick her up the next morning. Knowing she wouldn't sleep, she sat bolt upright and frightened, staring at the TV until dawn came. Very early that morning, she would be gone.

THIRTY-FOUR

BACK at her apartment Mary-Lou was forced to face the fact that soon she would no longer be able to afford it. She had some money in the bank but certainly not enough to maintain her extravagant lifestyle for much longer. Yet she loved her home, with its Italian sofas and modernist paintings and the whorish red and black bedroom in which she had spent so many happy hours. She stared at the view of the Huangpu River outside the floor-to-ceiling windows and for the first time in many years she felt like crying.

As a child she had been shunted from place to place by her shiftless parents and this was her first real "home." She had paid for it herself, admittedly with stolen money and stolen jewels, but it was all hers. She refused to end up like her parents who had trailed the city, dragging their few possessions and her with them, while they looked for the cheapest accommodation on the meanest streets.

She *knew* Lily had the necklace and now she regretted she hadn't stolen it while she had the chance.

Sitting at her chic little desk, she flipped through the messages on her laptop. There was only one and that was from the girl from the health club, whom she had no wish to see again. But when Mary-Lou worked with Lily, she'd had an expert hack into Lily's computer, so she would always know what was going on. Now, she typed in the password and suddenly she was looking at Lily's e-mail to Precious Rafferty in Paris.

Stunned, she realized that Lily was taking the necklace out of the country and that she must be going to ask her cousin, the antiques dealer, to find a buyer for it. She wondered for a moment what to do, but then she knew she had only one chance.

She called Cathay Pacific immediately and got a seat on the same flight as Lily. She knew Lily would be flying business and booked coach for herself. She also knew that first- and business-class passengers were always boarded before the others, and that their section was separated by the entry area, so there would be no chance of Lily seeing her. At the airports she would be sure to keep well out of sight and be amongst the last to board and disembark, and anyhow Lily would never suspect she was being followed. She'd be so caught up looking for her baggage and in a hurry to get out, she wouldn't even know she was there.

A while later she sat back on the black silk bedspread in her poppy red bedroom. The steam had gone out of her and now her plan seemed ridiculous. Even if she managed to find the necklace in Lily's hotel room, how would she sell it? She shook her head, despairing as all her wild plans seemed to disappear out the window, no doubt flying across the Huangpu River into the arms of the Dragon River Gods, who she was sure now were against her. She could not do this alone. She would have to go crawling back to Bennett. She would have to tell him she knew where the necklace was going to be and how they could get it, and take a fifty-fifty deal. Even though she didn't trust him it was her only chance.

She dialed Bennett's number, praying that he would answer. When he did, she was taken aback because she'd half-expected him not to.

"It's Mary-Lou," she said in a low scared voice. "I have something to tell you."

"I don't want to hear it," he said abruptly.

"It's about Lily . . . the necklace . . ."

"So?" He wasn't wasting words on her.

"She's running away to Paris. She's going to see Precious, she's taking the necklace . . ." The story poured out of her.

She told him she was following Lily to Paris, that she would get the necklace somehow; that they still needed each other; that they would go fifty-fifty as he had suggested . . .

"When does she leave?" he asked.

"Tomorrow morning. I'm booked on the same flight."

"I'll get the flight out via Singapore," he said. "I'll call you when I get to Paris."

"Bennett?" He still hadn't said what he planned to do, nor had he agreed to her fifty-fifty deal.

"I'll call you when I get there," he said again, and rang off.

Mary-Lou didn't trust him. She was afraid. She opened the bedside drawer and removed the Beretta. Then she remembered, of course there was no way she could take a gun on a plane. But she didn't trust Bennett. She *needed* a gun.

She was a very small cog in the wheel of Shanghai's crime machine, but she knew a man who was "connected." She called him now, told him what she wanted and that she would need it delivered to her in Paris. It would cost, but the deed was done.

Next she called the Paris Ritz and made a reservation. She could not afford it, but she needed access to Lily's room. Then she packed a bag and, like Lily, waited for morning to come.

THIRTY-FIVE

PARIS

UNUSUALLY for the time of year, Preshy had had a busy day, with a dozen potential customers, at least two of whom had expressed strong interest in her Etruscan bowl, even after she had told them honestly that though it had been broken and carefully pieced together, she believed it might be a later fake. No matter, the price was good and she was pleased. At four o'clock, with the cat under her arm, she ran up the stairs to her apartment, slamming the door quickly behind her to keep out the cold.

Maow sat on the kitchen counter, watching as Preshy fixed herself a cup of hot chocolate—from Angelina's on the rue de Rivoli, and the best in Paris. Throwing all thoughts of calorie counting to the wind, she piled on the whipped cream, gave it a stir and, with the cat at her heels, put on a CD of Joni Mitchell singing about her failures at the game of love. She sank into the cushy sofa with her feet on the coffee table, sipping the hot creamy, silky smooth chocolate, with her eyes closed, dreaming of a new life. One where she would be strong, and svelte and glamorous, and in charge of her own destiny. Hah! She drained the mug and sat up again. Unfortunately real life never worked out quite like that. It was much, much harder.

She went to her desk, did the day's necessary paperwork, thought about calling up a friend, going to a movie, decided against it, and turned on the TV. Bad weather was approaching, the solemn-faced forecaster said. Snowstorms were expected. She sighed. There went her business. She hoped the Etruscan bowl buyers came back before the storm began.

She checked her e-mails; the usual business stuff—but then something strange. An e-mail from Cousin Lily Song.

She read Lily's message. Then she read it again, still not quite sure she understood. *Lily* was coming to Paris? Book her into the Ritz—but under Preshy's *own* name? Why on earth would she want her to do that? It was "*imperative*" she speak to her. Something that "*involves*" her. . . .

Puzzled, she sat back in her chair, almost squashing the cat who had settled in comfortably behind. Of course it was exciting to think she would finally get to meet Lily, but why so mysterious? And why was it *imperative* she speak to her? And why the hotel room under *her* name? Since Lily would be arriving tomorrow, she guessed she would soon find out.

Feeling foolish, and a little like a fraud, she dialed the Ritz and booked the room as requested. She said she would be arriving tomorrow from Shanghai, and that she would stay one week.

Before she went to bed that night she pulled aside the curtain and checked the sky. It was clear and starry. With a bit of luck the forecasters had gotten it wrong again and Lily's flight would arrive on time. She couldn't wait to meet her and find out what this was all about.

THIRTY-SIX

At ten o'clock on the freezing January Saturday morning that Lily was to arrive, Preshy was in the crowded café near the rue de Buci breakfasting on her usual double café crème. Inside, the café's windows were steaming up, and outside the first flakes of snow were beginning to fall. Shoppers at the street market wrapped their woolen mufflers tighter and walked a little faster.

Preshy's newly short hair began to frizz in the steam and she dragged her fingers exasperatedly through it. She'd imagined being short it wouldn't frizz, but no such luck.

Today was the last of her Pity Days and she thought with relief she was finally getting over it. Or at least coming to terms with what had happened. She had called Daria and Sylvie and told them

Lily was coming, and they'd both thought it was interesting and were dying to know what she was like, and what she wanted.

In fact Preshy was looking forward to Lily's visit, even though her e-mail was mysterious. Looking worriedly at the now heavily falling snow, she hoped it wouldn't delay Lily's flight, and she made a quick call to Cathay Pacific just to make sure it was still on time, which it was.

She drained the last dregs of coffee and stood up to leave, wrapping her winter coat closely around her. Actually, it was Grandfather Hennessy's old sheepskin, a shapeless olive green garment that reached down to her ankles and could easily have wrapped twice around her, but it kept her warm and that was all that mattered. She pulled a Russian-looking fur hat with droopy earflaps over her newly shorn hair, momentarily regretting the loss of the long curls that had at least kept her neck warm. Then with a goodbye wave to her regular waiter, she prepared to brave the elements.

Head down against the blowing snow, she switched her thoughts to the cheese she would buy from her favorite market stall. Ten minutes later, carrying a paper parcel carefully wrapped and tied with string and containing a slab of fromage de montagne and a Banon from Provence prettily encased in chestnut leaves, and with a crusty loaf fresh from the baker's oven under her arm, she headed for home, tearing off bits of the bread to eat on the way.

The pretty apartment seemed to welcome her. Its tall narrow windows let in streams of snowy gray light and the old-fashioned radiators hissed warmth into the long L-shaped room. The cat unfurled herself from the cushioned window seat and ran toward her, slender legs crisscrossing, elegant as any runway model. Preshy crouched, allowing the cat to put her two front paws onto her shoulders, then leap up.

"Okay, Maowsie," she murmured. "Time for work, though I don't think we'll be getting many customers today."

She was right. Traffic down the usually busy street was light and the snow was already settling on the narrow sidewalks. In the shop, the cat parked herself on a cushion in the window, watching the snowflakes falling and loftily acknowledging the admiring smiles of the few passersby who stopped to say hello through the glass, while Preshy dusted her stock then took care of some paperwork. At five, without a single customer, not even those interested in the Etruscan bowl, she closed up the shop and, carrying Maow, who was trying to catch the fat snowflakes, went back upstairs.

She put a match to the kindling in the fireplace, waiting until it caught before arranging a couple of small logs over it, then went into the kitchen and cut a slab of the montagne cheese. "Heaven in the palm of my hand," she said, biting into it.

She and the cat established themselves on the slouchy gray linen sofa watching the flames dance and the snow falling even more heavily outside. Sighing, Preshy picked up the phone and dialed the airline one more time, resenting the unknown Lily for potentially dragging her out on a lousy Saturday evening when she would much rather have stayed home. But this time she was told that the airport was closed and that the Cathay Pacific flight had been diverted to Frankfurt.

As soon as she put down the phone, it rang. Lily, she thought, snatching it up. But it was Daria calling from Boston.

Before Preshy could even speak, Maow had climbed onto her shoulder and was yowling, Siamese-style, down the line.

"Oh my God," Daria groaned, "now the cat answers the phone."

"Actually," Preshy said, "I'm teaching her to say Mama."

"What?"

"Mama. She already says Maa . . . all she has to do is repeat it."

"Jesus, Presh, you really need to get a life."

"I can't," she said gloomily. "It's snowing, the airport's closed and I'm waiting for Lily to show up. I thought it was her calling, but it's only you."

"Thanks a lot! Here I am taking time out of my busy life to call internationally to see what's up, and you wished I was someone else."

Preshy laughed and Daria joined in. "It's your final Pity Day," she said. "I see you're making the most of it."

"No, no, really, I'm fine," Preshy said, hoping it was true. "I'm just bored, Daria," she added wistfully.

"So, close the shop for a few days and fly back here again."

"I can't. Besides, I told you, the airport's closed. And anyhow, I'm supposed to wait for Lily to contact me. Last I heard the flight was diverted to Germany."

"Then there's no point in waiting in, is there? At least call Sylvie and go out for a drink."

"It's Sylvie's busy night—Saturday—though I guess in this weather the restaurant won't be *that* busy. Still, I know her, she won't leave until closing time anyway, just in case some stragglers brave the storm and show up."

"So why don't you go over there for dinner?"

"I can't go alone, Sylvie would worry about me."

Daria laughed; she knew Preshy was right and that Sylvie would be hovering in and out of her kitchen, checking to see if there was anyone suitable she could introduce her to.

"Listen, sweetie, I meant it when I said why not come back here for a few days, after Lily's visit. Tom's going off to St. Louis for a conference, Grandma can take care of Super-Kid—and you and I would be free. We could do a spa weekend, get ourselves fit."

"I am fit," Preshy said. "And anyhow I can't just close up shop and leave."

"Why? Is business that brisk in snowy weather?"

Preshy had to admit it wasn't, and even Paris's everlasting fairs and conventions, fashion weeks and aircraft shows didn't really affect her business. Interior designers to the rich, and well-heeled tourists who fell in love with something displayed in her window, were her sort of customers.

She twirled a short strand of hair in her fingers. Even with Lily's surprise visit, a long gray winter seemed to stretch interminably in front of her and she was tempted. Maow shoved her nose against her face and she stroked her absently. "Anyhow, I can't leave Maow," she said finally. "And the airport's closed and when it reopens flights will be impossible."

Daria sighed. "I'll accept the second excuse, but not the first. Perhaps I'll just come out and see you instead. Meet Lily."

"Great. Except—no flights."

"Okay, okay, I'll wait and see. Meanwhile, I love you, baby."

"Love you too. And thanks."

Preshy's thanks were not only for Daria's offer but also—thanks for loving her. She needed all the love she could get, and unfortunately there seemed to be too little of it around.

She thought about Sylvie. After being jilted at the altar, she hadn't so much as felt like looking at another man, but Sylvie, good friend that she was, hadn't let it rest there.

"It's like getting back on the horse after you've taken a fall," Sylvie had said, dark eyes flashing. "I know I'm not one to talk," she'd added, hands on her plump hips, "but hey, I'm a chef and I have an excuse. My hours are hell and the only men I ever meet are other chefs. With their egos who needs that! But you, Preshy Rafferty, have no excuse."

"Maybe I don't like nice guys," Preshy had told her gloomily. "I'm doomed to fall for the scoundrels."

But now, despite what she'd said to Daria, she was lonely.

She decided to call Aunt Grizelda. Mimi answered.

"What are you doing home at eight o'clock on a Saturday night in Paris?" she demanded.

"Mimi, it's snowing."

"And since when did a little snow stop a girl from having a date?"

Preshy sighed. "It doesn't, Mimi. The fact is, no one asked me." She heard her answering sigh.

"I give up," Mimi said and went off to find Grizelda.

Aunt Grizelda got on the phone. "Darling, why don't you get on a plane and come down here? I'll throw a party for you," she said loudly. She always spoke loudly on a phone, never, Preshy believed, having gotten over the notion that the further the distance the louder one must speak. "I promise there are all kinds of fascinating people here at the moment."

Yeah, and all of them sixty-five or over, Preshy thought, gloomily. She had to give Aunt G credit for trying though. She explained about the snow and the airport closing, and then she told her about Lily.

"You mean after all these years she's just showing up?" Grizelda said, astonished. "But why?"

"I've no idea. All I know is that she said it was imperative she speak to me. And she had me book her into the Ritz—under my name."

There was silence at the other end while Aunt G thought about it. "I don't like it," she said finally. "The woman's after something, trust me."

"But *what,* Aunt G? I have nothing she could possibly want. The only thing we have in common is Grandfather Hennessy and that our mothers were sisters. Oh, and that we both deal in antiques, of course."

"Hmmm, she wants *something,* Preshy, you can be sure of that. We haven't heard a word from the Song family in fifty years and now all of a sudden your cousin's showing up on your doorstep."

"Actually, she's not. Her flight was diverted to Frankfurt. I haven't heard a word from her since her e-mail."

"Well, I have no doubt you will. Meanwhile, why not forget about her and come on down here? I don't like to think of you being alone on Saturday night."

"You sound like Mimi's echo," Preshy said, smiling as she promised to think about it. Then she said goodbye, blowing her aunt and Mimi a special kiss.

Alone in the quiet apartment with the clock ticking and the snow still falling she was almost tempted to take her aunt up on her invitation, simply pack the cat into her carrier, fling some clothes into a duffel and just take off. But her little Smart car, which looked like a regular small car but with the back chopped off making it even smaller, though a dream for city parking was certainly not meant for long sorties down the Autoroute du Soleil to the South of France in the snow.

She prowled the apartment restlessly. It was too quiet. The cat, curled up on the back of the sofa, snuffled gently as she slept; a log slipped in the grate, sending a low blue flame spattering into the embers; and the radiators hissed into the silence. Preshy thought forlornly about the bread and the cheeses and the glass of wine awaiting her in her lonely kitchen. The hell with it, she wasn't *that* French. She needed comfort food. She needed steak and fries.

She grabbed her bag, slashed on the new pink lipstick, ran a comb through her short hair, slung on Grandfather Hennessy's ancient olive green sheepskin coat and thrust her feet into her old furry après-ski boots. Dropping a quick kiss on the cat's sleeping nose, she headed out in search of food and . . . well, other people, she supposed.

THIRTY-SEVEN

FRANKFURT

LILY was waiting at carousel 5 in the baggage claim at Frankfurt-Main. She tapped a French-manicured fingernail impatiently against the metal cart, searching the vast hall, half-expecting to see Bennett materialize.

She had the uneasy feeling of being followed, that someone's eyes were on her. Her black Tumi bag slid down the ramp and she grabbed it. Then, tight as a drum with nerves, she hurried through the green customs light and into the arrivals terminal, wondering, since Paris was out, what to do next.

She looked at the departure destinations listed on a flickering screen. Many flights had been canceled. But she didn't want to stay in Frankfurt in case she was right and she was being followed. She would have to go south where there was no snow. There was a flight to Venice departing in an hour. It was the last place Bennett would ever think of looking for her. If she were quick, she could make it, otherwise she'd be spending a nervous night in an airport hotel.

Glancing nervously over her shoulder and pushing the luggage cart, she ran to departures. She was lucky, they had not yet closed the gate, and she was able to buy a ticket. Tension flowed out of her as the plane took off. She leaned back, eyes closed, thinking about the last few days. But she still didn't feel safe.

At Venice's Marco Polo Airport she called the Bauer Hotel. It was out of season and they were quiet, and she was able to get a room. She took a water taxi there, hardly noticing the beauty all around her because she was too busy watching a second water taxi she suspected was following her. But when she got out at the hotel, it went right on past, and again she breathed a sigh of relief.

Exhausted, she fell into bed. She would call Precious later and they would talk business.

She slept like a dead woman.

WITH THE UNEXPECTED DIVERSION AND then Lily's quick decision to take a flight to Venice, it hadn't been easy for Mary-Lou. Still, by always keeping to the back of the line and many rows away on the aircraft, somehow she managed it.

She had followed Lily's *motoscafo,* instructing the driver to go on past when Lily got out at the Bauer. A half hour later, she returned there, checked in and got a room on the same floor.

She called Bennett, who she found had been diverted to Lyon and told him what had happened and where they were. Then, exhausted, she lay on the bed thinking of what to do next.

Suddenly she sat bolt upright. She had forgotten about the gun. It was to have been delivered to her in Paris—and now she was in Venice. Without even taking into consideration the time difference, she called her contact in Shanghai. He warned it would cost her extra, and, as she knew, his financial dealings were always paid up front. Wire him the money, he said, and she would have the gun the next day.

Mary-Lou made the arrangements, depleting her savings even further, and then went back to bed. She was worn out and she knew she would need all her strength and all her wits, to pull off what she was about to do.

THIRTY-EIGHT

PARIS

LA Coupole was one of the few places in Paris to remain open in the storm, and despite the bad memories it held for Preshy, it was a good place for a woman alone.

Snow blistered her windshield as she crawled nervously down the boulevard du Montparnasse, but for once parking was easy because anyone with any sense—and who wasn't lonely—had stayed home.

The place was almost empty and she took a seat in a quiet corner, well away from where she had sat with Bennett. She ordered a half carafe of red and the *steak frites,* and was sipping the wine, wondering where Lily was and when she would contact her, when the waiter showed a man to the table next to her.

Of course he wasn't Bennett, but nevertheless her stomach

did a few somersaults. Her eyes met the stranger's briefly, then indifferent, he looked away.

Preshy sighed with relief. This man was no beautiful Bennett James. He was very tall and thin and wiry, brown-haired and brown-eyed behind gold-rimmed glasses, with a narrow face, a stubbled jaw and a bitter expression. She noticed he wore a wedding ring. Hah! No, no, no! *This* man was certainly not out to pick her up. He probably had a nice little wife waiting at home somewhere in, she guessed, the U.S.A. Chicago perhaps. Or Oklahoma. He probably worked for an international law firm and was here on business. The only thing that marked him as different from her analysis was that he wore jeans and a black turtleneck sweater under a leather jacket, and that he ordered oysters, Belons, and a double vodka on the rocks that he downed about as fast as she'd ever seen a man do before, then immediately signaled for a second.

Hmmm . . . a man pissed off at the world if ever she'd seen one. He then proceeded to order a fish called Saint-Pierre, one of her own favorites, thereby redeeming himself in her eyes for the glugging of the first vodka. The second was going down rather more slowly, though he'd also ordered a bottle of good Bordeaux, which was far too heavy for the fish and established him in her mind, part Frenchwoman that she was, as a philistine.

Looking around the almost-empty restaurant though, she wondered uneasily why he had chosen to sit next to her. But then she told herself she was being ridiculous; it was just a coincidence. After all it was a public place and anyone could sit anywhere they wanted. It was her newfound paranoia clicking in, that was all.

She sipped her wine, thinking gloomily of the icy drive back to the rue Jacob in her tiny Smart car, and her lonely apartment. She wondered again where Lily was. Taking out her cell phone she checked her messages. Zero. She tasted her steak and poured the last of the wine into her glass.

"Do you mind?" The stranger spoke. He was holding up a pack of Marlboros, a question in his eyes. She didn't like it, but this was France and smoking was permitted, and she shrugged it was okay. Behind the glasses his eyes were dark, intense. And weary. And he *was* American. She pushed the straggling bangs out of her eyes, wishing she'd spent a little more time on her appearance before dashing out into the storm, then she asked where he was from.

"Charleston, South Carolina," he said, surprising her, though now she recognized the soft slow drawl. She told him she was American and had gone to college in Boston.

He glanced indifferently at her. "I'm stuck here in Paris thanks to the weather," he said. "No flights out—no flights in."

"If you have to be stuck somewhere, Paris isn't so bad." She glowered at him from under the untidy bangs, resenting him for casting even an implied slur on her beautiful city.

"I should never have come here in the first place."

He stared into space, sipping the good Bordeaux and smoking his cigarette, looking, she thought, like a man who couldn't wait to get out of there. A silence had fallen between them and she returned to her fries, always a treat. She was definitely a carb addict. Except she also liked lobster and caviar, and then there was cheese of course. . . .

"Why are you so pissed off?" She asked the question in that direct way she had, wishing immediately, as she always did, that she had not said what she'd just said, because it was really none of her business.

"Why am I pissed off? Hah!" He laughed bitterly. "I just spent three hours sitting on a plane, on the runway, waiting for the wings to be de-iced. Turned out there were insufficient de-icers and by the time our turn came it was too late, a full-blown blizzard was blowing. I was disembarked and thrown out into the unwilling arms of Charles de Gaulle, along with thousands of other abandoned travelers—and all of them in search of a hotel room. Of course, there were none."

Preshy's "oh" was sympathetic.

"Someone gave me the name of a second-rate—okay let's call it a *third*-rate—joint, where I finally got a room. If you can call it that. It's no more than a cubicle really, with a plastic shower jutting from one corner and a cell containing a toilet and the smallest washbasin known to man."

He paused and took a gulp of his wine, eyeing her. "Since I'm six three this only added to my torture. There was a kind of a bonus, however. Normally traffic would have been zooming past my window but thanks to the snow—and it's the only thing I can thank the snow for—only a few cars and trucks managed to chug past. But there was no bar where I might have drowned my sorrows, no restaurant where I might have assuaged my hunger. So—here I am." He looked at her again. "So much for fuckin' Paris," he muttered under his breath, but still Preshy heard him.

"Ohh," she said again, a little nervously. "Well at least you found La Coupole," she added, trying to brighten things up.

"I've been here before," he said curtly. "I knew it was a place where you could get a solid drink, a decent bite and a bottle of good wine. I guessed it was open. If not, I was about to slit my wrists."

She stopped in midbite, looking at him, alarmed, but to her relief he smiled.

"Sorry," he said, "it's been a long day. A long week."

"Ohh," she said again, busying herself with her steak, which was blood-rare, thin as a washboard and almost as tough, but that was the way the French liked it.

"So, what d'you do, here in Paris?" He asked the question as though it was a mystery what anyone did in Paris, besides, she supposed, the tourist concept of femmes fatales and fornication.

"I work," she told him brusquely. "Antiques."

His eyes swiveled her way. He seemed to take her in properly for the first time. As though she were actually a real person, she thought resentfully. But then she thought, *Hey, it's okay, at least he's not like Bennett.* But she wasn't going to go there. Her Pity Days ended at midnight.

"I own Rafferty Antiques on the rue Jacob," she said, suddenly chatty. Loneliness and the wine were getting to her; here she was picking up a total stranger again. "I deal mostly in early artifacts, Etruscan, Roman, Greek."

"Then you must be quite knowledgeable."

"I like to think so. I learned at my grandfather's knee, you might say," she added. Then, while he ate his fish, she went on to tell him the story of Grandfather Hennessy and the family history, and about the Aunts, and about how she came to live in Paris. It must have been the wine talking, she thought, draining her glass, because she also told him the story of the Songs and the mysterious message out of the blue from Lily.

"So what d'you think she wants?" he asked, lighting up another cigarette.

Preshy said she had no idea, frowning as she wafted away the smoke. He apologized and put the cigarette out, then picked up the half-full bottle of Bordeaux, took a clean glass, poured the wine and set it before her. Sliding him an approving glance, Preshy thanked him. Crass smoker and vodka guzzler he might be but he was generous and at least he knew not to serve good wine in her used glass.

"And what do you do?" she added, suddenly curious.

"I'm a writer."

"So what do you write?"

"Novels."

"Really?" She eyed him respectfully. "Should I know you?"

He threw her a withering glance. "Why?"

"I mean, well, know your name?"

"It depends on whether your taste runs to mysteries."

"So what *is* your name?"

"Sam Knight."

Of course. He was well known. "My best friend Daria's your biggest fan," she said.

"And what about you?"

"Oh, I never have time to read." It was his turn to grin. Of course it wasn't true but mysteries were simply not her style.

"Just what every author wants to hear," he quipped, refilling his glass. He lifted it in a toast. "To the solving of the Lily mystery," he said with a smile that lifted his face from the lines of bitterness into a sudden boyishness. "And anyhow, what's your name?" When she told him, he laughed. "I could never call any woman 'Precious,' " he said. "And besides, you don't look like one. You're definitely a Rafferty."

"Okay," she agreed, pleased that he didn't see her as a wimpy Preshy. She wondered how old he was. In his forties obviously, but which end of forty? "And here's to your stay in Paris," she said with a smile that she hoped lit up her own face with a new girlishness she certainly didn't feel.

"A stay I could live without."

"At least you have to admit we have good wine."

He laughed again, a deep throaty laugh that made her join in. "I should never have come here in the first place," he said.

"Then why did you?"

His eyes behind the gold-rimmed glasses searched hers for a moment. He was not laughing now. "I was looking for the past," he said quietly.

Then he got up abruptly, said he was off to the bar to have a cigarette in peace, and left her sitting there, as alone as when she came in, and wondering what on earth he could have meant.

She finished the glass of wine, which was as good as it gets, and when Sam Knight came back, knowing there would be no taxis, she offered him a lift to his hotel. "It's on my way," she said when he told her it was on the rue de Rennes.

She noticed him grin when she put on the ancient sheepskin

coat, and she felt sure he was still grinning behind her as she clomped her way out in her gigantic furry boots. Embarrassed, she thought he might at least have done it to her face.

Outside, Sam Knight stared at her little Smart car. "This is it?" he said in a stunned voice. And it was her turn to snigger as he attempted to fold his lanky frame into it. He didn't grumble though, *and* he waited patiently while she checked her messages again. Nothing. If Lily was in Frankfurt she certainly wasn't telling her about it.

"No luck?" he asked, as she crawled and slid in low gear down the empty boulevard, and onto the rue de Rennes.

"No *Lily*. And therefore no solution to the mystery," she added with a grin. She knew she would never see Sam Knight again but she was glad she'd met him. He'd helped take her mind off Lily and also off her awful sense of "aloneness." If she stretched things a little she could even tell Aunt G and Mimi she'd had a date tonight.

She felt sorry for Sam, though, when she stopped the car outside his seedy hotel. Almost sorry enough to offer him the sofa at her place, but then she told herself quickly she didn't even know the guy. It flashed through her mind again that it was odd he'd come to sit right next to her in the half-empty restaurant. He might be another Bennett after all.

Sam got out of the car. He leaned back in to her, looking into her eyes, almost as weary as his own by now.

"Thanks a lot, Rafferty," he said. "I appreciate the lift. Without you, I'd have had to walk all the way back."

"You're welcome. And thanks for the company."

"Good luck with the mysterious Lily Song." He straightened up to close the car door. Then he bent back in again. "Why don't you give me your phone number?" he said, coolly. And Preshy thought if ever a man was cool it was Sam Knight. *Impenetrable* might have been a better word. "Just in case I ever get back to Paris," he added. "Then you'll be able to fill me in on the Lily story."

"Everybody's got a story," she said, and he smiled.

Still, he had a good smile, Preshy thought as she scrambled in the general chaos of the car looking for something to write on. She found an old card from the local florist and wrote her name and number on the back of it. He put it in his pocket, slammed the door and with a brisk wave was gone.

BACK HOME AND IN BED with Maow snuggled on her pillow, she called Sylvie and told her all about her evening.

"About time you met a guy" was her friend's tired response.

But Preshy knew Sam Knight was only a traveler, passing through on a snowy winter's evening.

THIRTY-NINE

SHE was awakened by the sullen gray light filtering through the curtains. Struggling from sleep, she remembered Lily and immediately called the airline. She was getting pretty fed up with the whole thing by this time. She was told the flight had landed in Frankfurt the previous evening and that all the passengers had disembarked there. Charles de Gaulle had now reopened but there was a backlog due to the canceled flights and it was complete chaos. And no, Ms. Song had not contacted the airline to try to reestablish her flight to Paris.

As she put down the phone, Maow leapt onto the bed, making the little grunting sounds that meant she was hungry, so she got up and filled her dish—an Hermès dish, a gift, of course, from Aunt Grizelda. Then she showered, dressed and went out for her coffee, slushing through the piled snow, smiling and feeling like a little kid on a no-school day. She expected Lily would contact her sometime soon. Lily did not, but Sam Knight did.

SAM WAS LYING ON THE narrow hotel bed, a half-empty bottle of vodka on the nightstand next to him.

He groaned, turning to the look at the limp orange curtains and the glimpse of steel gray sky behind them. He thought about his beach house on North Carolina's Outer Banks, raked by cold winds and storms at this time of year, but always beautiful.

It was the place where he used to do his writing, away from the social whirl of New York where he had an apartment on Gramercy Park. But he had not written anything in three years, and who knew if he ever would again.

He reached for the vodka and took a long drink. Another long, empty day in Paris—a city he had no rapport for—stretched interminably in front of him. Except now he had made contact with Precious Rafferty. He thought about her, in her ancient green sheepskin overcoat and big boots, blond hair tangling over her eyes, which he was surprised to find he also remembered were an icy aquamarine blue. He remembered her direct questions, her big hands and her high girlish laugh, and . . . He thought for a minute, searching for the exact word. The *innocence.* That was it. But was she as innocent as she looked? That was the question.

Retrieving the florist's card from his jacket pocket, he dialed the number she'd scribbled on it.

She picked up on the first ring. "Lily?" she demanded breathlessly.

"Rafferty, you're not still waiting for the mystery woman are you?" he said.

"Yeah." She obviously recognized his voice. "I'm getting sick of it though. Anyhow, why are you still here?"

"I can't get a flight out to New York. How about I take you for lunch instead? After all, it's Sunday."

Preshy didn't hesitate. "Pick me up in half an hour," she said. "I know just the place for a day like this."

FORTY

THE snow was pure and crisp underfoot and there were flurries in the air, whispering past Sam's face as he walked to the rue Jacob. The golden city of Paris had turned to silver, sparkling with a magical icy refracted light, but Sam did not notice. In fact he would rather have been anywhere else with or without snow.

He found Preshy's place easily enough and stopped to look in her shop window. He thought the place looked like a grotto with its soft light and faded pink walls, though he did admire the marble head of a boy. He looked innocent, the way he had himself when he was that age, he supposed with a wry smile. Now he was forty-two, not old yet, but the years and life experience had left their mark on him in the tight lines that ran from nose to mouth, the creases around his eyes, the weariness. It seemed a long time since he was young. Was it really only three years?

Shrugging off the past, he pressed Preshy's bell and was buzzed into the courtyard. She was waiting for him at the top of a flight of stone stairs that he guessed led to her apartment.

"Look," she called joyously, pointing to the paulownia tree. Every branch was rimed with a line of snow and thin icicles dripped like candles from the tips. "Did you ever see anything so beautiful?" she asked reverently. "I wish I could preserve it like that forever." Then she laughed and said with a little shrug, "But I say that every spring when the buds are bursting, and then again when the petals fall. I just love my tree."

He stood looking at it for a long moment. "It is," he said finally, "the loveliest thing I've seen in Paris."

"Hmm." She surveyed him from the top of the steps, arms folded over her pale-blue-sweatered chest. "Then perhaps you ought to try looking a little harder. After all, you're in the most beautiful city in the world."

He climbed the steps toward her. "Oh? And who says so?"

She laughed. "I do, of course. Who else's opinion would you trust?"

He found himself laughing with her. "Okay, so what if I buy you lunch and you show me some of your particular bits of Paris that you think are so beautiful."

"It's a deal." Preshy beamed. He was a bit of a downer but he had possibilities and that beat "charm" anytime. No chance of being swept off her feet here. "Meanwhile come in and meet Maow while I get my coat."

The cat was sleeping in her usual place on the window seat overlooking the street. She opened an indifferent eye and she and Sam surveyed each other for a brief moment before she closed it again. He was equally indifferent. He was a dog man himself and in his opinion cats were alien beings, too cool for their own good. He helped Preshy on with the sheepskin coat that weighed, he said, astonished, about a ton.

She explained that it was her grandfather's, and that he had been as tall as Sam but much heavier. "He wore it every winter of his life, as far back as I can remember," she said. "But it's still the best coat for weather like this." She smoothed it doubtfully with her fingers. "I hope you don't think I look too scruffy."

Sam laughed out loud. He couldn't remember a woman ever saying anything like that. Usually they just wanted to know how good they looked. "Not *too,*" he said, still grinning, "but we'd better not go anywhere smart just in case they want to throw you out."

She laughed then too, wrapping a long blue woolen muffler jauntily twice around her neck, leaving the ends to dangle to her knees. She noticed he was still wearing the turtleneck and jeans and leather jacket from the night before. "Anyway, you don't look so hot yourself," she said, inspecting his stubbled jaw.

He ran his hand across it, apologizing. "They threw me off the plane but my luggage stayed on. All I have is what was in my carry-on, enough to get me through an unexpected stopover, but I forgot the razor."

She studied him again for a long moment, head to one side, making him wonder uneasily what she was thinking.

"It's cute," she said. "You might want to think about growing a beard."

"Hah!" he said. "It's obvious you've never read any of my novels, otherwise you'd have noticed the author photograph. The one with the beard?"

"Ohh, well . . ." She beamed at him. "There you go. That's why I didn't recognize you in La Coupole."

He took her arm protectively as they walked down the icy steps and across the courtyard. "I get the feeling," he said, "that you have an excuse for everything."

"You're probably right. Daria says I lack a sense of reality, that's why I ended up . . ." She stopped suddenly. She'd been about to say, "that's why I ended up dumped at the altar in Venice," but she suddenly remembered she was talking to a stranger and it was none of his business.

"Ended up . . . what?"

"Oh, ended up with an antiques store. I guess it's easier dealing with the past."

"Not always," he said curtly.

It was her turn to stare. He'd mentioned the past last night, said he'd been looking for it in Paris. She wondered again what he meant.

"I thought we'd go to a little place I know on the Île St. Louis," she said. "It's a bit of a walk but it's so lovely, and it's a treat to see a traffic-free Paris."

"As long as they have good wine."

"They do, as long as you promise not to drink a good Bordeaux with your fish."

"But I like red wine with my fish," he protested. "Whenever I'd go fishing off the Outer Banks, I'd grill my catch on the beach and we'd share a bottle of good Carolina red. They make some pretty decent wines in Carolina now, you know. Maybe not like Bordeaux, but good."

They lingered on the Pont de la Tournelle, watching the barges and the strollers along the edge of the slow-moving brown river. It reminded Preshy of the tour boat and the night she'd met Bennett.

"Have you ever taken a tour of Paris on a *bateau mouche*?" she asked Sam abruptly.

He gave her a withering glance. "Isn't that for tourists?"

She'd had this conversation before—only with the roles reversed. "And you're *not* a tourist?"

"Not exactly. I am—no, I *was*—a man on a mission."

He was watching the boats emerging from under the bridge and she stared at his profile, wondering what he was all about. He was surely not giving anything away. In fact all she knew was that he was a mystery writer and that he liked good red wine.

"It's fun to be a tourist sometimes," she said wistfully.

He turned his head and their eyes met. "I remember," he said. "I was a tourist, once upon a time." He took her arm. "Come on, it's too cold to linger here. Where's this restaurant you like so much?"

It was a dark little cave of a place. The wooden door opened onto a small black-and-white-tiled foyer with a pair of swagged red velvet curtains sheltering the dining room from the drafts. Old blackened beams crisscrossed the low nicotine-yellow ceiling and clumps of fake red roses topped tables that were covered with sheets of white butcher's paper. Small-paned windows had red velvet pelmets and a fire blazed in a big rough-stone chimney. It smelled of roasting lamb and wine-rich gravy and was as welcome on a freezing Sunday as Santa at Christmas.

It was the kind of place where a bottle of the house red already waited on the table and to Preshy's surprise, Sam did not send it back and request a wine list. Instead he poured it into their glasses without even tasting it first. "Remember, I'm trusting you," he said with a smile as they clinked glasses. She watched him anxiously as he took the first sip. The responsibility was weighing heavily.

"Almost as good as the Carolina red," he said, making her laugh.

The proprietor, small and pale and skinny and not at all a good advertisement for his food, bustled forward with the daily menu. "You must have the soup, *madame*, *m'sieur,*" he said. "It's lentil with ham, very good for a cold day like this. And then I recommend the lamb, the whole leg roasted *à point,* until it's just pink with the juices flowing. Of course it comes with the *flageolets,* the little flat green beans, and a *tian* of potatoes *forestière,* cooked with garlic, onions and mushrooms in a little stock."

Sam's eyes met Preshy's. "Let's do it," he said and she nodded enthusiastically.

The soup was as good as the owner had promised and sent little squiggles of heat from her mouth all the way down to her toes, and even to the tips of her fingers. She could feel her cheeks growing pinker and she took off the muffler and put it on the chair next to her bag. She looked at Sam, still with a question in her mind. "So, you know all about me," she said. "Now, how about you?"

"What do you want to know?"

"Hmmmm . . . well, who you are."

"You already know that."

"No, I don't. I know what you are, what you do. But I don't know *who* you are."

He gave her a withering look. "And you're telling me I really know who *you* are, Precious Rafferty, antiques dealer with a Paris apartment and Grandfather's coat, a cute haircut and a pair of aunts who sound like Auntie Mame in duplicate?"

Of course he was right; she hadn't told him *who* she really was. After all, they were practically strangers. "Maybe I was getting too personal," she admitted. "But you know where I live. Can't you at least tell me about that house on the beach where you drank Carolina red?"

He sat back as the proprietor removed their empty soup dishes. "I've owned that house for ten years," he said. "It was love at first sight and I bought it with my first royalties. It's outside of a small village—I guess you'd call it a small town—one of those strings of little places that line the coastline. The house is kind of isolated, set back on stilts above the dunes in a patch of saw grass and sea pinks, sheltered from the wind by a shaggy border of the tamarisk trees I planted myself, and that are now ten feet tall. It's just a gray-shingled cube, fronted with glass to catch every nuance of that ever-changing sea, and with a wraparound covered porch for long lazy summer evenings."

He fell quiet and Preshy thought he must be feeling homesick.

"You speak like a writer," she said. "The house is coming to life as you tell me about it."

But when he looked at her, his eyes behind the glasses were sad. "The house is as simple inside as out," he said. "Bleached wood-plank floors, pale rugs, a comfortable sofa or two. A giant urn filled with twisted branches stands in the fireplace in summer, and in winter, like here, the fire seduces you into sitting before it, watching the flames instead of its rival, the ocean, that you can hear pounding savagely on the sand while the wind whistles through the tops of the trees. The house is like an island," he added softly, "my own personal island, where everything is perfect and nothing can ever go wrong."

"And did it?" As usual, the question was out before she even thought about it. She apologized hurriedly. "Sorry, you just described it so evocatively, I felt as though I was in the middle of a story."

"You were, though it's not a story that will ever be written." He refilled their glasses as the proprietor bustled back with their lamb, then returned to the kitchen and came quickly back with the steaming dish of potatoes and a sauceboat of *jus.*

Looking at Sam's wedding ring, Preshy was dying to ask about his wife, but this time she had the sense not to. If he was such a devoted husband he would have mentioned her by now.

Sam tasted the lamb. He looked up and smiled at her. He was a different man when he smiled. "This is wonderful," he said.

"Didn't I promise you?"

"I can see you're a trustworthy person. Even the beans are good, and I was a kid who hated vegetables."

"But now you're all grown-up you've got more sense."

He laughed. "Looks like it. But you know what? I forgot to ask about Lily."

Lily's name came at her out of the blue and Preshy was surprised to find she had also forgotten about her. "Haven't heard a word," she said, tasting the potatoes under their thin golden crust and smiling with delight. "I have no idea where she is. She might at least have called, Frankfurt is not exactly a million miles from here. But she was so mysterious anyway, I wouldn't be in the least bit surprised if she never showed up. Except . . ." She thought for a moment. "No, that's not true, I *would* be surprised if she didn't show. She said it was urgent. That she *had* to speak to me. It was something that involved me, she said." Preshy shrugged. "Though since we've never even met, how it could be anything involving me I simply don't know."

"It'll be some family thing," Sam said. "She's probably heard you inherited Grandfather Hennessy's coat and wants to get her hands on it."

They laughed together, really laughed this time, clinking wineglasses again across the table.

"I'm enjoying this." Sam glanced approvingly at the now-crowded little room. "It's real, not at all like that big 'Paris' out there."

"But that big Paris is made up of hundreds of little places like this. It's like your Outer Banks, you have to know it to appreciate it, other than just its beauty of course. And you can't deny that my city is beautiful."

He stared at her across the table, taking in her flushed cheeks, the steep slide of her cheekbones, the light eyes under the tangled golden fringe that was beginning to curl slightly in the heat. "I admit, Paris is beautiful," he agreed.

"And when you finally get a flight to New York, will you go directly to the beach house?"

To her surprise, he lifted a dismissive shoulder and said, "I haven't been there in years." Then he signaled for a second bottle of wine, changing the subject abruptly to what they should order for dessert.

"There's only one thing," she exclaimed. "The apple tart, of course, with vanilla ice cream. I happen to know they get their ice cream from Berthillon, right here on the Île St. Louis. It's simply the best."

They enjoyed another glass of wine and their apple tart with the best ice cream in the world, though Sam said, personally, he was a Häagen-Dazs fan, then they lingered over rich dark coffee into which he poured enough sugar, she said, to stand a spoon in.

FORTY-ONE

A while later, they shook the beaming proprietor's hand, promising to return, then wandered out into the gray light of a chilly late afternoon. This time they didn't linger on the cold bridge but hurried back through the maze of small streets to Preshy's apartment.

She stopped at the courtyard door and turned to look at him. "Thank you for a lovely lunch," she said. "It was fun."

"Surprisingly, it was. Thanks for coming, Rafferty. You were good company."

"Good company for a lonely man," she said, recognizing that, in fact, that was exactly what he was. He gave her a long bleak look, then he turned and walked away.

Again, she had said the wrong thing and, feeling bad, she called after him. "Look, you can't just go back and spend the evening in that awful hole of a hotel. Why not come on up? We'll have some more coffee, play some music, maybe watch a little TV. Whatever you need to pass the time in Paris until your flight." He stood, looking at her, obviously undecided. "No obligation," she added, giving him a winning smile, hoping he would come because she was lonely too.

He walked back to her. "Thanks," he said.

As they crossed the courtyard the concierge emerged from her ground-floor lair. "A package came for you, Mademoiselle Rafferty," she said. "Special courier delivery. And on a Sunday. It must be very important," she added with a sniff. "Anyway, I told them to leave it outside your door, and naturally I signed for it."

Surprised, Preshy thanked her. She wasn't expecting anything, but there was the parcel, actually a crate, about three feet by two, addressed to her. There was a lot of Chinese writing on the labels and she saw it came from Song Antiquities in Shanghai.

"It must be from Lily," she said, opening the door as Sam hoisted the crate and carried it inside.

He deposited it on the kitchen floor and Maow came running to see what it was. Crates and boxes were the cat's specialty, new places to jump into, to curl up in, to hide. She sniffed it suspiciously, then sat back on her haunches looking expectantly at Sam, waiting for him to open it, while Preshy rummaged in a drawer and came up with a screwdriver.

"I'm dying to know what's in it," she said.

Sam got busy with the screwdriver while she fixed the coffee, setting out cups on a black lacquer tray, remembering he liked sugar, pouring milk into a little jug. She went into the living room and put a match to the fire, watching the smoke curl from the blackening paper, waiting for the kindling to catch before putting on a log. She thought it was quite the little Sunday domestic scene. She heard the crate crackling under Sam's onslaught and hurried back to the kitchen. He'd gotten it open and was removing a brown-paper-wrapped parcel.

"Oh, do hurry," she cried, excited. "This is like Christmas."

Sam peeled back the brown paper, uncovering yet another layer, this time a padded blanket. "Must be something special," he said.

It was a terra-cotta figurine and Preshy saw instantly it was a fake, a direct copy of the famous ones in Xi'an, China. She ran a hand over it, seeing the telltale marks of the commercial mold it had been cast from.

"Why would Lily bother to send me something like this?" she asked, puzzled. "They sell them in tourist shops around the world. In fact I'll bet you could even get them here on the boulevards where the North Africans sell all this kind of stuff. The expense of shipping it alone was more than it's worth. Oh well." She shrugged and picking it up, carried it into the living room, where she cleared a space on the shelf for it. She shoved it to the back where it didn't look too terrible. Then, glancing along the shelf of photographs, she frowned.

"That's odd," she said, lifting each one and looking behind it. "Where's Grandfather's wedding picture? It's always kept right here, next to Aunt Grizelda and Mimi."

"Did it have any value?" Sam asked.

"Only to me. The frame is silver, but only my housekeeper comes in here, and she's been with me for years. I trust her completely. Of course it's not something I look at every day. I mean it's just sort of . . . there. I didn't even notice it was gone until now so I've no idea how long it's been missing." She shrugged, putting it temporarily out of her mind. "Oh well, I daresay it'll turn up. Anyway, let's have our coffee, shall we?"

She carried in the tray while Sam prowled her living room inspecting the works of art scattered casually around, with the cat sniffing suspiciously at his heels. When he went and sat on the sofa she jumped onto the arm, fixing him with an unblinking blue stare.

He eyed it warily. "Is it always like this?"

"You mean *her*. And her name is Maow. Remember?"

Preshy set the tray with the coffee things on the tufted leather ottoman in front of him. It was already getting dark and she drew the curtains shutting out the frigid gray sky, then poured the coffee.

"I take it you don't like cats?" She offered him a dish of pastel-colored macaroons from Ladurée, the famous pastry shop just down the street. "Try them, they're good, as well as world-famous. And try to be nice to Maow. She's just not used to men."

Sam noticed her blush when she realized she had left herself wide open to further questioning as to exactly *why* there were never any men in her apartment, but she was saved from his questions by the phone ringing.

"I'll bet it's Aunt Grizelda to see why I'm not already in Monte Carlo," she said, answering it. But it was not. It was Lily.

Preshy didn't know whether to be glad or just relieved. "Lily!"

she said. "At last." Amazed, she added, "I was beginning to think you didn't exist." There was silence at the other end. "Lily?" Preshy asked, puzzled. "Are you still there?"

"Why did you say that?" Lily demanded, sounding upset.

"Say *what?*"

"That I didn't exist."

"Well, first you didn't show up, then you didn't call and I've never even met you." Preshy laughed. "But now you're here so it's okay. Now I know you *do* exist after all."

"Precious, you don't understand. Soon I might not *'exist.'* I'm being followed. Somebody wants to kill me."

"What?" Preshy's voice was pitched so high she could have sung soprano at the Paris Opéra, and both Sam's and the cat's ears pricked up. The cat stared at her while Sam pretended he wasn't listening.

"Here kitty." He held out a hand in an attempt at a diversion, but the cat eyed him disdainfully, then turned her head away as though she knew she was being used. "Smart cat," he said, just as he heard Preshy say.

"To *kill* you? What do you *mean,* Lily? Why would anybody want to *kill* you?"

Sam dropped all pretense and began to listen.

"I can't talk on the phone," Lily said.

"But where *are* you? And *who* is following you?" Preshy glanced worriedly at Sam. She shook her head, frowning, obviously puzzled.

"I'm in Venice," Lily said, and the mention of that fateful city sent a shiver down Preshy's spine.

"But I thought you were coming to Paris."

"I was. That's why I had you book me into the Ritz under your name. I thought he wouldn't know where I'd gone, that he wouldn't be able to trace me. I thought he'd never look for me in Venice. . . ."

"Just stop for a minute," Preshy said, bewildered. "Think about it first then tell me exactly what you're talking about."

"I'm talking about murder, Precious."

"Murder?" Preshy's eyes bugged. All she'd thought was that Lily was coming to visit and that maybe she wanted something from her. "But *why* would anyone want to murder you?"

"I have something he wants and he'll kill me to get it. And this also involves you. Precious, you might be the next to be killed."

"What?"

"I'm in great danger. I need your help. You must come here immediately. Please, *please,* I'm begging you to meet me in Venice. Only you can help me—"

"Lily, I can't just—"

"But you *must.*"

Preshy heard real terror in her voice.

"I'm at the Bauer Hotel," Lily said. "I'll wait for you there." There was a long pause and then, "It has to do with the man you know, called Bennett."

The line buzzed in Preshy's ear as Lily rang off. Shocked, she turned to look at Sam.

"What kind of long-lost-cousinly talk was that?" he said.

She sank into a chair, hands tightly clasped between her knees. "I could hear the *fear* in Lily's voice," she said, stunned.

"What exactly did she say?"

"That somebody is following her. That he wants to kill her because she has something he wants. She said *I* might be next." She shook her head, still disbelieving. "She wants me to meet her in Venice, as soon as I can get there. She said she's in Venice because she thought he'd never look for her there."

"And did she say who *he* was?" Sam asked. Preshy shook her head, and he said, "Of course she didn't, they never do."

"You mean crazy people. But I'm telling you, Sam, she's not crazy. She's terrified. Besides," she added quietly, "she said it also concerned a man I knew. His name is Bennett. We were getting married and he left me at the altar. In Venice. Just a couple of months ago."

FORTY-TWO

MAOW yawned loudly into the silence, stretching out along the back of the sofa. Preshy got up and took the fire tongs, poking at the smoldering logs. She stood with her back to Sam, staring into the flames.

"That's probably more information than you needed to know."

"It was very brave of you to tell me. You needn't have."

"It's the simple truth. I was ditched at the altar by a man I believed loved me. He disappeared without a trace. Aunt Grizelda tried to find him but the detectives said he must have been using an assumed name. He lived in Shanghai, or at least that's where he told me he lived."

"He worked there?"

"He claimed to have an export business, James Export Company, but it turned out not to exist. He told us he manufactured components for furniture companies in North Carolina."

"I know people in that line of business. Want me to check on him?"

Preshy shrugged. "I don't care anymore, except about Lily. The real mystery is I've never spoken to her before. I don't even know how she knows Bennett's name."

"He probably has several. Men like that usually do."

"Men like what?"

"Con men, criminals." Sam shrugged. "Do you really think Lily believes it's this Bennett who's going to kill her?"

Preshy shook her head and said, frowning, "Oh no, it couldn't be him. Bennett was a gentle man, he was never violent."

"And do you know what it is she has, that someone is willing to kill for?"

Preshy shook her head, she had no idea. She slumped into a chair and took a gulp of her coffee, thinking. It all sounded crazy, but there was no doubt Lily was terrified. And if it had something to do with Bennett she needed to find out.

"Lily's in trouble," she said to Sam. "She's my cousin and she needs my help. I'm going to Venice to meet her."

"And exactly how do you propose to get there? Have you forgotten the airport's closed."

"Then I'll drive."

"In *that* little car? In *this* weather?"

She gazed defiantly at him. "I'm a good driver, I'll get to Monte

Carlo, stop off at Aunt Grizelda's. I can get a flight out from Nice."

"I'm not driving all that way in that Smart car," he said coolly. "We'll have to rent one."

Preshy gawped at him. "You mean you're coming with me? Why would you do that?"

"Hey, I'm stuck here in Paris anyway, so why not Venice? At least I'll get a better hotel room." He grinned disarmingly at her. "Besides, I can't let you go alone, not after an intriguing story like Lily's. So . . . Venice here we come."

FORTY-THREE

SAM took Preshy's car and went to pick up a rental while she called her aunts. She knew the two women always raced to be the first to the phone, and this time they picked up simultaneously.

"Hi, Aunts," she said, smiling. "You'll be pleased to know I've decided to come visit you after all."

"When?" they asked, in unison, then Mimi got off the phone and let Grizelda do the talking.

"I'm leaving right now, driving through the night. I'll be with you by lunchtime tomorrow."

"But Presh, you can't drive all that way alone."

"I'm not alone. I'm bringing a man with me."

"What *man?*" Aunt G sounded pleased.

"Oh, just some guy, an American writer I met in La Coupole last night."

She heard Aunt G yell to Mimi, "She picked up a man in La Coupole again last night." And then Mimi yell back, "It's becoming a habit, I hope he's better than the other one."

"I hope he's more trustworthy than the last," Aunt G said. "Anyhow, how long can you stay?"

"I don't know if I can, we might go straight on to Venice. But I'll definitely get to see you." She winced, wishing she hadn't told her about going to Venice, now she would have to explain everything. Well, maybe not *everything,* but some kind of explanation was needed.

"She's off to Venice," she heard Aunt G say in a shocked aside to Mimi. "With the new man." Then, to her, "But *why* are you going back there?"

"It's Lily. Her flight got diverted. She ended up in Venice and said she needed me, it was important." Preshy hesitated then took the plunge. "She said it was something to do with Bennett."

"You mean Lily *knows* Bennett?"

"All I know is what she said; that it has to do with the man I know called Bennett."

"But can it possibly be the same man?"

"Who knows? That's why I have to go to Venice, to find out."

"Wait just a minute." Preshy heard Aunt Grizelda in urgent muffled consultation with Mimi, then she got back on the line.

"Okay, so we'll expect you tomorrow. We'll discuss this then. Call us when you get close and we'll meet you in Nice. Le

Chantecler at the Hôtel Negresco does a good lunch. You can introduce the new pickup and tell us all about it."

IT WAS SUNDAY AND PRESHY knew Sylvie would be at home so she gave her a call to fill her in on what was going on. Sylvie also answered on the first ring. She listened, horrified, while Preshy told her the Lily story, and what she'd said about Bennett.

"You can't go," she said firmly. "You absolutely must *not* go, Presh. I forbid it."

"It's okay, I have a 'protector,' " Preshy said. "I'm taking him with me."

"Him? *Who?*"

His name's Sam Knight. I met him yesterday at La Coupole—"

"*Merde,* Presh, are you completely mad?" Sylvie's voice rose to a shout. "Don't you ever learn? You met a man last night and next thing we know he's driving to the South of France with you, and helping you investigate some lunatic who says she knows Bennett and that somebody wants to kill her and you? Are you crazy, Preshy Rafferty, or what?"

"I promise you it's okay," Preshy said soothingly. "Sam's a bit of a mystery man, I admit, but he's a nice guy. And he's one of Daria's favorite writers. I mean, he's not like Bennett, he's very well known, so there can't be anything wrong with him, can there? Besides," she added as an afterthought, "he's married."

She heard Sylvie groan. "So you're going off with a married

man to find what Lily has to say about Bennett, and who Lily's so-called wannabe killer is? Tell me right now, Preshy Rafferty, does this sound like a nice normal scenario to you?"

Preshy giggled. "It sounds exactly like the basis for a Sam Knight mystery story," she said. "Now I think of it, that's probably the reason he offered to go with me. The writer on the scent of a good plot."

"More likely he wants to seduce you."

"Well if he does, it must be the new haircut. And anyhow I'm currently unseducible. Once bitten, a dozen times shy."

"How long are you going for? I want to come with you." Sylvie sounded really worried.

"No need, I'll be back in a couple of days."

"So where will you stay?"

"Lily said she's at the Bauer, so I guess I'll stay there too."

"Hmm, just make sure you get a single room," Sylvie said. "And promise to call me when you arrive, okay?"

Preshy promised and rang off. She shoved the reluctant Maow into the travel carrier. Grumbling, the cat twirled a few times before settling down, just as Sam returned with the rental car.

"What's that?" he asked, eyeing the carrier suspiciously.

"It's Maow, of course."

"You mean the *cat's* coming with us?"

"Maow comes everywhere with me. Anyhow, what else would I do with her at this time on a Sunday?" He gave her an exasperated stare and she said, "Let's get this straight, Sam Knight. Where I go, Maow goes. That's all there is to it. You don't like it, you know what to do."

He rolled his eyes but said nothing, so she picked up the cat and led the way downstairs to the street where the rental car was parked.

"Here." She handed him a pack of folding travel litter boxes and the bag of litter. "Put one of these on the floor by the backseat," she instructed. "Then fill it with litter."

Sam groaned but he did as she asked while she arranged the carrier on the backseat. She wedged her own hastily packed duffel next to it and Sam put his small bag, that he'd picked up from the hotel, next to that.

Preshy made to get in the driver's seat but he grabbed her arm. "Nope," he said, guiding her back to the passenger side and opening the door for her. "I'm driving."

"But I know the road well," she protested.

"But I don't know how you drive." He got behind the wheel, then he glanced sideways at her and gave her a grin. "Okay, Rafferty, so we'll take turns," he said generously.

She was fastening her seat belt when she had a sudden flash of the crusty bread and the good cheeses still sitting on her kitchen counter.

"Hang on," she said, sliding out again. She ran back through the courtyard and up the stairs, grabbed them and a couple of glasses, plates, knives and a bottle of wine, then ran back again.

"Just in case frostbite sets in and the Saint Bernards can't reach us," she said, stuffing them into the already crowded backseat, before sliding into the passenger seat next to him again.

Sam was silent as he followed her directions, negotiating his way out of snowy Paris's complicated one-way system onto the *périphérique,* then onto the autoroute. For once, the cat was also silent.

On the motorway Preshy thought there was something very intimate about driving through the dark frosty night, the two of them alone in the quiet cocoon of their car. She rummaged in her bag and found the CD *Zucchero & Co.,* her current favorite. Zucchero was the Italian singer-composer, whose mix of classic and pop reminded her of long-ago summers in South of France beach clubs with her aunt. Soon her eyes closed and she fell asleep.

When she awoke a couple of hours later it took a few seconds to remember where she was. She glanced quickly at Sam's profile as he drove, concentrating on the road. He looked stern and she realized she knew virtually nothing about him except that he was a writer with a house on the Outer Banks. Remembering Sylvie's words of warning, suddenly suspicious, she wondered exactly why he'd bothered to come with her, but then supposed he was simply bored waiting for a flight to New York.

Still, she thought he was kind of cool in his narrow blue jeans and black sweater. She peeked at him again from under her lashes, taking in the broad forehead, the shock of spiky brown hair, the firm stubbled jaw—he still hadn't managed to have a shave. Even the gold-framed glasses were kind of retro chic. He was definitely growing on her.

The CD had finished and all was quiet. She was still thinking about him and wondering what his story really was. "Tell me about your wife," she said into the silence.

He turned his head fractionally to look at her.

"I thought you were sleeping."

"I was."

He said nothing.

"Sorry," she said, "I don't mean to pry, I'm just curious about you."

"Her name is Leilani," he said. "I met her on one of those author's jaunts organized by the publisher's PR department. I was in Santa Fe, signing books. Leilani came in, she stayed around and we got to chatting." He shrugged. "Three months later we were married."

"How romantic."

"Yes. It was." He fell silent, concentrating on the road.

"What does she look like?"

He was silent for a long while, then finally he said, "She's kind of low-key beautiful. Half Hawaiian; long black hair; golden skin; slender; graceful. She's an artist, that's why she liked living in Santa Fe. There's a big artists' colony there. We bought a house out in the desert a little bit. Just the two of us with my dog, a German shepherd by the name of Cent. Leilani painted and I wrote. It was ideal for her, but I'm a Low-Country boy born and bred and I pined for the smell of the ocean. I missed the way the rivers flow slowly through the marshlands, and the sigh of the reeds and grasses in the wind. I missed the call of the seabirds and the scudding of the low clouds in the gray skies, and I yearned for the brilliance of the sun glinting off the ocean. It's in my blood and I needed it for my peace of mind, for the energy of my writing. So, though she hated the ocean, Leilani agreed to move, and we bought my dream house on the beach."

"And that's where you've lived ever since."

"I have a place in New York; an apartment on Gramercy Park."

"The best of both worlds," Preshy said, wondering why he was in Paris without his beautiful wife, Leilani. "Any children?" she asked instead.

"No kids."

She refrained from asking why not, thinking of him returning to New York, and of Leilani waiting to greet him at JFK. "I guess you'll be awfully glad to see her again," she said.

He pulled off the road into an autoroute café. "Time for coffee," he said.

Preshy let Maow out of her travel bag, waiting while she daintily used the litter box. Then she put the cat back in her case, and carried her into the café, where they lingered over coffee and their cheese and bread, talking about the Lily situation and not coming up with any answers.

Back in the car she said it was her turn to drive, and for the next two hours there was silence while she took charge and Sam dozed. Then the roles were reversed, until they stopped again and repeated the performance. Finally, they were on the Autoroute du Soleil, heading along the coast. When they passed the turnoff to St.-Tropez, Preshy called her aunt and they arranged to meet at Le Chantecler in Nice in half an hour.

FORTY-FOUR

THEY arrived a few minutes early and took the opportunity to freshen up in the Negresco's posh restrooms before Grizelda and Mimi arrived. Studying her face in the mirror, Preshy thought she looked okay considering she had driven all night and was in desperate need of a shower, though right now a glass of wine was even more appealing.

Leaving Maow in the care of the concierge, she and Sam made their way into Le Chantecler restaurant, where they ordered glasses of champagne.

She had warned Sam not to be surprised when he saw two old Las Vegas showgirls coming their way. Nevertheless, Sam's eyebrows rose in surprise when Mimi strutted across the ornate gilt dining room, Riviera-smart in a pale pink wool suit and platform shoes that made her still-fabulous legs look even longer. Her blond hair was sleeked back into a chignon and her rows of diamond bracelets glittered as she shook Sam's hand.

"*Enchantée,* M'sieur Knight," she said, sinking with a heartfelt sigh into a chair. "Stilettos are a tall girl's answer to a prayer, and a short girl's best friend," she added. "But they are surely hell on the feet."

"There you are." Grizelda slinked toward them in a clinging red dress with a little sable jacket that had belonged to her mother-in-law, and that she swore was older than she was. She was also carrying a beautiful white Valentino coat, which she handed to Preshy. "I knew you'd be wearing that green 'horror,' " she said. "So I brought you this. It'll be cold in Venice and you'll need it." She held out her hand to Sam. "I hear you picked up my girl in La Coupole." Like her niece, Grizelda always got directly to the point.

Sam smiled. "Should I apologize?"

She considered him. "I don't think so," she decided finally. "Come, sit down. Oh, you've already got champagne, good." She signaled the waiter and ordered two gin fizzes. "They know us here," she confided to Sam. "They understand exactly how Mimi and I like them." Then she turned to Mimi. "What d'you think, darling? Is he good enough for our girl?"

"Oh God!" Preshy shrank back in her chair. "Would you please stop it, Aunt Grizelda!" she said, but Sam just laughed.

Mimi tasted her drink, turning to give the waiter a pleased thumbs-up. "So—what's all this about Lily?"

"Let's order, we'll talk later," Grizelda decided. "They've driven all night, they must be starving."

They all decided on the same thing: the filet of beef with capers and potato ravioli, then cheese, and a quince tart with Granny Smith ice cream. With it they would drink a Provençal rosé.

"Now," Mimi said when that was taken care of, "let's get down to business."

So Preshy told them the whole story again, and that Bennett was involved. "And that's the reason I have to go back to Venice," she finished. She looked warily at them, waiting for them to say she was the crazy one, but Grizelda frowned.

"I never told you before," she said, "but I met the Songs years ago, at the casino in Macao. Henry had already lost his looks to drink and cigarettes. He looked gaunt and pasty and old. His eyes were permanently narrowed into slits from smoking, and his fingers were stained yellow from the nicotine." She shuddered. "The man looked as though he lived under a stone, never seeing daylight or breathing fresh air. And his wife, poor Grandfather Hennessy's spoiled-rotten daughter was wearing an unfashionable dress and cheap shoes. She looked worn out. She told me Henry Song had lost all their money, and I told her she should leave him. 'Apologize to your father for running off with that playboy in the first place,' I said. Of course her father would have taken her back but the poor woman was besotted with her husband. I could see he was some kind of a control freak. He had her under his spell, *and* he was addicted to alcohol as well as to gambling. And besides, they had the child by then. Poor little Lily."

"That's the other reason I have to meet her," Preshy said. "Grandfather would have expected me to help her."

Grizelda had to admit she was right. "But you're going to have to be very careful," she said. "I don't like the sound of this. Not one little bit." She glanced sharply at Sam. "Can I trust you to take care of her?"

Sam's eyes met hers. "I'll do my best," he said calmly.

She heaved a grateful sigh. "That's all a man can do," she said. "It's a pity you don't have the time to visit, I would have thrown a *petite soirée* for you, introduced you to some of my friends, though I must remind you, Preshy, never to drive the Corniche road when you come to Monaco. I haven't driven it myself, since I was almost forced off the edge of the cliff by some madman. It was just after you and Bennett visited us," she added, looking at Preshy. Then she clapped a hand over her mouth, embarrassed at having mentioned the past. "What am I saying? I'm sorry, my dear."

"It's okay, I'm over him," Preshy said, still sounding a little uncertain about it.

Sam listened while Grizelda told him what had happened on the Corniche road. He asked if she'd reported the incident to the police and she said she had, a couple of days later when she'd gotten her nerves back together, but of course by then it was too late to try to trace the white van. And it had cost a fortune to fix the Bentley.

"And this was right after Bennett was here?"

"Bennett and Preshy had already left and flown back to Paris. He was going straight on to Shanghai. This incident occurred a couple of days later."

"So as far as you knew he wasn't in the country?"

Puzzled, Grizelda said she didn't think so, and the subject was dropped.

Sam had managed to get them seats on the four o'clock Venice flight and they walked outside to say their goodbyes, leaving Maow with the aunts.

"Well?" Grizelda asked, her green eyes alight with curiosity as she hugged Preshy goodbye, while Sam went to get the car.

"Well—*what?*"

"Ohh—*you know,*" Mimi said, exasperated.

"If you mean am I interested in him, the answer is no. We are two strangers passing in the night who happened to get acquainted, that's all."

"Then if 'that's all,' what's he doing here with you?" Mimi said. "In my opinion that shows some 'interest.' "

Preshy groaned. "Will you two stop with the matchmaking. He's just a guy I know. And anyhow, he's married."

"What!" Two pairs of stunned eyed stared at her.

"You mean you didn't notice the ring?"

"So where's the wife?"

"I don't know. In fact I don't know much about him at all. I told you, we're just like ships that pass in the night. He simply offered to come to Venice to help me with the Lily situation. And to tell you the truth I was kind of glad he did."

"Hmmm . . . me too," Aunt G said, thoughtfully, "though I do wonder why he did. Be careful this time, Preshy," she added. And to her surprise, this time Preshy knew she meant be careful of Sam, not of Lily in Venice.

FORTY-FIVE

VENICE

It was dark when they landed in Venice and Marco Polo Airport brought back a slew of memories of the last time Preshy had arrived there with Sylvie and Daria, carrying her beautiful wedding dress and the golden cape with the fur-trimmed hood, and of how elated she had been. And later, of the sad departure with her friends instead of with her new husband.

"I guess this brings back some difficult memories," Sam said out of the blue.

"It does," she admitted. "But I'm not going to think about it." Still, she closed her eyes so as not to catch a glimpse of the illuminated dome of the Santa Maria della Salute as they passed.

"This place is a real live Canaletto," Sam said.

She smiled. "Sometimes I wonder if he painted it first and they built it after, it's just so perfect. I forgot to ask," she added, surprised at herself, "is this your first time in Venice?"

"My first, but looking at it now, it's probably not my last."

The *motoscafo* idled to a stop at the Bauer Hotel's private embarcadero, the landing stage, where their luggage was whisked away and they were escorted inside.

The luxurious hotel overlooked the Grand Canal, and though impeccably refurbished, its salons and rooms were redolent of the romance of another era. They checked in—separate rooms and on different floors—everything very correct. Then Preshy told the desk clerk she was expecting to meet a Miss Song, who was also staying at the hotel, and asked if there were any messages for her. The clerk checked but there were none.

Sam said he wanted to see something of the city and was going out for a walk but to her surprise, he did not ask her to go with him.

In her room, lonely again, she drew back the curtains. And there across the Grand Canal was the Salute, its dome moonlike in the night sky. It seemed there was no escaping the past, after all, and saddened, she went off to drown her sorrows in the shower, where her tears mingled with the water. She wondered if the heartache would ever really end, and what Lily had to tell her about Bennett.

FORTY-SIX

It was already evening when Lily awoke from a deep sleep that left her unrefreshed. She glanced at her phone, then remembered she had turned it off and of course there were no messages. Sitting up, she glanced nervously around the darkened hotel room. She still didn't feel safe, still felt as though eyes were watching her, still felt threatened, even though, logically, no one could possibly know where she was. Except for Cousin Preshy, who, she fervently hoped, was on her way to meet her.

A short while later, showered, dressed and hungry, she contemplated room service, but then told herself she was being ridiculous. She was in Venice, one of the wonders of the world, a city she had never seen. She had never even been to Europe before. At least she should see its glory and taste its food.

She walked through the narrow busy streets until she came to the Piazza San Marco with its magical views across the Grand Canal to the lagoon and its magnificent Basilica. Hearing music, she went inside, peering through the half-light at the beauty all around her. Then suddenly all the lights came on, flooding the great church with a golden glow. A mass was about to begin and she stood watching and listening, awed by its majesty, by the mosaics and the glitter of gold; by the Madonnas and the saints in their arched niches, the great altar, and by the soaring singing of the choir. All at once the shameful memories of those secret freezing nights in ancient burial grounds, and of the stolen artifacts, of the treachery and the violence, of threats and terror, left her. At that moment she felt a sense of peace and serenity that she prayed would stay with her forever.

After a while she left the Basilica and walked alongside the canal, thinking about the past, about all the years of striving to make a living, and about her future once she had sold the necklace. A whole new world would open up to her. She hoped Cousin Precious would get here soon because she wanted so badly to talk to her, not only about the necklace, but now about so many more things.

Turning down a narrow side street, she came across a small restaurant. Liking the look of its simple dark-wood interior, she went in and took a seat, ordering pasta with clams and a glass of white wine. Afterward, she lingered over an espresso, for once at peace with herself, sure at last that she was not being followed.

It was dark when she left and there was no one about. Quickening her pace, she made for the bigger street alongside the canal, smiling when it came in view, gleaming under an almost full moon. She stopped to look, taking a deep wondering breath, admiring the silhouetted skyline with its domes and pinnacles and the dark water sliding silently past. This was something she would never forget.

The blow to the head took her completely by surprise. She cried out once, then lifted her hands. The warm blood trickled through her fingers. Suddenly all around her it was growing dark, it was as though the lights of Venice were being extinguished, one by one. The push to her back sent her staggering. She teetered on the brink, another push and she was in the canal. And then everything was black. The dark water closed over her head with barely a ripple.

A perfect murder.

FORTY-SEVEN

RESTLESS, Preshy decided to go for a walk. She flung on some clothes—jeans, a sweater, boots. It was cold out and she put on the winter white wool coat with the impressive label that Aunt G had given her.

She wrapped her long blue woolen muffler twice round her neck with the ends dangling almost to her knees, just the way she liked it, though no doubt her aunt would have said she was ruining "the line" of the expensive coat. Then she went downstairs and out the Bauer's street entrance.

She wandered idly through the narrow *calli,* shivering in the icy night wind. Every corner brought back a memory. The very stones under her feet and the peeling stucco walls seemed to breathe romance. There was the scent of coffee and of wood fires, aromas of pizza and bread and wine. The lit shop windows offered a million temptations, and everywhere there was the sound of water lapping eternally at the edges of the sinking city. It was like walking through history.

Turning the corner she found herself in front of the Palazzo Rendino. Her feet had simply taken her there without her even thinking. It wasn't lit up, though, the way it had been for her wedding festivities, and the little square was in darkness. She closed her eyes, feeling the stab of pain in the place where her heart used to be before it was broken. Then, as she opened her eyes, she caught a glimpse of a tall dark-haired man in a long black coat, disappearing around the corner. *"Bennett!"* she cried. *Oh my God . . . could it really be him?* She ran to the corner but there was only an old woman walking her dog. She must have been hallucinating. It was being back at the Palazzo that had triggered her imagination, that was all.

She walked slowly back to the spot by the Palazzo's entry where she and Bennett had stood with their arms wrapped around each other the night before the wedding. She remembered saying, "Tomorrow, my love," and she had kissed him. "Tomorrow," he'd replied. And then he had walked out of her life.

Even so, she still secretly wished it was Bennett she had seen now. She wanted to believe there was still, somewhere, a flicker of hope, that there was a logical explanation and that everything would be all right. She wanted so badly for Bennett to apologize to her, to tell her again that he loved her, and that everything would be the way it was before. But of course, that could never be.

FORTY-EIGHT

LONELY, she wandered on, emerging from the narrow shadowy street into the glorious open vista of St. Mark's Square. It was filled with light and the flutter of pigeons, and busy people. Music wafted from the rival *caffès,* Quadri and Florian. The grandiose illuminated Basilica dominated to her left, and on her right, the ancient stone arcades gleamed in the lamplight, the color of molten honey. And in front was the most magnificent view in all of Venice: the Grand Canal, with, beyond, in the mist, the islands and the lagoon.

In summer the *caffè* chairs and tables spilled across the square, but the cold January weather had forced everyone indoors. Except, that is, for the aggressive tribes of pigeons. "Rats with wings," Aunt G called them.

Deciding that the Venetian specialty, a double espresso fortified with grappa, was exactly what she needed on this cold night, Preshy pushed through the etched glass doors into Quadri's gilt and rosy velvet rooms. And into a fog of cigarette smoke, of conversation and laughter and music from the string quartet playing Cole Porter, another sometime Venice inhabitant, though "Night and Day" sounded squeakily different on a violin.

Hearing her name called, she looked up and saw Sam at a table by the steamed-up window, with what looked like a double vodka on the rocks in front of him.

"Hi." She beamed, hurrying over and taking a seat next to him.

"It seemed to me it was about time for a drink," he said. "What d'you say?"

"Espresso with grappa. When in Italy . . ."

He called over the busy waiter, and watched amused as she unraveled the long muffler. He remarked admiringly on the white coat. "You look very Italian."

"I should, it's Valentino. Aunt G's," she added. "She couldn't stand the sheepskin."

"Oh I don't know, it kind of grows on you. Like moss."

To her surprise they were laughing together, like two people on holiday without a care in the world, instead of a pair of wannabe detectives out to solve a mystery.

"Still no Lily," she said. "She really is the most mysterious woman."

"A combination of Greta Garbo and Mata Hari," he agreed. The waiter produced her grappa-ladden coffee and they clinked glasses and said *"cin cin,"* Italian style, then she asked what he thought of Venice.

"Are there words to describe it?" he asked. "You can never understand that such a wonder of the world truly exists until you see it for yourself. Even Canaletto could only show us a glimpse. Beautiful buildings floating on silver water, a low sky that seems to hover over the city, as though a ladder to heaven awaits 'all who enter here.' "

She stared admiringly at him. "You put into words things I can only think."

"Words are a writer's job."

He sipped his vodka, something she noticed he drank quite a lot of, while she called the hotel and asked if there was a message. There wasn't, so they lingered, exchanging impressions of Venice, before venturing out again, into the cold.

The fog was rolling in over the lagoon, great soft woolly waves that left droplets sparkling in their hair. Sam put his arm around her and they huddled together, chilly intimate strangers. To her surprise, she found she liked the way it felt. "I'm hungry," he said. "And since Lily's still not around, let's have dinner."

So they caught the *vaporetto* to the Rialto and she took him to a small place she knew, an old monastery where, under an arched stone ceiling lit by sconces, they dined on tiny spider crabs and the Venetian classic, calves' liver with onions. Sam said Preshy should choose the wine and she picked a simple Pinot Grigio from the hills of the Veneto that, he admitted, went perfectly with everything. And she was so busy talking about Venice that she forgot all about Lily.

FORTY-NINE

MARY-LOU was on her third espresso, sitting opposite Bennett in the hotel bar.

Signaling the waiter, Bennett ordered a second grappa. He ordered one for her too. "You look as though you need it," he said with a contemptuous lift of his lips that, she assumed, was his real smile, and was quite different from the practiced sensual charm of the one he had always used on her before.

Nevertheless, she downed the liquor, shuddering as it hit her stomach. Her black suede purse was on the table in front of her, with the Beretta nestled in its shocking pink satin lining. She picked the purse up and placed it on her lap. It gave her a feeling of security.

Bennett said, "Our only hope is that Lily's hidden the necklace in her suitcase, or in the room safe." He fixed her with that hard implacable gaze. "We have her room key. We will go upstairs together, go through her things. If the maid sees you, she'll assume you are Lily."

Mary-Lou knew he wasn't about to allow her to go alone. He'd made it obvious he was not going to let her out of his sight. Shivering, she ran the tips of her fingers over the bump that was the Beretta. She hated Bennett. She would shoot him rather than hand over the necklace.

They walked together to the elevator, then down the corridor to Lily's room. The maid on duty gave them a passing glance and a *buona sera.* A lamp was lit and the bed had been turned down. Everything was in order. Lily's suitcase was on the luggage stand. She had obviously not bothered to unpack and Mary-Lou went quickly through its contents.

She glanced up at Bennett, standing, arms folded, watching her. "Not here," she said.

"Try the safe."

She did. It was empty.

Lily had fooled them.

Mary-Lou sat on the bed and suddenly she began to cry. She had gone to the limit—and for nothing.

Despising her, without a further word, Bennett walked out of the room, and out of the hotel. Mary-Lou was of no more use to him. She wasn't even worth the risk of killing. She was too involved now to go to the police. She would say nothing. She had served her purpose and would go home like a good girl, and he would never hear from her again.

He walked the darkened back streets of Venice for hours that night, trying to figure out what Lily might have done with the necklace. Suddenly the answer came to him. Of course, she had been on her way to Paris. She would have sent it to her cousin. Preshy Rafferty must have it.

FIFTY

BACK at the hotel, Sam and Preshy went up to her room to check the phone for messages. The red light was not blinking. Preshy called Lily's room. No answer.

She sat on the edge of the bed, looking at Sam. "What shall we do now?" she asked, worried.

He threw up his hands wearily. "I suggest we get some sleep and check again in the morning."

They said good night, but still worried and unable to sleep, Preshy called Daria in Boston and filled her in on what was going on. Of course Daria was as alarmed as Sylvie had been, especially when she told her about Bennett.

"Presh, why did you go to Venice?" she said. "This is Lily Song's problem, not yours. It sounds dangerous to me. Especially the Bennett part. That's all over for you."

"But I'm the only one who can help her. She truly has no one else," Preshy said. "Anyway, I need to know what she has to say about Bennett. And besides, I'm not alone. I have a new friend with me. His name is Sam Knight. You might have heard of him," she added with a little smile in her voice.

"What? You're with *Sam Knight*? Jesus, Presh, how'd you meet *him?*"

"You're not going to believe this. In kind of a repeat performance, I picked him up in La Coupole Saturday night, in a snowstorm."

"You picked up *Sam Knight?*"

"Sure. Why not? He was stranded in Paris—no flights, airport closed. . . . Why? What's wrong with that?"

Daria's sigh gusted ominously down the line into Preshy's ear. "I have to give you credit," she said. "You surely know how to pick 'em."

"For God's sake, what is it?"

"You mean you don't know the story?"

"*What story,* dammit."

"I don't think you're going to like this," Daria said, "but I think you should know. About three years ago Sam Knight's wife disappeared."

"Disappeared?" Preshy's heart did a little jump. "What do you mean *disappeared?*"

"Here's the story. Sam told the police the last time he saw his wife was at their beach house. He'd gone out fishing. He had a small boat and he said he often fished at night. She didn't like the sea and never went with him. He told the police he'd left her alone in the house, with just their dog, a German shepherd called Cent for company. See, I even remember the dog's name; the story dominated the media for weeks. . . ."

Preshy gripped the phone tighter. "What happened to her?"

"There was no sign of violence, nothing was disturbed, no robbery. The dog, who Sam said was devoted to her, was still there. The bed was unslept in, the TV still on. She had simply disappeared. It was exactly like one of his mystery novels.

"Forensics took that Outer Banks house apart and came up with nothing. And to this day, Leilani Knight has not been found. I believe Sam is still 'a person of interest' to the police—which is what he was always referred to as, never as an actual *suspect.* But they suspected he'd killed her all right. Everyone did. And Leilani Knight has never been found."

"I don't believe it," Preshy said, shakily. "Of course he didn't kill her." Yet, when she thought about it, why else was Sam so mysterious about his past? "Perhaps she ran off with another man." She was grasping at straws, still unwilling to believe that Sam had anything to do with his wife's disappearance.

"Do you seriously think she wouldn't have been found by now if she'd run off with somebody? It's been *three years,* Presh. And I'll tell you something else, Sam Knight hasn't written a word since then."

Preshy had the phone in a death grip now. She knew the story was true. That was why Sam was reluctant to talk about Leilani . . . because maybe he had killed her. Tears strangled her words as she said in a small tired voice, "Life used to be so uncomplicated, Daria. I'm here with Sam, looking for Lily—and now I'm wondering exactly *why* he came with me. Do you think he can know something about her? About *Bennett*? I don't know what to do."

"Be careful," Daria warned. "And get the next flight home. *Alone*. I'm begging you, Preshy, get out of there, and without Sam Knight."

Promising she would, Preshy said goodbye. She turned out the lamp and lay, rigid with shock, staring into the darkness.

Sam's lean face came into her mind; the brown eyes behind the glasses, his stern aloof profile as he drove down the autoroute that long dark night. She thought about the coincidence that he had come to sit next to her in La Coupole, even though the place had been half-empty. *Exactly the way Bennett had.* And how he had said, so quickly, that he was coming with her to Venice. Now she asked herself why. Was there something Sam knew that she didn't? Could he possibly be involved in this Lily saga too? As well as in his wife's disappearance?

Oh my God. She was in Venice with a man suspected of murder, searching for another man who might also be involved in murder. *What had she done?*

FIFTY-ONE

FOR Sam, sleep was a lost art. He had been drinking all night and it was still dark when, a little after six a.m., he left the hotel and retraced his steps along the *fondamenta,* the canal-side walkway. There was no one around and the water seemed to lap in sync with his lonely footsteps.

After a while it began to rain, icy needle-sharp slivers that chilled him to the bone. He turned up his collar, zipped the jacket and walked on, uncaring. It was only him and the feral cats, thin shadows huddled near the fountains and on the church steps, waiting for the dawn and for life to begin again.

There was some activity on the canal though, the fruit and vegetable delivery boats heading for the Rialto market; a garbage boat; the mostly empty *vaporetti*. And a police boat, blue lights flashing, just ahead of him.

A small crowd had gathered and he watched as the police recovery team grappled with something in the water, then hauled it in.

"Probably some tourist," he heard an Englishman in the crowd say. "The guy on the fish delivery boat spotted her. An Asian woman. She must have been in the water for some time by the look of her. Probably got drunk, fell in. It happens," he said. "Or else her boyfriend pushed her," he added with a laugh that rang hollowly from the silent buildings.

Sam turned and walked quickly down the maze of little lanes until he came to an open *caffè*-bar. He stood at the counter alongside men in suits and overcoats, newspapers tucked under their arms, grabbing coffee and *cornetti* on their way to the office. He ordered a double espresso, piled in the sugar, drank it down and ordered a second. He lit a cigarette, wincing at the acrid taste. Smoking was a habit he'd kicked years ago and resurrected only recently. The cigarette tasted like ashes and he ground it out, sipping the espresso instead. He had a third, waiting for the caffeine to kick in and clear his liquor-overloaded head. It was almost eight before a cold gray dawn broke over Venice and he headed back to the hotel.

He stopped at the concierge's desk and asked him to get a seat on the Paris flight and then on to New York.

Back in his room he called Preshy. It was obvious from her befuddled voice that he'd woken her, but she snapped to icy attention when he said who it was.

"Isn't it a bit early to be calling?" she said coldly.

"I need to talk to you," he said. "There have been some developments."

"It's only ten after eight. How could there have been developments?"

"Rafferty, get your clothes on, I'm coming up. I'll give you five minutes." He put down the phone, lit up another cigarette, grimaced, ground it out. He glanced at the empty bottle of vodka, then at the minibar. No, he wasn't going in that direction again. He had things to take care of.

FIFTY-TWO

SHE answered the door in jeans and a T-shirt. Her short hair stuck up in coppery spikes, her pale eyes were ringed with shadows and she looked exhausted.

Without speaking, she led the way into her room, then sat looking at him as he dusted off his soaked leather jacket and smoothed back his wet hair. "Well?" she said distantly.

Sam thought *frigid* was the word that might best describe her attitude. He wondered what had happened. He pulled up a chair and sat opposite her. She looked away and he leaned forward, knees apart, hands clasped loosely. Their faces were just inches away. When finally she lifted her eyes reluctantly to his, he said, "The police found the body of an Asian woman in the canal this morning."

Her chin shot up and her shocked eyes locked on to his.

"I'm guessing it's Lily," he said.

"Oh my God," she whispered. "I *knew* it. I *knew* something was wrong." Her eyes narrowed with sudden suspicion. "How do you know about this?"

"I happened to be there when they fished the body from the canal, very early this morning."

"Oh. Right. You *just happened* to be out walking, before dawn, when the police found a body? That *just might* be Lily's? Isn't that a bit of a coincidence, Sam? I mean, you still can't find your wife but you find Lily right away. What exactly *happened* to Leilani, Sam? Was it something similar to what's happened to Lily? Or can't you admit to it?"

Sam shrugged. Now he knew the reason for her iciness. "You've obviously heard the story, so why bother to ask?"

"Because I need to hear it from you."

"The truth and nothing but the truth," he said bitterly. "It's going to haunt me for the rest of my life."

"Yes," she agreed. "I believe it will."

He got up and walked to the door. He hesitated and stood thinking, then he turned to face her, hands in his jeans pockets, staring silently down at the floor.

Finally, he said, "My wife, Leilani, was a depressive. She was a fragile soul, shy and insubstantial as a wood nymph; serene one minute, in the depths of despair the next. She left me that night, just as she had threatened to do so many times before. She didn't want to 'trouble' me any longer, was what she would say. What 'trouble,' I'd ask, angry that she didn't understand I loved her and that was all that mattered. But Leilani hated the ocean. She was afraid of it. It was the reason she had left Hawaii, she couldn't bear the noise of the surf. Santa Fe was a landlocked island of peace for her, and selfishly, I took her away from that.

"I don't know what happened to Leilani, only that she was not there when I came home from my fishing trip the next morning, but I guessed she had done what she'd always threatened to do. Left me so she wouldn't be any 'trouble.' She left no message, no note to explain."

He lifted his eyes to look at Preshy. "She was such a very private woman, I couldn't shame her by sharing her personal torment with the world. The media would have had a field day. So instead I said nothing, and I took the rap." He shrugged. "It was only right. After all, I was the guilty party. I'd taken her from the place she felt secure, to live in the place that finally drove her mad."

Despite Preshy's misgivings, he sounded so—defeated—her heart went out to him. "You think she . . . ?" She couldn't bring herself to say "killed herself."

"I don't think about it," he said abruptly. "At least I try not to. In my waking moments, that is."

She knew what he meant. At night, alone in the dark, memories had a way of coming back to haunt you, all the whys and why nots, and if onlys. "I understand," she said, wanting to believe him, but still unsure.

His eyes behind the glasses were steely as they met hers. "Do you?" he asked indifferently, as though he no longer cared what people thought. He shrugged, then he came back and sat opposite her again. "We have to talk about Lily," he said.

FIFTY-THREE

HE took off his glasses and rubbed his eyes wearily. "You'll have to go to the police," he said. "Tell them you were supposed to meet your cousin here, and that you think the body might be hers." His eyes met hers. "They'll want you to identify it."

Preshy gasped, horrified. "But I've never met her. I can't identify her, I don't even know what she looks like."

"Her passport will be at the desk, or in her room." He didn't add that anyhow a drowned woman who'd been in the water for any length of time would be bloated beyond all recognition and would look nothing like her passport photo, and that fingerprints and dental records might be the clincher on her identity.

Preshy's hand shook as she poured a glass of water from a

half-empty bottle of San Pellegrino. It was warm and flat and she wrinkled her nose in distaste.

"There'll be an autopsy immediately, of course," Sam said. "To establish the cause of death. Then the body will be released. To you," he added.

Preshy put her head in her hands. She would have to identify the body, take care of everything, send Lily home to be buried. She wanted this nightmare to end. But it wasn't going to go away just yet.

Sam glanced at his watch. "Better get going," he said. "Get it over with."

Getting a grip on her nerves, Preshy threw on Aunt G's beautiful white Valentino coat and wound the blue muffler twice around her neck. Lily was her cousin. It was her duty to take care of her. Grandfather Hennessy would have expected it.

"You'll be okay," Sam said.

She glanced quickly at him. "You're coming with me, aren't you?" she said, suddenly worried.

"I can't," he said quietly.

She stared, stunned, at him. He was involved in this . . . he couldn't just walk away, leave her to pick up the dreadful pieces.

"You're looking at a man who's been there before," Sam said. "I can't go through it again. Knowing what you know about me now, you have to understand. I'm flying back to New York tonight. I'm sorry, Rafferty, but you're going to have to deal with this alone."

They stood, silently, looking at each other for a long moment. Then he shook his head and walked out of her room. And also, Preshy thought with a sudden pang of sorrow, out of her life. Forever.

FIFTY-FOUR

SOMEHOW Preshy pulled herself together. She called Aunt Grizelda on her cell phone and told her the terrible news.

"Do nothing" was Aunt G's horrified response. "Mimi and I will be there with a lawyer in a few hours."

Pacing her room, Preshy went over and over again what Sam had said. Of course she knew what he meant—that a man suspected of one murder could not afford to be involved in another—in which, because of his past, he might again become a suspect.

Uneasy, she wondered *why* Sam had gotten involved with her. And what about Bennett? Could he know something about him that she didn't? And what was it Lily had possessed that someone wanted badly enough to kill for? And now she was dead, did that person have it?

She was going crazy. Nerves jangling, she threw on her coat and went in search of coffee. Her head ached and she wished she had never heard from Lily, or met the mystery man Sam Knight, whose past anyhow was as murky as Lily's. *How could he leave me? He was there when they found the body. He was a part of this, the bastard. He had no right to skip town.*

Huddled in Florian's over her ten-dollar cup of coffee, she wished she were anywhere else but Venice, which, for her, was now beginning to sink under bad memories.

AUNT G ARRIVED A COUPLE of hours later on a private plane "borrowed" from a friend, with a lawyer, Maître Hugo Deschamps, in tow. "You look terrible, *chérie,*" were her first encouraging words. Her second were "And where's the Knight in shining armor?"

"I *feel* terrible." Preshy burrowed her face in Aunt G's scented shoulder as the tears finally flowed. "And the Knight's gone back to New York. He left me to face the music alone. I can't blame him," she added, lifting her wet face and look blearily at her aunt. "He's been through all this before when his own wife disappeared into thin air and never came back."

"What?" Mimi let out a shriek and Aunt G gasped, and now Preshy was forced to tell them Sam's story.

"So you see," she concluded, "he's a suspect in his own wife's disappearance or possibly murder. 'A person of interest' is what the police call it."

"Imagine, a nice man like that," Mimi marveled, thinking of the pleasant lunch at Chantecler. But Grizelda snorted and said as far as she was concerned men were all alike and none of them were to be trusted, especially by Preshy, who certainly "knew how to pick 'em."

"Of course Maître Deschamps is an exception," she said with a sugary smile at the lawyer: a tall, imposing, silver-haired Frenchman with forty years of criminal law under his belt, including several famous murder trials.

"Thank you for that, Countess," he said with a courtly bow. "But now I must accompany Precious to the *polizia.* And you, my dear," he said looking sternly at Preshy, "will not say one word. You will leave it all to me."

Preshy promised to keep her mouth shut, and Maître Deschamps informed the Aunts that they could not come along with them because he feared Grizelda would say too much, and he knew from past experience he had no control over *her.* They arranged to meet later at Harry's Bar and he and Preshy headed off to the police station.

Thanks to Maître Deschamps, the interview was not as traumatic as Preshy had feared. As he'd promised, he did all the talking, merely saying that Precious was to have met her cousin from Shanghai, glancing every now and again at her for corroboration of the story.

The police captain in charge of the case said there didn't seem to be much mystery about a tourist falling into the canal and drowning, and that she'd probably had too much to drink. Meanwhile the autopsy would take place tomorrow and the cause of death established. He thanked them for their help, promising the results of the autopsy the following day.

SO WHAT D'YOU THINK?" Preshy asked Maître Deschamps, en route by *motoscafo* to Harry's Bar.

"Of course it all depends on the autopsy. If there is evidence of foul play then we have to rethink your situation. But if the cause of death is established as an accident"—he lifted a dismissive shoulder—"then I doubt we'll hear anything further from the police. And after that, my advice to you is to forget all about Lily Song." The Maître helped her out of the *motoscafo* outside Harry's. "Now, let's try one of those famous Bellinis, shall we?"

THEY SIPPED THEIR BELLINI COCKTAILS—a drink made famous by the then barman Harry, consisting of champagne and pressed fresh peaches, though in winter these had to be of the bottled kind. No matter, they were delicious and Preshy's slid like silk down her tight throat.

Sam, you bastard, you left me all alone, she thought, already on her third Bellini. *I know why you did it, but it was a cowardly thing to do . . . and anyhow I don't trust you . . .*

"You're too quiet," Aunt G said suspiciously. "What are you thinking?" She was her usual flamboyant self in a black dress with thirties diamond leaf-shaped clips at the sweetheart neckline, and her Rita Hayworth red hairdo sliding over one wickedly bright emerald eye. A taupe Fendi mink lay on the seat beside her and she wore high heels that were completely unsuitable for walking on Venice's cobbled alleys.

"I was thinking how great you and Mimi look," Preshy lied, "especially considering you had so little notice and got here in record time."

"*Chérie,* you know I can pack in ten minutes flat and be ready for any occasion." Grizelda gave her a warm smile. "But that's *not* what you were thinking."

"My guess is she was thinking about that *snake,* Sam," Mimi said, having gone full circle on him.

Sighing, Preshy admitted it was true. "I can't help it," she said sorrowfully, "I just seem to find the bad boys."

Maître Deschamps looked at his watch then got to his feet. "My advice to you, mademoiselle," he said, as he paid the check, "is to forget about him. And forget about the other one. Bennett, wasn't it? Allow your aunts to introduce you to some nice gentlemen. They have a lot of friends, and I'm certain they will make perfect matchmakers."

The Aunts beamed at him and Grizelda told him that piece of advice alone was worth any money she was going to have to pay him.

"Don't worry, I'll send you the bill," he promised with a smile. "I'll wait to hear from the police tomorrow, then I'll call you and discuss what our next moves should be."

"There," Grizelda said relieved. "I knew Hugo would take care of everything. There's no need to worry anymore, *chérie.* You'll be all right."

"But what about poor Lily?"

"We'll face that tomorrow, darling," Mimi said. "Meanwhile, let's behave like tourists and order Harry's hamburgers. I hear they're divine."

FIFTY-FIVE

SAM'S flight to Paris was half-empty. He asked for a vodka and drank it down as they flew over the Alps and grassy rural France, deliberately emptying his mind of the events of the last few days.

Looking round, he noticed an Asian woman, an exceptionally attractive woman who gave him a fleeting glance from almond-shaped eyes the color of warm amber, and whose short black bob bounced as she walked past. He wondered what *she* had been doing in Venice. Of course it was ridiculous to think she might have known Lily simply because they were both Asian, but he noted the coincidence.

He'd left Rafferty in Venice for two reasons. He could not afford to get involved, and there was nothing more he could do. It was over. Or was it? The question haunted him the entire flight.

He thought of her dealing with the police, taking charge of Lily's belongings, coping with shipping the body back to Shanghai to be buried.

He had another drink but still couldn't get Rafferty out of his mind. Even full of liquor as he was, he could hear her voice saying, "You're coming with me, aren't you?" Even with his eyes closed he could see her aquamarine eyes widen with suspicion, and remember the smudge of freckles across her nose.

The plane made a bumpy landing in a still storm-tossed Paris and he strode through the terminal to Delta to check in for the New York flight. Halfway there, he changed course and went instead to Cathay Pacific, where he managed to get a seat on a flight departing the following afternoon for Hong Kong and from there to Shanghai.

He canceled New York, then went to the shopping area where he bought T-shirts and boxers, a couple of shirts, a cashmere sweater and a warm coat. At another shop he found a lightweight bag into which he put his new purchases. After that, he checked into the airport Hilton, ordered a room service hamburger which he ate while watching the usual bad news, in French, on TV. Then he showered and fell into bed. And this time he slept.

The next day the Cathay Pacific flight went as far as Hong Kong and took over eleven hours. After a four-hour wait, he took a Dragonair connecting flight to Shanghai.

FIFTY-SIX

VENICE

PRESHY'S dreams were filled with the image of a woman's body floating just below the surface of the canal. The water lapped over her face and she could not see who it was, but the arms were outstretched, palms up as though asking for help.

She shot upright, sweating. She glanced at the clock and groaned. Four-thirty. She got out of bed, poured herself a glass of water and sat huddled in a chair, gazing at the blank TV screen. There were hours to be gotten through before Maître Deschamps had the autopsy answer from the police captain. Hours before they would know if the body was really Lily's. Hours before she might be asked to identify a woman she had never met.

She pictured the cold morgue, imagined the smell of formalde-hyde, the covered female shape on the steel slab, a tag tied to her toe; the attendant lifting the sheet from the dead face . . . *She couldn't do it.* But she must. There was no one else.

She took a shower and thought about going back to bed. What would she dream of this time? More bodies? Bennett? She shuddered. At least awake, she had some control over her thoughts.

She contemplated a cup of coffee but there was already so much caffeine flowing in her veins she figured it would only bring more bad dreams. She thought about Sam, on his way to New York. So much for that Knight in shining armor.

She glowered into her empty glass for a while, then got up, walked to the window and pulled aside the curtain. The sky had cleared and the dome of the Salute glimmered white under a silver moon, bringing memories of Bennett and her nonwedding.

Exhausted, she climbed back into bed and turned out the light. It would be a long sleepless wait for morning.

AT TEN O'CLOCK, SHE WAS in the Aunts' suite, having breakfast, when Mâitre Deschamps called.

"You can relax," he told her. "There's no need for you to identify the body. They were able to do it from her passport, and from fingerprints. It is Lily Song, I'm afraid. Apparently she must have slipped—the cobblestones were slick from the damp. They deduced that she fell, hit her head and rolled unconscious into the canal. Death was from drowning. It *was* an accident after all. And my advice to you is to forget what Lily said to you on the phone. Simply take her home and bury her and leave it at that."

"Well," Preshy said to the Aunts, putting down the phone, "they are releasing the body to me. Now all I have to do is arrange for Lily to be shipped home to Shanghai for burial."

"But *who* will bury her?"

"Her family, her friends . . . surely there must be someone. Lily couldn't have been all alone in the world. We should look in her address book, find out who her friends were."

Mimi was put in charge of arranging for a mortuary to pick up Lily's body and provide a coffin suitable for transportation, while Preshy called the airlines about shipping it to Shanghai. Then she went with her aunt to Lily's room.

Lily had not unpacked and all her things were still in her suitcase. Looking at the small pile of underwear, the black suede pumps, the sweater, Preshy thought how pathetic they were; the leftover belongings of a dead woman. Tears pricked at her eyelids.

"I can't let her go home alone," she said. "I have at least to go to her funeral."

"Then I'll go with you," Aunt G said quickly.

But Preshy knew that no matter how much she denied being "old," the journey would be too arduous for her aunt. "No need," she said. "I'll represent us. I'll take care of everything."

Grizelda found Lily's small black leather address book on the nightstand. "It's from Smythson, the good shop on Bond Street in London," she said approvingly. "Cousin Lily had good taste."

"Expensive taste, you mean," Preshy said, examining it. A few business cards were tucked into the flap behind the front cover. Most were Lily's own. The others were all in Chinese, except for one with the name Mary-Lou Chen, which had the same address as Lily's but with a different phone number.

Figuring Mary-Lou must work for Lily, she called the number. There was no answer. She couldn't just leave a message saying Lily was dead, so she hung up. She would try again later.

Meanwhile, Mimi had arranged for the body to be collected from the morgue and prepared for shipping the following day. Preshy couldn't bear to fly on the same plane so she got a seat on a flight via Singapore that would get her into Shanghai at around the same time. Grizelda booked her into the Shanghai Four Seasons, and then the Aunts departed, on their private plane, for Monte Carlo.

Preshy left Venice later that day for what she hoped would be the last time, on a flight to Frankfurt and from there to Singapore, then a connecting flight to Hong Kong and on to Shanghai. Bennett's city.

FIFTY-SEVEN

SHANGHAI

SAM guessed that Aunt Grizelda was not going to allow her "daughter" to stay in any old fleabag, and when he arrived at Shanghai's Pudong Airport, he called around the hotels, starting with the five-stars. He'd guessed right. At the Four Seasons he was told Miss Rafferty was expected tomorrow. And yes there was also a room available. He took a taxi there right away.

Once installed, he ordered flowers to be delivered to her room. "Something exotic," he told the florist. "Orchids and peonies, that sort of thing." He wrote a card saying, "Welcome to Rafferty," then he went to the steam room for half an hour to clear his head. After that, he got dressed, put on his warm new coat, and had the concierge look up the address and phone number of

Song Antiquities, whose name he remembered from the parcel Lily had sent to Paris. Then he took a taxi there.

The area of the French Concession was an odd mixture of old-fashioned charm, high-level noise, speed and urban blight. But the broad leafy avenues had retained some of their glamour, and the narrow lanes, the *longtang,* were crowded with small businesses and stores, clubs, bars and teahouses where to his astonishment, birds in little bamboo cages hung in the trees and were fed live crickets by their doting owners. Tile-roofed houses were hidden behind arched stone gateways called *shikumen,* set in rows along the alleys, with wooden doors that opened inward onto small courtyards.

The rain started as he walked down the lane where Song Antiquities was located. When he came to it he stepped back to take a look. Over the tall gate he could see a red-tiled roof, the tops of some columns and a fretwork art deco verandah. The house seemed larger than most, and he guessed Lily lived and worked out of it. There was a small seedy-looking nightclub on one side and a busy noodle shop on the other. He rang Lily's bell and waited. No one came, but then he had expected that.

Walking briskly, he went back to the main avenue, ducking out of the rain into a teahouse where he ordered what he was told was the specialty, *longjing* tea, and some of the sweet crescent-shaped dim sum stuffed with pork, known as *shenjian bao.* He bit into one, wincing as he burned his mouth on the scalding-hot broth inside. It was good though.

He looked round at his neighbors, all of them talking Mandarin Chinese, a language he had no hope of ever understanding.

Occasionally one would glance his way, unsmiling. He realized he was the only foreigner and feeling like an intruder, presently he got up and left. He hailed a cab and told the driver to take him to the market.

It was evening and the streets were jammed with noisy people. The scent of incense from the nearby temple mingled with the aromas from the roadside stands, where all kinds of snacks were being barbecued or fried or boiled.

Sam pushed his way through the throng, dazzled by the thousands of flashing neon signs and the harsh rattle of the language, by the music, the gongs and drums, by the children carrying balloons, yelling and darting, and by the crowds streaming in and out of the ornate red-columned temple, where fortunes were told in separate little booths.

He walked over to where the wise men of fortune-telling plied their trade and read the PR written in English for tourists like himself, and the faded newspaper clippings tacked on the walls that proclaimed their excellent ability to foretell a man's future.

One newspaper clipping boasted that this was the son of the most illustrious fortune-teller in China, and that he now carried on the tradition of his famous father. "Tycoons and billionaires and society ladies consult him on a daily basis," the newspaper clipping said, "so they will know how to plan their day and which will be the most auspicious time for that important business move, or for catching the man they want."

On an impulse, Sam pulled aside the bead curtain and stepped inside.

The fortune-teller was a small, middle-aged man with narrowed eyes and smooth skin. He was sitting behind an empty table and he waved Sam to a chair opposite.

Sam expected him to take out a pack of cards, or at least a crystal ball, but instead the fortune-teller studied his face intently. Sam offered his palm to be read but the man said, "Not yet," and continued to search his face. Uncomfortable, Sam looked away.

"I am reading your cranium," the fortune-teller said finally. "Your face tells me your story. I see that when you were a child you suffered a life-threatening sickness."

Sam glanced at him, startled. He had indeed been very sick when he was only five years old.

"Your mind is quick, facile. You are a creator," the fortune-teller told him, accurately again. "Success comes easily to you. Money sticks to your fingers." His eyes narrowed to mere slits as he looked into Sam's face. "But tragedy stalks you," he added, softly. "Images of violence and death have kept you in their thrall. And there is more even now, far from your home."

Startled, Sam said nothing; watching; waiting.

"Mystery surrounds you," the fortune-teller continued. "You are always looking for answers."

Finally, he took Sam's hand, gazing intently at the palm. "The life line is long, but there are breaks in it." He pointed to the wisps of conflicting lines. "Here, when you were very young, and here again." He looked up at him, eyes narrowed. *"Now,"* he said.

Sam didn't like the sound of that, but he thought the fortune-teller had come close to the truth with the childhood illness and the mysteries. He said, "I'm searching for two people. I want to know if I'll find them."

The man's narrow eyes met his. "The first person you seek is a woman. And the answer lies in your own soul," he said quietly. "For the second, the answer lies with another woman."

Sam paid his money and pushed his way out from behind the bead curtain. Sweat beaded his forehead as he stood, thinking about what the fortune-teller had said. Incense wafted from the temple; the spicy food smells were overwhelming, and the noise of the crowd swelled. He couldn't take it any longer. He hailed a cab and went back to the hotel, where he went to his room and fell into a deep sleep, only to dream of Rafferty, who would be here tomorrow. With Lily's body.

FIFTY-EIGHT

ALMOST twenty-four hours later, Preshy emerged groggily from the elevator that took her up to the Four Seasons hotel, where she checked in.

"Madame, a gentleman is waiting at the bar for you," the desk clerk told her. "He wished me to tell you as soon as you arrived."

Her brain still reeling from hours of travel stuffed into a steel cylinder, breathing bad air and obliterating the bad memories with champagne, Preshy wondered uneasily who it could be. She headed into the bar and her heart did a double flip. It was Sam.

"What are *you* doing here?" she demanded.

"Waiting for you, Rafferty, of course," he said.

She squeezed onto the leather stool next to him. "Why?" she

asked, looking into his eyes. They were red-rimmed behind the glasses.

"Because you need help. And I can't let you go through this alone."

"Hah!" She lifted a shoulder in a disbelieving shrug. "The last time we spoke you didn't want to be involved. Anyhow, you look like crap."

"It's merely a reflection of the way I feel. By the way, what would you like to drink?"

She glanced disparagingly at the double vodka in front of him. "Perrier. With lime."

He said, "I had the opportunity to rethink my position on the flight to Paris." He raked his hands through his short brown hair, offering a smile. "Let's just say I changed my mind."

"Oh? And what part did Leilani play in that role reversal?"

He stared blankly at her, then he shook his head and said sadly, "You didn't have to go there, Rafferty."

The waiter delivered the water and she looked, shamefaced, into her fizzing glass. "Sorry," she muttered. "I didn't mean it." Her voice trailed off and her shoulders sagged with weariness. "It *was* Lily in the canal, of course," she said. "They've shipped her body back. I came here to bury her, but first I need to see if she has any relatives, find her friends."

"I knew you would. I came here to help you."

She glanced at him. He looked a bit worse for wear, but then she figured she probably did too. And she still didn't know whether to trust him. After all a man didn't just fly halfway round the world to come to help her bury a cousin, unless he had a motive.

"Thanks. But you don't have to." She slid from the stool. "I can take care of myself."

"Good. I'll see you around then."

"Maybe."

She glanced back at him as she trailed from the crowded bar, wanting to believe him. Of all the men in all the world, she thought, I have to bump into him. Wasn't that a quote from *Casablanca*? Or was it "of all the bars in all the world . . ." She was too tired to remember.

And then there were the beautiful flowers waiting in her room. "Welcome to Rafferty," the card said, and her heart melted. Just a bit.

FIFTY-NINE

IN her room, Preshy saw there were three messages waiting. Casting off her clothes, she showered, put on a robe, then flung herself on the bed, picked up the phone and listened.

The first was Aunt Grizelda, saying she must call and let her know she had arrived safely, and tell her what was going on. She said that Maow had completely taken over the apartment in their brief absence and now the two dogs sat on the floor at the cat's feet, while it lolled lazily on the sofa, keeping a beady brilliant-blue eye on all of them.

The second was Daria. "What the *fuck* were you doing in Venice, involved in what Sylvie tells me (via Aunt G) might have been Lily Song's death? And what the *fuck* are you doing in Shanghai, burying the poor woman? Why can't you leave well enough alone, let her family and friends take care of it?" There was a pause, while Daria thought, then she added, "If she has any. And if Super-Kid didn't have the chicken pox, I'd be on the next flight, but soon as she's better, I'm coming to get you, wherever you are in the world. And for your sake, Presh, I'm praying it's Paris. I'm so worried, Preshy, please, please, *please,* tell me you're okay."

The last was Sylvie. "Aunt Grizelda told me all about it," she said sternly. "I can't tell you how reckless your behavior is. Why do you feel you have to be involved with this woman? Her problems were her own, not yours, and now you might be in danger." *Oh my God, Sylvie was crying!* "I'm getting a flight tonight, I'll be in Shanghai tomorrow. I hope you are still alive, or that at least I don't have to resuscitate you. *Merde,* Preshy, I love you, you silly bitch."

Despite her fatigue and her worries, Preshy laughed. They had always called each other "silly bitch" when they did something stupid.

Clicking off the lamp, she lay back against the pillows, trying to adjust her aching travel-weary back to the soft comfort of the bed. Had she not been so tired she would have had a massage to remove all those travel crinkles from her spine . . . but she was just so sleepy . . .

IT WAS FIVE O'CLOCK THE next morning and still dark when she awoke. She pulled back the curtains and stared out at the blinking neon of the foreign city, wondering what the day would bring. She thought of Sam, hunched over the bar, glass in hand, and wondered how he was feeling. He was probably out to the world. Still, he had come all this way to help her—and she could certainly use some help. She thought for a minute, then smiling wickedly, she picked up the phone and ordered a full breakfast for two, right away. Then she called Sam's room.

It rang and rang, then at last, *"Wha . . . ?"*

She grinned. Sam wasn't sounding too alert. *"Bonjour,"* she said.

"What?"

At least he'd added a consonant to the end of the word. "I said good morning," she replied. "Perhaps you didn't recognize it in French."

"Jesus!" She heard him groan, imagined him falling back against the pillows, eyes still shut. "Rafferty, do you know what time it is? *Five a.m.* Isn't that a *teeny* bit early for a telephone conversation, complete with good morning in a foreign language?"

"You said to call as soon as I was ready . . . so . . . here I am. I've ordered breakfast for us," she added briskly. "Should be here in ten minutes so you'd better get your act together. I thought we would have a meeting, discuss procedure."

"Hmm, quite the corporate woman today, aren't we? Last night I thought you never wanted to see me again."

"Like you, I changed my mind," she retorted. See you in ten," and she put down the phone.

He was there in fifteen, arriving with the floor waiter with the breakfast. She inspected him while the waiter arranged the table. His hair was wet from the shower but he was unshaven with that stubble growing in again. And his eyes behind the gold-rimmed glasses looked sunken. Booze did not become him.

"Try the orange juice." She handed him a tall chilled glass. "I hear it's good for hangovers."

He drank it down then gave her a level look. "We each have our own way of dealing with our demons," he said. "Mine is drink. Yours, I assume, is cats."

Preshy laughed. "You're right," she said, suddenly missing Maow's sinuous Siamese presence.

They sat across from each other at the table. She poured coffee and ignoring the bacon and eggs Sam helped himself to a croissant from the basket.

She handed him the little black leather address book. "You'll find all Lily's contacts in here. I thought about going through it, calling them one by one. But then I came across this card."

He read it. "Mary-Lou Chen. And the same address as Lily."

She stared at him astonished. "How do you know that?"

"The concierge got it from the telephone directory. I went over there yesterday to check it out. No one was home."

She would never have thought of anything so simple, not when everything else seemed so complicated. "Well, anyway," she said, "my guess is Mary-Lou is Lily's assistant, so she's the first one we should call."

He glanced at the clock. "At five-thirty in the morning? Somehow, I don't think Ms. Chen would be too pleased about that. She probably doesn't start work until nine."

"Okay, you're right. I was just so fired up and ready to go . . ."

"I know, I know, Rafferty." He reached across the table and patted her hand. "But after what happened to Lily, I think we'd better tread more carefully."

"You sound like a writer," she said impatiently.

"Probably because I used to be one."

"Used to be?"

He shrugged. "Somehow I've lost the knack."

Looking at his haggard face she felt pity for him. "I'm sorry for what I said last night. About Leilani." She swirled the coffee dregs in her cup, avoiding his eyes. "I don't know what came over me, but I honestly didn't mean it. And I want to thank you for coming here to help me."

"That's okay." He got to his feet. "I'll meet you back here at nine-thirty. Then we'll call Ms. Chen and see what she knows." He grinned at her from the door. "Better take a shower," he said, "you look like crap this morning."

SIXTY

MARY-LOU did not look too good either. She rummaged through her closet trying to decide what to wear. By rights she should wear white, the color of mourning, but she couldn't do that until Lily was found. If she ever was. Weren't there tidal currents in Venice that swept things away? Debris, possessions, bodies . . . She prayed it was so.

She finally put on a pair of khaki pants and a white shirt, tying it in a knot at the waist. She added a coral necklace and chunky bracelets and gold hoop earrings. She brushed her short black hair and applied her usual scarlet lipstick. She was not satisfied with the result. Murder, she thought, did not add luster to a girl's looks.

Throwing on a red leather jacket, she took the elevator down to the garage, got in the little car she hated and drove to the French Concession. Life must go on. She must act as though nothing was wrong.

She let herself into the courtyard, parked next to Lily's SUV, walked up the shallow steps onto the verandah and unlocked the door.

The old house seemed eerily quiet. Not even the ticking of the clock disturbed the silence. The clock had been Lily's mother's, brought over from France. She had stolen it, along with the necklace, and it had always been there, like background music to Lily's life. Now it had stopped.

Superstitious, Mary-Lou shivered. She opened up the case, and gave the hands a little push. The clock still didn't tick. She searched in the drawer underneath, found the small key and wound it. There was a faint whirring then the clock fell silent. It seemed like a bad omen and she flung the key back into the drawer and slammed it shut.

She glanced round wondering where Lily's canary was; at least its song would bring life into the place. But the bird was not there.

Thinking of the necklace, she remembered that Lily kept her own jewelry in the small wall safe in the back of her closet. She knew where the key was hidden—under a pile of sweaters third shelf from the top.

There wasn't much, only a large diamond ring Lily had worn occasionally. About five carats, she estimated, and a good color. She put it in her pants pocket. There was also a heavy gold necklace with a matching bracelet; some gold and jade bangles, and a pendant or two. A bundle of documents that she saw were the deeds to the house. Not such a big haul. Deciding that for the moment she had better leave the bangles and the gold necklace in case anyone came inquiring, she stuffed them back in the safe along with the documents, locked the door and was heading down the rickety wooden cellar steps to the big safe when her phone rang.

"Yes?" she said impatiently.

"Am I speaking to Miss Chen? Mary-Lou Chen?"

It was a woman's voice, but no one she knew. "Yes," she said in a tone that indicated she was busy and not happy about this interruption.

"Miss Chen, this is Precious Rafferty speaking. Lily's cousin from Paris."

"Ohh." Shock hit her first, then fear.

"Miss Chen, I'm here in Shanghai—"

"You are in *Shanghai*?"

"I arrived last night. I need to see you. I have some important news."

Mary-Lou realized immediately that Precious must know about Lily. "What kind of news?"

She heard Precious sigh, then she said, "I prefer to speak to you in person, Miss Chen. I can be there in half an hour, if that's okay with you."

Mary-Lou hesitated. If she refused it might look suspicious, after all she was Lily's partner and best friend. "I'm happy to meet any relative of Lily's," she said, adding a warmer note to her voice. "Lily mentioned that she had a cousin in France. I'm sorry she's not here to greet you personally, but by a coincidence she is in Europe."

"I know," Precious Rafferty said, sending new chills down her spine. "In half an hour then, Miss Chen."

Despite the surprise phone call, Mary-Lou hadn't forgotten all that money stashed in the basement safe, Lily's profits from the selling of the illegal treasures. She still had half an hour. Just enough time to pack it into a suitcase and into the trunk of her car. And speaking of cars, Lily's was much better than hers. The keys were probably still in it. She would take possession of that later.

SIXTY-ONE

SAM said it would be better if Preshy met Ms. Chen alone, so leaving him in a nearby teahouse, she walked down the lane crammed with small houses behind big arched stone gates. Lily's gate was painted green. Preshy rang the bell and waited. Mary-Lou Chen answered on the intercom and buzzed her in.

The big old house with its Chinese garden, its fragrant lotus pond with the goldfish, and the cool trickling fountain made her feel as though she were entering another, more tranquil world. Mary-Lou was standing on the verandah steps waiting for her.

"Won't you please come in," she said. "Lily will be so sad to have missed your visit, but I hope I can make up for it with some small hospitality."

She waved Preshy into the living room, indicating a chair, then excused herself while she went to get the tea.

Curious, Preshy looked around, noting the spare furnishings, the shiny bamboo floor, the altar table with the golden Buddha. It was simple and quite beautiful and for the first time she wished she had known her cousin.

Mary-Lou was back in an instant and Preshy thought admiringly how lovely she was, with her shiny black hair and wonderful amber eyes, and that full scarlet mouth in a shade of lipstick she would never have dared to wear.

Mary-Lou poured the tea into small handleless blue-glazed cups. She said, "It's really a great pity. Lily would have liked to have met you. You are her only relative?" She looked inquiringly at Preshy as she offered her a cup.

"I'm her only *European* relative. I don't know about her father's family."

"Lily hated her father," Mary-Lou said bluntly. "She and her mother had no contact with the Song family after he died, and that was many years ago. Lily is very much on her own," she said, sounding regretful. "I've tried often—oh so often, more than you will ever know—to get her to socialize, to attend parties and functions with me, but Lily is a loner. She's dedicated to her work," she added, smiling candidly at Preshy. "Lily has exquisite taste in antiques, but of course most of her business is with the tourist trade copies."

"Fakes," Preshy said.

"If you wish to put it that way, though they are never sold as authentic, they are always described as replicas." She lifted a delicate shoulder in a shrug that made Preshy wonder if she was even capable of making an ungraceful move. It was like watching a lithe young panther as she walked across the room and picked up a small plaster figurine.

"This is the kind of thing Lily sells," Mary-Lou said. "It makes us our living."

Preshy looked at her. "I have some bad news for you, Miss Chen."

"Bad news?" She frowned, looking concerned.

"Lily was in Venice. There was an accident. I'm sorry to tell you, but Lily drowned."

Mary-Lou shrank back in her chair. Her small face puckered and her eyes glittered with tears. She wrapped her arms across her chest, clutching her shoulders as though to protect herself.

"But *why* was Lily in Venice?" she said. "I thought she'd gone to Paris. . . . She even mentioned she hoped to see you . . ."

Preshy wondered why Mary-Lou hadn't told her that earlier, but she thought perhaps it was just the Chinese way and that she had not wanted to discuss Lily's personal business with a stranger, even though she was a relative.

"I'm so sorry," she said gently. "But the fact is I've brought Lily home to be buried." She put the piece of paper with the address and number of the Chinese funeral home on the low table between them and told Mary-Lou they needed instructions. "I was hoping you could help," she said. "I don't know the Chinese customs and traditions, I don't even know about her family, or who her friends are."

Mary-Lou seemed to pull herself together. She said, of course she would take care of it. That there was no family, or close friends, only her. And if Miss Rafferty would excuse her now, she was a little upset and needed to be alone. But she needn't worry, everything would be done for Lily.

Promising to call later, Mary-Lou saw her out. At the gate, Preshy turned to say goodbye but the door was already shut. Poor thing, she thought. It's been a terrible shock.

Sam was waiting at the teahouse, sipping a brew he said was called *longjing* tea, that he was becoming quite fond of.

"Beats vodka," Preshy said, tasting it.

"What are you, Rafferty? Some kind of reformer?" He glared at her.

"Sorry, sorry . . . no need to be so huffy." She grinned at him. "And anyway, it's true." He gave her a withering look and she said, "Well, anyway, Mary-Lou Chen is a beauty, and a sweetheart. Oh, Sam, when I gave her the bad news that lovely young woman just seemed to shrivel in front of my eyes. She looked like a frightened child."

"Why frightened? I would have expected shock."

She stared at him. Of course he was right. "I don't really know," she said. "But she agreed to take care of the funeral arrangements. She's going to call me later."

MARY-LOU DID TAKE CARE OF the funeral arrangements, and very efficiently and quickly, before any more questions could be asked.

"The burial will be tomorrow," she informed Preshy in a phone call that afternoon. "At the temple where Lily's mother already rests. If you would like to attend, please be at the temple at noon. And please do not wear black. It is not our custom."

SIXTY-TWO

LATER that evening, Sylvie arrived, jet-lagged and furious. "You don't deserve me," she said as Preshy embraced her in the Four Seasons lobby. "I'm a martyr to your emotions," she added dramatically.

"Good," Preshy said, "I could use a martyr. It'll make a change from a boozer."

"What boozer?"

"Sam Knight. He's taken to drink."

"I'm not surprised, being around you." Sylvie stopped and gave her a sharp look. "What's Sam Knight doing here? I thought he'd gone back to the States."

"He changed his mind." Preshy tried to look modest, then she laughed. "Either he's got something to do with it or he's succumbed to my fatal charm."

"Well, it certainly turned out fatal for Lily," Sylvie said. "And hasn't it occurred to you to wonder why women keep disappearing when Sam Knight is around, and maybe turning up dead?"

"Actually, yes it has."

"And did you not stop to wonder whether *you* might not be next in line?"

They rode in silence in the elevator to Preshy's floor, then walked, in silence, down the lushly carpeted corridor to her room, which Sylvie was going to share.

Preshy said, "Sylvie, I'm in Shanghai for two reasons. One was to bring home poor Cousin Lily. The other is because this is where Bennett lived. And Lily said this whole thing had to do with Bennett."

"So?"

"I want to find him, but I've never had an address, or a phone number, only his cell phone. But now I have Lily's address book. I haven't had time to look through it yet but I'm hoping to find something in there."

While Sylvie showered away the travel blues, Preshy went through the book page by page, but found no Bennett James.

"There's nothing," she said, disappointed, when Sylvie emerged from the bathroom, wrapped in a robe, with her hair in a towel.

Sylvie sighed as she picked up the phone, called room service and asked for tea and toast. "Sourdough toast," she instructed, "and make sure it arrives hot. And a little smoked salmon too, please. A salad? No, I don't think so. . . . Fifteen minutes? Thank you."

She sank wearily into a chair and looked through the address book. "It might not be under Bennett's name," she said. "For instance, here's a Ben Jackson. And then there's a Yuan Bennett. They might be worth a try."

While Sylvie ate her toast, Preshy called the two numbers. The first was an antiques dealer who said he did business with Lily and was sorry to hear that she had met with an accident. Mary-Lou Chen had told him about it and he would be at the funeral the next day.

The second number no longer existed. "But there's an address," Preshy said, deciphering Lily's untidy scrawl. "Maybe I should go there and find out."

Sylvie threw her a warning look. "Oh no," she said. "Not without me you don't, and I'm going to sleep." She yawned. "Just don't do anything foolish until I wake up, okay?"

But when Sylvie was snoring, in about two minutes flat, Preshy put on her coat and went downstairs. As she'd expected Sam was in the bar.

"Not you again," he said, swinging round as she tapped him on the shoulder. "Can't a man drink in peace?"

"Not when he's with me, he can't. My friend Sylvie just arrived from Paris. I showed her Lily's address book. I might be on Bennett's trail."

She gave him the address and he looked at the page with the name Yuan Bennett. "You think this might be him?"

She shrugged. "Who knows? But obviously Lily knew him and this is the closest I can come to any Bennett. Anyhow the phone's disconnected. Maybe nobody's living there."

"Okay. So we'll find out tomorrow." Sam turned back to his drink.

Preshy hung around for a few minutes, hoping he would say Okay let's go now, but he did not, and he didn't ask her to stay and keep him company either. Finally she stalked off and went outside.

Shanghai glowed like a new planet under halogen arc lights, with illuminated skyscrapers shimmering like stars in the heavens. Hundreds of people crowded the streets and the cold night air was full of spicy aromas from the roadside barbecue stands. Signaling a taxi, Preshy climbed in and gave the driver Yuan Bennett's address.

It was a tall expensive condo building, built of shiny pink granite with a pair of rugged bronze lions placed at odd *feng shui* angles outside, to protect the good *chi*. A spotlit fountain played in the courtyard and a uniformed doorman opened the taxi door for her.

"I'm looking for a Mr. Yuan Bennett," she told him hopefully.

"So sorry, but Mr. Yuan no longer here."

So it was Bennett *Yuan* she was looking for, not Yuan Bennett, and therefore probably not *her* Bennett. Still, she needed to be sure. "I've come all the way from Paris to see him. Could you tell me where I can find him?"

"So sorry, miss, but Mr. Yuan left after his wife died."

"His *wife*?"

"Yes, miss. Ana Yuan was the daughter of a very distinguished Shanghai family. Mrs. Yuan was in Suzhou, a pretty place with many canals, like the Venice of China, people say."

"*Venice?*" Preshy repeated, stunned.

"Yes, miss. Unfortunately, Mrs. Yuan tripped. She banged her head and slipped into the canal. She was drowned, miss, and you never saw a sadder man than Mr. Bennett. He tried to find witnesses to her accident but there were none, and nobody knew why she went alone to Suzhou that day. They said Mr. Bennett was sobbing at the funeral, but he did not inherit his wife's money and could no longer afford this magnificent apartment. He moved out soon after, miss, and we have not seen him here since."

Preshy thanked the doorman and asked him to call a cab for her. Back at the hotel, she found Sam still in the bar. She slid onto the stool next to him.

He glanced at her. "I thought I was going to see you tomorrow. Don't tell me you've come back to preach."

"No, though I should. But Sam, you're not going to believe this," she said. And then she told him the Bennett Yuan story and how his wife had drowned in the Suzhou canal.

"I still can't believe it's *my* Bennett though," she said finally.

"Hah! What do you need, Rafferty? A signed confession? Of course it's him." Sam turned back to his drink. "And anyway, why did you go there alone? Anything might have happened."

"No, oh no," she said softly. "Bennett would never harm me. And I still don't believe it's him, it's just a trail of circumstantial evidence. We don't even know if it's the same man."

Groaning, Sam drained his glass. "Rafferty," he said, "you need your head examined."

"Maybe I do." She slid off the stool. "And I should have known better than to expect sympathy from you."

"You don't need *sympathy,*" he said, as she walked away. "You need a brain!"

Back in the room, Sylvie was snoring gently. Turning the TV on low, Preshy sat and watched Chinese programs until the early hours, her mind full of Bennett Yuan. Could the two drownings really be just a coincidence?

SIXTY-THREE

THERE were only a half dozen mourners at Lily's funeral and three of them were Preshy, Sylvie and Sam. Preshy wore Aunt G's white Valentino coat, and Sylvie her old beige Burberry, while Sam wore black because he had nothing else. The other mourners were Mary-Lou Chen, gorgeous in a long white brocade Chinese dress, wrapped against the cold in layers of pashmina shawls; Ben, the business friend Preshy had spoken to on the phone; and a frail old man with a stiff goatee beard and flowing hair, in worn gray robes.

At the temple they lit bundles of fragrant incense and thin bamboo sticks, watching the smoke spiral upward. They were told this would assist Lily's spirit on her journey to heaven. A small group of paid mourners walked behind the coffin on the way to the burial ground, banging on drums and cymbals and wailing a kind of song for the dead, followed by a troop of scruffy, laughing urchins and a stray dog. It was, Preshy thought sadly, the most lonely funeral anyone could ever have.

Tears streamed down Mary-Lou's beautiful face and she bowed her head sorrowfully. After the burial, the businessman went over to shake her hand and express his regrets, then left quickly. She stood by the grave with the old man beside her, but they did not speak. After a few minutes he turned away. He went over to where Preshy and the others were standing, bowing as he shook each of their hands.

"I came across Lily again only a short time ago," he said. His beard wagged as he spoke and his rheumy old eyes were soft with sorrow. "I was a friend of her mother, and before she died, she entrusted me with something for Lily, to be given to her on her fortieth birthday. This birthday, as you might know, took place only a few months ago, and so I went to see Lily. I gave her the necklace in its beautiful red leather box. I told her its exquisite story and explained its value."

They stared at him, surprised. "A necklace?"

He nodded. "Not any ordinary necklace, but a necklace with a history that is almost as valuable as the jewels themselves." Shivering in the cold he said, "But this is no time to be talking of jewels. I am sure you will find your grandmother's necklace amongst her possessions and then it will become yours."

He pressed a card into Preshy's hand. "I am at your disposal, Miss Rafferty," he said with dignity. And he bowed and walked away through the dripping misty trees, down the path to the gate.

"What can he mean 'grandmother's necklace'?" Preshy said. "Does he mean the one in the photograph?"

"The photograph that went missing," Sam said.

"Ohh . . . ," she said, realizing what he meant, and remembering that Bennett was the only other person who had been in her apartment.

"Here comes Mary-Lou," Sam muttered. "Just act natural."

Natural! Preshy hardly knew what "natural" was anymore.

Mary-Lou came toward them with that particular pantherlike stride, smiling sadly as Preshy introduced the others.

Dabbing at her eyes, in a low quiet voice she thanked them for coming. "We were childhood friends, Lily and I," she said, "two little half-Chinese outcasts in our all-Chinese school, so of course we bonded immediately. Now things are very different, it hardly matters who you are or who your parents were. Time moves on, you know," she added with a faltering smile. "But I would be pleased if you would do me the honor of returning to Lily's house to take some tea."

They had rented a car and driver and now they followed Mary-Lou back to Lily's home. When they got there she had discarded her shawls and was looking calm and beautiful in her Chinese floor-length white dress.

"I welcome you on Lily's behalf," she said in her low throaty voice, and even though she was covered from head to toe, Preshy thought somehow she still sounded sexy. A sideways glance at Sam confirmed that he had noticed too.

She and Sylvie perched on the edge of the low hard sofa, but Sam said he preferred to stand. Mary-Lou served tea with special round buns filled with a sweet lotus paste, then she took a seat on an elm-wood chair opposite them.

"I was sad to see so few mourners," Preshy said. "I'd hoped Lily would have had more friends to say goodbye to her."

Mary-Lou shrugged. "I told you she was a loner. She hated to socialize, she lived for her work."

"I'm surprised that manufacturing and selling replicas of Xi'an warriors could mean that much to anyone," Sam said, taking a sip of his tea. He was beginning to like the Chinese tea very much.

Mary-Lou seemed suddenly flustered. "It does seem a little odd. But both Lily and I grew up poor. Making money was her obsession, Mr. Knight, not the Xi'an warriors."

"And yours also?" His eyes lingered on the five-carat diamond on her finger.

She leveled her gorgeous amber eyes at him. "Of course. I did not find it pleasant to be poor."

"Then Lily must have left quite a legacy."

A flicker of irritation crossed her face. "I have not gone through Lily's things, Mr. Knight. But her world was very small. What you see here is all she had. As far as I know," she added.

"But she must have a lawyer, someone who took care of her affairs, prepared a will for her."

"Like all Chinese, Lily kept her personal business close to her own heart. I've never heard of her using a lawyer and I've worked with her for many years. However, I do know there is a safe in her bedroom. If there were anything private, anything she didn't want anybody else to know about, it would be there. And I *do* know where she hid the key. Lily kept changing the hiding place," she added with a half smile, "but she kept forgetting where it was, so she always told me. I believe currently it's under the sweaters in her closet." Getting to her feet, she said, "Why don't we go and see?"

They followed her into the bedroom and Mary Lou fished the key from under the sweaters and handed it to Sam. "You open it," she said, pushing aside the hanging clothes to reveal the small gray safe door.

There was very little inside. Some gold jewelry, jade bangles, and a bundle of papers, written in Chinese. Mary-Lou read them.

"These are the title deeds to this house," she said. "It belonged to her father's family, and eventually to her father. Her mother inherited it from him, and finally it became Lily's. Of course now it's quite valuable."

"What about bank accounts, safe-deposit boxes?" Sam was looking hard at her but Mary-Lou did not flinch.

"There is, of course, a business account. And you are at liberty, Mr. Knight, to go through this entire house and search for any other papers or valuables. Lily was only forty years old, she had no family, she didn't expect to die. I don't think making a will even entered her head."

"Then what will happen to her property?"

Mary-Lou shrugged, that simple feline shrug that was her habit. "Her property will go to her nearest living relative. Which means Miss Rafferty I suppose."

Preshy looked at her, surprised. "Oh, but I don't think . . . I mean you were her best friend, it should go to you."

"Let's talk about it later," Sam interrupted curtly. "Meanwhile, if you can find the time, perhaps you can go through the house and see if there's anything else. More papers relating to bank accounts, legal matters, things like that."

"Of course." Mary-Lou walked them to the door. "And thank you again for all you did for Lily. It was so tragic, drowning like that, in Venice of all places. I still don't know what she was doing there."

When they got back in the car, Sam said, "Of course she knew."

"Knew what?" Preshy and Sylvie stared at him.

"Knew what Lily was doing in Venice. Mary-Lou knew because she was also there. She was on my flight from Venice to Paris."

"Oh . . . my . . . God . . . ," Preshy whispered. "Do you think she had something to do with Lily's death?"

"Why else would she have been there? And you know what else? My bet is it has something to do with your grandmother's fabulous necklace."

SIXTY-FOUR

BACK at the hotel, it was decided that Preshy should call Mary-Lou and invite her for drinks so Sam could question her, and they arranged to meet at the Cloud 9 bar.

Mary-Lou arrived in a haze of expensive perfume, looking ravishing, and over drinks, she assured them she would search the house for any legal papers, though she doubted sincerely that there were any.

"I shall, of course, carry on the business," she added, sipping her usual vodka martini with the three olives.

Preshy thought she looked stunning in her simple black suit, with dangling jet earrings glittering beneath her shiny black hair. "Don't worry about it," she said, "take your time. And I wish you luck with the business."

"Thank you." Mary-Lou smiled modestly while taking a cautious glance around the large room. You never knew; Bennett might just decide to come back to Shanghai and show up here.

"What about the necklace?" Sam asked, noticing Mary-Lou's face tighten fractionally.

She took a sip of her drink, then said, "I'm afraid I don't know anything about a necklace. Lily never wore much jewelry, you know."

"I'm talking about her grandmother's necklace," Sam said, aiming in the dark and hoping for a hit. He didn't get one.

"I'm afraid I shall have to leave that up to Miss Rafferty," Mary-Lou said. "It has nothing to do with me."

A short while later, Mary-Lou said she must go, and they said goodbye, watching as she strode confidently through the now-crowded bar.

"Miss Chen," Sam called after her. She turned. "Can I ask you something?" he said.

She nodded. "Of course."

"Were you ever in Venice?"

Her eyes widened. "I'm sorry," she said quietly, "but I've never been to Europe." And she turned again and continued on her way.

"She's lying again," Sam said. "And I wonder why."

Preshy wondered too. And she wondered again about Sam. He was being so helpful. The mystery writer in search of a story perhaps? She was beginning to feel better about him; in fact she might even have fancied him. Under other circumstances, of course.

. . .

THAT NIGHT, NOT KNOWING WHAT else to do and to cheer themselves up and experience the Shanghai culture, they dined at the Whampoa Club at Three on the Bund, the chic dining and shopping address. Sylvie chose it because of its modern Chinese cuisine, and still discussing Mary-Lou, they feasted on crispy eel strips and drunken chicken and tea-smoked eggs, as well as Su Dongpo braised pork. Then they had double-boiled Chinese pears with almonds, silver fungus and lotus seeds, while tasting some of the forty infusions offered by the tea sommelier.

Sylvie pronounced it spectacular and went off to congratulate the chef, Jereme Leung, and to say she would be trying out some of his ideas at Verlaine.

"Well?" Sam asked, looking across the table at Preshy.

"Well . . . what?" She glanced back from under her eyelashes.

"So do you still think I'm a killer?"

The fiery blush heated her cheeks. "Oh, I never . . . I mean . . . I didn't . . ." She stammered to a halt.

"Don't lie to me, Rafferty. You've suspected me of having something to do with this all along. And I guess I've given you no reason to change your mind. Right?"

"Right." She nodded. Then blurted in her usual fashion, straight from the heart, "But I still like you."

Sam was still laughing when Sylvie came back.

But what Preshy had said was the truth. Despite everything against him, she really "liked" him.

AND THEN SHANGHAI WAS OVER. Mary-Lou was still a mystery; Lily had been buried next to her mother, and the next morning they were flying back to Paris. And Preshy hoped that her cousin would rest in peace. Though she knew *she* would not. Not until she had found out the truth.

SIXTY-FIVE

PARIS

BACK in Paris, Sam checked into the Hôtel d'Angleterre, just down the street from Preshy's store. He dropped his bag there and then they went back to her apartment.

She had called Aunt G to tell her she was on her way home, and knowing how much she missed the cat, her aunt had shipped Maow back, by special courier. The grumpy concierge had let the cat in and fed her and now she came running with a welcoming yowl. Preshy kissed and hugged her and spoke softly to her, and gave her some of her special cat treats. Then she fixed coffee and went and sat on the sofa opposite Sam, staring gloomily at the empty fire grate.

"We have no proof Mary-Lou was in Venice," she said.

"No, but the police could check the airlines and also immigration. We also have no proof that Bennett James, or Bennett Yuan, or whoever he is killed his wife, but I'd still bet my shirt on it. And one of them killed Lily."

"How can you say that?" She glared at him. "There's no proof of any of this. And anyway the autopsy showed Lily drowned. Her death was an accident."

"And so was Ana Yuan's. You have to go after Mary-Lou," Sam persisted. "Somebody killed Lily for your grandmother's necklace. And I *know* she was in Venice."

"But I *can't,*" Preshy said, feeling the tears coming. The past months had been grueling; she just couldn't take any more.

Sam ran his hands exasperatedly through his hair, groaning. "*Why not?* Are you afraid to know the truth?"

Her temper flared. "What do you mean?"

"Aw come on, Rafferty, admit it, you don't want to know if perfect Bennett—or sweet, beautiful and oh so sad Mary-Lou—had anything to do with Lily's death."

"Oh, stop it!" She turned away. "Just leave me alone, why don't you?"

Sam got to his feet. "The trouble with you, Rafferty, is that you always think the best of everybody."

"And the trouble with you, Sam Knight, is that you *never* think the best of anybody. And anyway, you were not exactly helpful to the police in finding out what happened to your wife."

They stared at each other across a chasm of animosity that had opened a space between them, like the shifting tectonic plates in an earthquake.

Sam nodded. "You're right," he said. "But you know the old saying 'two rights don't make a wrong.' Well, this time those old soothsayers were correct."

Preshy watched as he collected his coat from the back of a chair.

At the door, he turned to look at her. He was remembering the temple fortune-teller telling him, "The answer to your second question also lies with a woman," and he knew that woman was Rafferty. Only she could unravel this mystery.

"Call me—if you change your mind," he said, closing the door behind him.

Tears stung Preshy's eyes. She was exhausted from the long plane journey, battered by the events of the past few days. Sam had no right to treat her like that. She didn't even *like* him anymore. She would *never* call him. And if he called her, she would not even speak to him. Ever again.

Weeping, she called Boston.

"What's up?" Daria asked.

Preshy could hear the sound of dishes rattling, Daria was obviously in the kitchen, no doubt cooking something good. She wished she were there, where everybody was normal, comfortable, with no secrets and no murders. She told Daria the whole story, and exactly what Sam had said to her.

When she'd finished there was no more sound of pots and pans rattling. Instead there was silence. Finally Daria said, "And don't you think Sam has a point, Presh? After all, a woman is dead. I know they said it was an accident, but Lily's so-called friend *was* there, Sam saw her. And she's lying about it. And what about

Bennett's wife? If he is the same man, and Sam obviously believes he is even if you don't, Bennett never told you about *her,* did he? And *she* died the same way Lily did. Something's wrong, Presh. One of them killed her and it's time you faced up to it. And maybe did something about it."

Like what? Preshy asked herself miserably, later as she prepared for bed. Lying awake in the dark with Maow's warm comforting body curled on the pillow, her purrs in her ear, she thought at least the cat couldn't ask questions, and demand answers. And action.

SIXTY-SIX

SHE was in the shower when the phone rang the next morning. Ignoring it, she let the hot water soothe her bones, wondering why the message center wasn't picking up. It had been acting up for the past few weeks though.

But the ringing went on and on, and suddenly every bad thing that might have happened jumped into her head. Something must be wrong. . . . Had something happened to Super-Kid? Why else would anyone keep on ringing like this? Frantic, she stepped out of the shower, almost tripping over Maow, who was sitting right outside the glass door looking aggrieved. The cat didn't like the ringing either . . . and it was *still* ringing. . . .

Grabbing a towel, Preshy ran into the bedroom and reached for the phone, just as it stopped. She sank onto the bed, mopping at her wet hair. She waited a few minutes, but when it didn't ring again, she went back to the bathroom and began to rub lotion into her legs. She wondered whether to call Daria, but if it had been Daria, she was certain to call again. And anyhow it might have been her aunts, or Sylvie. Or Sam, though since she and Sam were no longer speaking that seemed unlikely. Unless, she thought hopefully, he'd been calling to apologize.

Looking in the mirror, she began smoothing on the face cream that was guaranteed to prevent the ravages of time. Maybe time, but what about stress? She could *count* those fine lines around her eyes now, and she had crow's-feet!

She jumped as the phone's shrill beep split the silence again. Maow yowled, and she stubbed her toe on the foot of the bed as she ran to answer it. Wincing with pain, hopping on one foot, and with the other foot clutched in her hand, she grabbed the phone. She just knew it was Sam and boy was she gonna let him have it for letting the phone ring and ring like that.

"If it's you, Sam Knight," she said frostily, "I don't want to speak to you ever again."

There was a long silence, then a familiar voice said, "Preshy, it's Bennett."

She stood for a minute, rigid with shock. The blood seemed to drain from her brain and she thought she would faint. Her knees gave way and she sank onto the bed, the phone still clutched in her numb hand.

"Preshy? Please speak to me," he was saying. "I need to talk to you. I need to explain. . . ."

Bennett was talking to her . . . he was saying that he needed to see her, to explain. . . .

"Speak to me, Preshy, please just *speak* to me," he said in that soft urgent tone that brought back a thousand intimate moments spent right here in her bed. "You may not forgive me but at least allow me to tell my side of the story. Please Preshy, please, my love, just talk to me."

"I don't want to talk to you ever again," she said, surprised to find that she even had a voice.

"I understand. Believe me, I know what you're feeling, but I want you to know this, Preshy, that no matter what happened, I always loved you. All I'm asking is that you see me, even if it's just for the length of time I need to explain. Preshy, I can't go through life with this burden of guilt on my shoulders."

She lay back against the pillows, eyes tightly shut. Tears trickled sideways across her cheeks and into her ears. *She hadn't expected to feel like this. She'd thought she was over him. No more Pity Days. . . . Move forward. . . . A new life ahead. . . . Life with a capital* L. . . . *And within minutes she had been reduced to a trembling wreck. . . .*

"I always loved you, Preshy," Bennett was saying urgently. "But I hadn't told you the truth, and that's what I couldn't live with. It's why I couldn't go through with it. And it was too late, I saw no way out. The truth is I had no money, Preshy. I was a poor guy faking it because I was in love. Remember that night we met? I told you I followed you? I fell in love in that moment, and nothing's changed. When it came down to it I couldn't cheat you, I couldn't marry you and live the lie I'd constructed around me. And I couldn't tell you the truth. It all became too much. The only answer was for me to leave. I didn't mean to hurt you. It just seemed the right thing to do."

She said nothing.

"Preshy, are you still there?" There was a long silence as he waited for an answer. "Speak to me, sweetheart," he said with a catch in his voice, as though, like her, he was crying.

"I don't know why you're calling me, Bennett," she said at last, sitting up and drying her tears. She wasn't going to be caught out again by his honeyed words and declarations of love.

"I must see you," he was saying. "You have to let me explain. You have to forgive me, Preshy, because only then can I . . . can *we* . . . go on. I'm here in Venice," he said. "The place where we were so happy. Meet me in Venice, my darling. I'm begging you. If only you could *see* me, Preshy. I'm on my knees *begging* you to at least meet me here and let me explain. You have to *trust* me."

She closed her eyes again, silent, imagining Bennett down on his knees, begging her. "There's something else," he said, in a suddenly quiet voice. "I know who killed Lily. And it wasn't me. Believe me. I'll tell you everything when you get here. But you are in danger too, Preshy."

Oh my God. What was he saying? She thought of poor Lily telling her she was in danger, and now Bennett was telling her the same thing. She had to see him. To find out the truth. And for her own peace of mind. To finally put this thing to rest. Or it would haunt her all her life.

"I'll meet you, Bennett," she said quietly. "I'll be there tonight."

His voice seemed to lift with joy and relief as he said, "Oh, sweetheart, it'll be so wonderful to see you again. You're gonna love it here. It's Carnevale time, the pagan festival when everyone wears masks and dresses up and pretends to be someone they're not. I know," he added, sounding inspired, "I'll get tickets for a ball. Why don't you bring a costume too? We'll pretend we don't know each other, start all over from the beginning, like two new people."

Preshy tried to imagine that but couldn't. The past was too fixed in her mind to pretend she was someone else. He seemed temporarily to have forgotten all about Lily, and her own danger, he was so caught up in seeing her again. "Give me your number" was all she said. "I'll call when I get there."

"I don't *still* love you, Preshy" were his last words before she rang off. "I always have."

And despite herself, despite all the progress she'd made, despite Lily, despite all the questions in her head, Preshy still wondered if it were true.

She sat on the bed for a long time, thinking about Bennett. She had no doubt she was doing the right thing. She needed to put closure to Lily's murder and this whole disastrous episode. And she also needed to know the truth about him, and who he really was.

SIXTY-SEVEN

QUICKLY, before she could change her mind, she called and got a noon flight to Venice. Then she began to pack. Maybe Bennett's suggestion of the carnival disguise was a good idea after all. She could watch him and he wouldn't know it was her.

Her wedding outfit still hung in the very back of her closet where she had buried it in its plastic shroud. Now she took out the fur-trimmed cape. It would be the perfect disguise; the wedding cape the groom had never seen. She rolled it mercilessly into a bundle and stuffed it in her carry-on. She was wearing black jeans, a black turtleneck and slouchy flat boots. She wouldn't need much else because she wasn't planning on spending time there. Which reminded her, she needed somewhere to stay.

She rang the Bauer but they told her that because of Carnevale they were full. All the hotels in Venice were full, they said. So she called Tourist Information and got the name of a small *pensione* near the Rialto. It would have to do.

She called the concierge downstairs and bribed her to come in and feed the cat again, then she considered who else to call.

She certainly wasn't calling Sam because he'd only interfere, and besides she wasn't speaking to him. And she needed to do this alone. She wasn't calling Sylvie for the same reason, and because she would raise hell and tell her she was mad, which she was, but that was the way it had to be. Nor would she call Daria. But she had at least to let Aunt G know where she was going. And why.

She was relieved, though, when she got no reply, because she knew what the Aunts' response would be. That she was out of her mind and absolutely must not go. The housekeeper, Jeanne, never answered when the Aunts were out because the messages were often in foreign languages and she got them muddled, so now the message center picked up.

"Hi, it's me, I just want to tell you that I'm going to Venice to meet Bennett," she said. "He wants to see me, to explain. He said he knows who Lily's killer is. And that it wasn't him. I have at least to give him that opportunity to prove himself to me. Don't I?" she added, sounding less sure than she'd meant to. "Anyhow, I'm going to Venice to meet him. I need to do this. It's Carnevale there and all the hotels are full so I'll be at the Pensione Mara, near the Rialto."

She left the number and then said, "I'm only there for one night. That's all it'll take to straighten this out. At least I hope so.

And I really need to know the truth about Lily. Don't worry though, I'm not going to do anything 'foolish,' " she added with a nervous little laugh. "I'll be fine. It's just something I have to do alone. Love you . . ."

Soon she would see Bennett again and as the plane circled over Marco Polo Airport, she wondered how she would feel about that.

GRIZELDA'S SCREAM BROUGHT EVERYBODY RUNNING. It came from her room and Mimi, Jeanne, Maurice and the dogs all arrived there at the same moments. Unable to speak, Grizelda was on the bed, wafting her face with a hand to stop herself from fainting. She pointed to the phone and mouthed the word *message.* Mimi pressed the button and Preshy's voice came on. *"I'm going to Venice to meet Bennett. . . . He wants to see me, to explain . . . said he knows who Lily's killer is . . . I need to do this . . ."*

"Oh . . . Mon . . . Dieu . . ." Mimi sank onto the bed next to Grizelda, while Jeanne rushed to get glasses of ice water and Maurice opened the windows for some air. "The silly little fool," Mimi exclaimed. "We have to stop her."

Grizelda nodded. "Call Sam," she said, gulping down the water. "Send a plane for him. Tell him we'll meet him in Venice."

Mimi did as she was told. Sam answered on the first ring. "If it's you, Rafferty," he said, "remember we are not speaking."

"Well soon you will be, I hope," Mimi said briskly. And then she told him the story. "Drive to the airport at Orly," she said. "A plane will be waiting for you. We'll meet you at Marco Polo. Right away, Sam."

She didn't have to tell him twice. He was in a taxi in less than five minutes, and an hour later was in a private four-seater Cessna on his way to Venice.

So were Mimi and Grizelda, though they were in a Gulfstream. For once they were tense and silent. Every now and then Grizelda would moan, "How could she be so stupid? How could she?" And Mimi would answer, "Because she still hasn't learned about men, that's why. The poor fool still believes she's in love."

At Marco Polo they waited an hour for Sam. Finally, he came racing toward them, lanky and lean in his black leather jacket and jeans. They took a water taxi to the Rialto and walked to the Pensione Mara, where they were told that the *signorina* had checked in, but she was not there right now.

Sam tried Preshy's cell phone but it was switched off, so Grizelda called the Cipriani and using her influence, got them rooms. While they waited by the canal near San Marco for the Cipriani's launch to pick them up, Sam called Preshy again. Again no reply.

At the hotel while the two aunts went to freshen up, he found the bar and sat brooding over a triple espresso. He was on the wagon—he'd need all his wits about him to get Preshy out of this one. He was very afraid for her.

AS DARKNESS FELL, VENICE CAME to life. Gondolas full of bizarrely masked and costumed revelers poled down the canals, and crowded motor launches sped back and forth in a surge of spray, with cargoes of beak-nosed plague doctors and redheaded harlots in fishnet tights with scarlet plumes in their hair. Music pounded as the parties started and the narrow streets teemed with masked revelers. Laughter and song bounced from the old walls, echoing across the lagoon, and fireworks split the sky into a million stars. It was Carnevale in Venice.

Sam was on his second espresso when he dialed her number again. *Nothing.* He called her at the *pensione.* Nothing. Grizelda and Mimi had rejoined him and were sitting silently, watching the fireworks without really seeing them. Their faces were drawn with worry and he had no words to comfort them. "I don't know where she is," he said, "but I'm going over there."

They jumped up. "We're coming with you."

"No. No, you can't." He didn't want to scare them by saying it might be dangerous. "Please," he said. "Let me take care of this. I'll call as soon as I know anything."

"Promise?" they said together, and he nodded, but he thought that unless he could get her on her phone, his chances of finding Preshy in a city whose narrow crowded streets were filled with anonymous revelers, were less than slim. But anyway, the Aunts didn't take him at his word. Instead they took the next launch to the Piazza San Marco. They were right behind him.

SIXTY-EIGHT

VENICE

PRESHY was sitting in Quadri's, but she wasn't thinking about Bennett, she was thinking about Sam. She was even sitting at the same table by the window where they had sat together, bickering, over their drinks. She almost wished he were here with her now. *Almost,* she thought, but not quite. She was her own woman now and she needed to prove to herself that she could do this alone.

She was wearing the brocade wedding cape with the fur-edged hood thrown back and a feathered eye mask. With her new short hair, she doubted Bennett would even recognize her, and that suited her just fine. Of course *she* would know *him.* How could she not when every aspect of his face and body were permanently engraved on her mind?

Nervous, she took another sip of the hot grappa coffee. Now

she understood why Sam drank. He was looking for Dutch courage, drinking just to get through day-to-day since his wife disappeared. Except unlike Leilani, Bennett had come back.

It was dark outside now and the mist was starting to roll in, the way it did over the lagoon in winter, in great curls of gray vapor, like something from the black-and-white mystery movies of the fifties, about Zombies, and creatures from Black Lagoons.

She took her phone from her bag, switched it on and called Bennett's number. He answered immediately, as though he'd been waiting.

"Preshy," he said, in a husky voice, filled with emotion. He'd known it would be her; he'd been waiting for her call for hours. "I'm so happy, I can't wait to see you."

She did not respond to that. "Where shall we meet?" she asked instead.

"You'll never guess where the ball is. At the Palazzo Rendino. I thought it would be a perfect place for our reunion. Why don't we meet there? And then we can talk."

She nodded. "Okay."

"I'll be in costume, I hope you brought yours?"

"I did."

"I'm a Plague Doctor," he said with a laugh in his voice. "Like about a thousand other guys tonight. Black cloak, black britches, tricorne hat and a white face mask. Think you'll recognize me?"

"How could I not?" she said.

"And what's *your* disguise?"

"You'll have to wait and see. I'll meet you at the Palazzo," she said, and rang off.

Her phone rang again immediately. She didn't answer. After a few minutes though, curiosity got the better of her and she listened to the message.

"Rafferty, where the fuck are you?" Sam yelled. "Your aunts told me what happened. Are you completely out of your mind? I've tried and tried to call you and now I'm in the middle of the lagoon on my way over to the Piazza San Marco. I *know* you're there. Call me. And don't do anything even dumber than what you already have."

He was in Venice. "Don't do anything dumber!" he'd said. Like meet *you,* she thought. Sam had the knack of rubbing her the wrong way. It would almost be soothing to be back in Bennett's company. At least he'd always been nice to her. Before he dumped her, that is.

SIXTY-NINE

Bennett paced the alley that ran down the side of the Palazzo Rendino, linking the small cobbled square with the canal. Music blared from the open windows and lanterns glimmered in the fog that hovered like a gray cloak, just inches above the water. Every now and again party boats and gondolas filled with drunken young people burst through the mist in a shout of noise and laughter. Everyone was masked, everyone was anonymous. It could not have been a more perfect setup for what he wanted to do.

His costume was based on the outfits worn by the doctors who'd tended the plague victims in the great epidemic that swept Venice in the Middle Ages, and he also carried the "plague stick," a rod they had used to touch their patients when they were examining them, in order to avoid catching the disease. Except Bennett's stick was heavier, though playfully disguised with pretty ribbons. It was not so different from the one he'd used when he killed his wife, Ana, and then Lily.

He glanced at his watch. It had been almost an hour since he'd spoken to Preshy. He was anxious for her to get there.

THE PIAZZA SAN MARCO WAS erupting with a surging mass of dancing people. A stage had been erected for the band and the sound of trumpets blared from massive speakers, echoing off the old walls. The entire city was partying in the grand piazzas, and at the palaces and on their boats.

But the narrow side streets leading off were empty. The shops and restaurants were closed and the fog swirled like cotton wool, pressing so close to Preshy's face she could hardly see a foot in front of her. Her gorgeous wedding cape billowed behind as she hurried on, the low heels of her slouchy black boots ringing on the cobbles. After a few minutes she stopped and looked around. She saw only anonymous gray walls, padded with fog. She didn't recall coming this way before, but tonight everything looked different, as though Venice itself was wearing a disguise. There were no partygoers here and, nervous, she hurried on. Surely she would come to a landmark soon, a caffè, a shop she knew.

As she crossed a tiny stone bridge she heard footsteps behind her. Suddenly a Plague Doctor burst from the fog, followed by half a dozen other masked men and women. He brandished his stick at her, and terrified, she cried out, but their laughter only mocked her as they ran off again.

Less sure now that she had made the right decision, she wished she had asked Sam to come with her. Taking her phone from her jeans pocket, she dialed his number. He answered immediately.

"Please tell me where you are," he said. "I'm begging you, Rafferty, just tell me."

"I'm on my way to the Palazzo Rendino. I'm supposed to meet Bennett there. There's a Carnevale ball. He's wearing a plague doctor costume with a white mask. I thought it would be all right, but now I'm scared."

Suddenly, at the end of the alley, she spotted the familiar square. "I'm here," she said, as relief made her realize how frightened she had really been. "I'll be okay now, it's just that I got frightened, alone in the back streets."

"Stay right there!" Sam ordered. "Wait for me. And Rafferty . . . whatever you do, do *not* talk to Bennett. Do not go anywhere near him. Okay?"

"Okay," she said in a small voice, as he rang off.

Sam's phone rang at once. It was Grizelda. "Where are you?" she demanded.

"On my way to the Palazzo Rendino, she's meeting Bennett there."

"Not without me, she's not," Grizelda snapped, and rang off.

Preshy hesitated in a corner of the little piazza. She was wondering what her next move should be when she felt a pair of arms snake round her and breathed the familiar smell of Bennett's cologne. "There you are, my lovely Preshy," he whispered in her ear. "At last."

She swung round in his arms—and looked into the terrifying

white mask of the Plague Doctor. But it was Bennett's fierce blue eyes blazing at her from behind it, Bennett's voice saying how happy he was to see her, Bennett telling her she was so good to come here, allowing him to explain like this . . . and that he could explain everything, and he would take good care of her, protect her from Lily's killer.

Hypnotized, she stared back at him.

"You look so beautiful," he said, "even though you're masked, I recognized you by your walk." Her hood fell back and he put up his hand and touched her golden cap of hair. "But you cut off your hair," he said, sounding sorrowful. "It was the first thing I noticed about you. Remember I told you, Preshy?"

She stared at him, like a small animal caught in the headlights of his eyes. Music filtering from the Palazzo buzzed in her ears. It was as though she were not herself, not really there, that this was some other woman listening to Bennett, falling under his spell all over again.

In the back of her mind she heard Daria's voice. *"Thirty 'Pity Days,' "* it said. *"Thirty day when you can cry and moan. . . . and then it's all over. . . . Move forward . . . A new life ahead . . ."* And she heard Sam telling her she wasn't a Precious. *"You're definitely a Rafferty," he'd said. She was strong, she was a new woman. She was herself, and she was no longer Bennett's puppet.*

She jerked out of his arms. "Tell me what you brought me here for. And make it good, Bennett, because I don't trust you. I want to know exactly why you left me at the altar. And I want to know who killed Lily. Tell me the truth about yourself. Explain it all to me. I'm listening."

A flower-filled launch blasted its horn as it sailed by. The partygoers tooted their blowers at them, but Bennett ignored them, his eyes still fixed on hers.

"I'll tell you exactly why I'm here," he said in that soft persuasive tone he'd always used with her. "Of course I love you, I told you that, and that I was ashamed. And I'll tell you about Lily. But first, you have something I need."

Suddenly, he grabbed her gold cape, throwing it back, staring at her neck as though expecting to see something. Then "Tell me where the necklace is," he said, still in an oh-so-quiet voice that sent chills down Preshy's spine.

Frightened, she took a step back. Of course! That was why he wanted her to come to Venice. He thought she had the priceless necklace. *Oh God, Oh God,* and fool that she was, she had fallen for it! She wondered desperately where Sam was. She glanced quickly round the deserted piazza, looking for an escape. The Palazzo and its partygoers were so close, but they might have been a million miles away for all the good they were to her now.

"I don't have the necklace," she said, stalling for time.

"Yes you do. I *know* Lily gave it to you." He put his arms round her again, holding her in a grip so tight this time she couldn't move. "It's for us, Preshy," he said. "I have a buyer for it. We'll be rich and I can marry you without shaming you. All I'm asking you to do is tell me where it is."

"It's in my room at the *pensione,*" she lied. Then immediately wished she hadn't because if they went to the *pensione* then Sam would never find her. And she couldn't telephone him. *Where, oh* where *was he?*

Bennett grabbed her hand. "We'll take a boat there," he said, and dragging her with him, he walked to the steps leading to the canal. Spotting an approaching empty gondola, he let go of her hand for a second to flag it down. Preshy didn't know how, but in that instant it was as though she flew from him. With her cape billowing behind her like wings, she was racing up the alley and past the Palazzo.

She kept on running down dark silent alleys. The fog pressed against her eyes. She could barely see. Out of breath, she had to stop. And then she heard footsteps.

She turned, running alongside the canal now, retracing her path. She *had* to meet Sam at the Palazzo. It was her only chance. But now she was lost again. And were Bennett's footsteps in front of her? Or behind?

The lights of the Palazzo glimmered suddenly from the fog, and with a thankful cry she ran toward it.

Bennett darted from the alley. He got her in an armlock, pressing against her throat.

She was choking, gasping for breath, her eyes bugged from her head. He was talking to her again, and the evil words just seemed to erupt out of him, telling her the truth finally.

"I felt *nothing* for you, Precious," he said. "*Nothing at all.* Of course I wanted your money, but I planned to kill Grizelda first to make sure you got it. Then I would have killed you. Grizelda managed to escape, but anyway when I found that she wasn't leaving you her money and there was no paycheck, I walked. You are a meaningless woman, Preshy," he said in the low, smooth silken tone. "Just like all the others. You don't count in life. You offer nothing, just another scrap of DNA swept away in a canal.

Your only value is that necklace. Now be a good girl, Preshy, and tell me where the *pensione* is, and where you've hidden the necklace. Or I'll kill you right now."

Bennett's words fell on her like blows. All her past beautiful dreams lay in ruins. There was nothing left to grieve for except her own selfish stupidity. He had never loved her. He didn't even hate her. She was nothing to him. He had killed Lily. And now he was going to kill her.

Anger hit her in a shot of adrenaline. She was damned if she was going to die. But she wasn't strong enough to fight him off and escape. She had to think quickly. If she told him where the necklace was he would kill her. And if she didn't tell, he would kill her anyway. Panicked, she struggled to get free but his arm tightened on her throat so she couldn't even scream. She heard footsteps approaching, the feminine clack of high heels trotting along the alley in back of them.

Bennett heard it too. He turned his head for a split second . . . and found himself looking at a gun.

Aunt G stood there, wrapped in her second-best mink, the dark blue sheared one, holding what looked to Preshy like a pearl-handled revolver. Mimi was next to her, all in white and silver, her blond hair glittering with fog drops, looking like an avenging Valkyrie. The pair were like something out of a sixties James Bond movie.

Grizelda's voice had a slight quaver to it as she said, "Let go of my niece at once or I shall shoot you."

"Go ahead. Shoot." Bennett had Preshy positioned in front of him, her arms pinned behind her. "Though why you want to shoot me I don't know. I was just telling your niece how much I loved her.

I apologized to her and explained what happened. All she has to do is tell me where the necklace is and then she's yours."

Peering into the shadows beyond him, Mimi stalled for time. "What necklace?" she demanded.

But Bennett saw where her gaze went. He turned to look, just as Sam launched himself at him. He let go of Preshy and she hit the ground with a thud, with Bennett on top of her and Sam on top of Bennett. Grizelda ran to them, still waving the gun and Mimi shrieked for help.

Preshy wasn't sure what happened next. Flattened, with her face in the cobblestones and all the breath knocked out of her, she heard shouts that somehow were mixed up with music, and the sound of running feet. *And then a shot.*

Oh My God. Aunt Grizelda had killed him.

She got to her feet and saw Grizelda staring at the smoking gun in her hand, and Mimi with her hands over her ears, screaming, and Sam running after Bennett.

He'd reached the canal, but Sam was right behind him. An empty party boat waited, moored to the blue-striped pole at the Palazzo's embarcadero. Bennett jumped for it, caught his foot on the edge and slipped and fell, cracking his head on the striped pole. He staggered to his feet, swayed, then with a splash, fell backward into the water.

Preshy ran with the others to the canal. The cold black water rippled gently. The gray fog pressed down on it like a shroud. There was no sign of Bennett. It was the perfect accident.

SEVENTY

I shot him," Aunt Grizelda said in a trembly voice.

"You didn't shoot Bennett, Grizelda, you shot me." Sam took off his jacket and pointed to the blood slowly oozing from his arm.

Grizelda clapped a shocked hand to her mouth. "Oh, I'm *so* sorry. Oscar always said I was a terrible shot and that I'd kill somebody someday."

"But not today, thank God." Sam looked at Preshy, still staring into the water. As though, he thought angrily, she expected Bennett to be resurrected any minute. God, would she never learn? The man had just tried to kill her.

Remembering to be gentle, even though she'd gotten them all into this mess that would now have to be played out with the police one more time, he said, "Come on, Rafferty. Bennett's gone, and none of us should be regretting him. I have no doubt he killed his wife, and Lily. The man was the most dangerous kind of sociopath. He would have killed anybody that got in his way."

"I know," Preshy said bitterly. Bennett's words still burned, and she shook her head, trying to unremember them. All she *should* remember was the evil that had been hidden behind those intense blue eyes and behind that soft voice that knew how to say such sweet things, and behind that charm that he'd made into an art form.

"I'm sorry I got you all into this," she said wearily. "It was my fault and I accept responsibility." She took her phone from her pocket. "I'll call the police and tell them everything."

Sam grabbed her arm. "Oh no you don't. You'll take Mimi and Grizelda and go back to the hotel. I'll take care of the police."

Preshy recalled him saying he couldn't afford to be connected to another murder mystery, but now he was going to take full responsibility for dealing with the police. She could just see the headlines: *"Murder suspect involved in another death."*

"I can't let you do that," she said.

"You have no choice. And for once, Rafferty, you'll do as you are told."

"But what about your arm?" Grizelda asked, worried.

"I'm glad to say Uncle Oscar was right about you. I've seen more blood from a nosebleed. Now, go. All of you. I'll see you in a little while. And remember, this was an accident. You know nothing. You were never here. No one will even ask you of course, because your names won't be mentioned. But just stay cool. Okay?"

The three women drifted slowly back toward Piazza San Marco where they caught the Cipriani launch. Up in Grizelda's suite they ordered coffee and a selection of little sweet cakes because, Mimi said, they needed a sugar fix after what they'd been through. Then Preshy told them exactly what had happened with Bennett, about how he was the one who had tried to run Aunt G off the road, and what he'd said to her.

"I felt so . . . worthless," she said tearfully. "I was just another scrap of useless DNA was what he said. Which, if he'd killed me, was all I would have ended up as."

"It's men like Bennett who are worthless," Mimi said fiercely. "He's never cared for anyone in his life, except himself."

"And just look where it got him." Grizelda went to sit next to Preshy. She put her arms around her and said, "*Chérie,* you cannot possibly believe what that dreadful man said. Every word was intended to hurt you. He was throwing verbal spears at you, bringing you down so he could manipulate you. I'm glad he's dead, Preshy. And you know what? I wouldn't even have cared if I *had* shot him. Maître Deschamps would have defended me. A *crime passionné,* he would have called it and I'm sure he would have gotten me a couple of years in one of the prettier jails. I would willingly have taken the rap for you, my little girl."

"But now Sam's doing it instead," Mimi said.

And so they ordered some more coffee and more of the little sweet cakes. "After all that's happened, I think we need a change," Grizelda said thoughtfully to Mimi. "A world cruise, perhaps?"

"We'll have to go shopping," Mimi said. "And just think of all the good things we can buy at bargain prices in China."

"Mimi!" Grizelda glared at her.

"Oh, well, perhaps we'll skip China," Mimi said hastily. "They say Japan is the best for pearls, though."

Mimi always put her foot in her mouth, Grizelda thought resignedly.

SEVENTY-ONE

It was dawn when Sam finally left the *polizia* after making his report. He'd told them he'd seen a man fall into the canal near the Palazzo Rendino. He believed his name was Bennett Yuan or Bennett James. The police questioned him, inspected his passport, asked his occupation and what he was doing there and where he was staying.

"I'm with the Countess von Hoffenberg at the Cipriani," he said. "I was on my way to the ball at the Palazzo when I saw this happen. Of course I ran to see if I could help, but it was too late. There was no sign of him."

It was all true, Bennett had died in an accident of his own making, he thought wearily, as he made his way back through the party-littered alleys, past tired couples still in their fancy dress, past the band packing up their instruments in Piazza San Marco; then into the launch to the hotel, floating over the canal that had claimed Bennett James Yuan's life in a final justice that his wife's Chinese family might find fitting. The evil Dragon River Gods had claimed him and made him their own. And neither Sam nor Rafferty, nor the Aunts had any responsibility toward him.

Back at the hotel the three women were sitting in a row on the sofa, coffee cups clutched in their hands, eyes wide and alert, waiting for him, when Sam walked in the door.

"Well?" Grizelda spoke for them all.

"It's okay. Everything's worked out. The cop said his wouldn't be the only body fished from the canal this morning. People get drunk, they fight, it happens at Carnevale."

Mimi poured him some coffee and he sipped it gratefully. He felt empty inside, drained. Rafferty could have been killed and it would have been his fault for leaving her all alone. Just the way he had with Leilani. Suddenly near rock bottom with emotion and fatigue, he slumped into a chair.

As he drank his coffee, he told them everything that had been said at the *polizia,* and that they were free to leave.

"But what will happen to Bennett?" Preshy asked in a small voice. She couldn't help it, she had to know.

"When they find him, then they will identify him. They'll ship him back to Shanghai, I guess." He shrugged. "It's no longer our problem."

Preshy felt the weight lift from her heart. She was about ten pounds lighter, a bit like when she'd had all her hair cut off.

"Let's go back to Paris," she said wearily. "I need to go home."

. . .

BENNETT'S BODY WAS FOUND THE next morning and identified through his passport and immigration. He was traveling as Bennett Yuan and the Chinese consul informed the Yuan family of his death. After the autopsy, his body was to be returned to the Yuans in Shanghai.

Ironically, Bennett would be buried like the rich man he'd always wanted to be in life.

SEVENTY-TWO

SHANGHAI

MARY-LOU heard the news about Bennett when she bumped into the girl from the health club.

"Tragic," the girl said, eyes brimming, "and him so handsome, so charming. Why do bad things always seem to happen to the good people?" she asked sorrowfully.

"Why indeed," Mary-Lou said calmly, though inside she was trembling.

Of course Bennett Yuan's death was reported in the media, but unlike his wife's, it was played down, as was his burial. Mary-Lou felt nothing. Only relief. She wondered what had happened to the necklace but remembering it was the cause of all her troubles, decided she didn't want to know.

She had her own life now, running Lily's antiques business. No one else had come forward to claim it, so she had simply taken over, and since Lily's death she had lived alone in the pretty little house where once she had plotted her friend's downfall.

If Mary-Lou had a conscience she would have considered it clear. She had stolen a few dollars here and there—so what? She had not killed anyone, had she? And now she was dating someone Lily had known, a Swiss guy who acted as an agent for rich art collectors. If only she had the necklace now she would have had it made.

SEVENTY-THREE

VENICE

PRESHY sipped a brandy, trying to pull herself together. She still felt pretty shaky. It had all happened so fast, she was only now beginning to recall in detail the sheer horror of being trapped by Bennett, knowing he intended to kill her. The only good thing to come out of it was that she had not fallen all over again for his fascinating blue eyes and his honeyed words of love. She had stood up to him, told him she didn't want to hear it. What she had wanted was the truth, and thank God that was what she had gotten. It had shocked her to her senses, and Bennett had gotten the end he deserved. An end for which only he was responsible. And Sam, dear Sam, whom she had so unjustly suspected of being involved, had been her hero. He, and the Aunts, had saved her life.

Her eyes met his over the rim of the glass and she gave him a smile. His answering smile was filled with tenderness.

And then the phone rang. And the moment was lost.

Sam answered it. He said very little, asked no questions. When he put down the receiver he turned to them.

His eyes met hers again. "That was my agent, calling from New York," he said in a dead calm voice that made Preshy uneasy. "He told me a red jacket was found on the rocks near the beach house. The police believe it was my wife's. They want me back there. I gather it's a question of my going voluntarily, or they will take me in for questioning."

Preshy heard gasps from the Aunts. "What will you do?" she asked, shocked.

"I'll go of course. I know the jacket. It *was* Leilani's, but it was heavy and why she would have been wearing it on a warm summer night, I don't know."

Preshy didn't hesitate. "I'll go with you." She heard the Aunts gasp again.

"No you won't."

"Why not?"

"Because I don't want you involved. Besides, you've been through enough."

"I *am* involved," she said fiercely. "I'm involved with *you,* Sam Knight. You just saved my life. Do you really expect me to walk away when you're in trouble?"

"Hey"—he shrugged—"no obligation."

"I'm coming, and that's that," she said finally.

"Quite right," Aunt G chimed in.

"We would come too, for support," Mimi added, "but you're probably happy with just Preshy."

Sam shook his head, smiling as he thanked them. "I'll be fine," he said. "Alone," he added, looking at Preshy.

"She's coming with you," Aunt G said briskly. "Go now, right away. Get it over with. I'll have a plane waiting for you at Marco Polo."

He tried to protest but she refused to listen. "And Sam," she said, as they left. "Our hearts go with you."

SAM WAS VERY QUIET ON the plane flying back to his home. His eyes were closed and Preshy hoped he was sleeping. He looked exhausted. Drained, in fact, like a man who had reached the end of his rope. He was no longer drinking. Those days of Dutch courage were over.

SEVENTY-FOUR

OUTER BANKS

THEY finally touched down at the small local airport. From there Sam went straight to the police station, while Preshy checked into a motel. She would be there for him when he needed her.

She lay on the bed, watching CNN, and watching the clock tick the minutes past, thinking about Sam and how they had met quite by chance, and how their lives now seemed to be so inextricably entangled.

Closing her eyes, she saw his narrow lined face, his caring brown eyes behind the retro glasses, his tall lean body, comfortable in jeans and the old leather jacket, now with the rip in it from Aunt G's wayward bullet. Sam was not the kind of man who would ever let a woman down, and that was why she knew without a shadow of doubt that he would have protected his gentle Leilani with his life. Just the way he had protected her.

The phone rang. "I'm coming to get you," Sam said, sounding weary. "We'll pick up some food, go to the beach house. If that's okay with you?"

Preshy said it was and went outside to wait for him. When the black Mustang rental pulled up beside her, she hopped in and took a quick look at his face. It was grim.

"How was it?" she asked.

"Okay." He shrugged. They drove a couple of blocks in silence, then he pulled up at a convenience store and they went in and bought bread, butter, milk, coffee, and a couple of cans of gumbo.

The drive along the coast road was wild and windy, with the ocean surging and foaming, advancing and retreating in the beginning of a winter storm. They turned off down a sandy lane that led between the rows of tamarisk trees Sam had planted ten years ago, to the simple gray-shingled house with its wraparound porch and its wide-open view across the dunes to the sea.

Sam's shoulders sagged. Different emotions played over his face: pleasure, relief, despair. He straightened up and looked at her.

"Welcome to my home," he said quietly. And then he took her hand and they walked together, up the wooden stairway into his house.

Inside was simply one big room with a massive stone fireplace in the center, and walls lined with large somber paintings, done, Preshy guessed, by Leilani.

But when Sam opened the electric steel shutters that protected the house from hurricanes and winter storms, it was instantly filled with a magical clear gray light that felt, she thought, the way the first dawn must have. So translucent and pearly, so clean and clear; it was like being on the prow of a great ship in the middle of the ocean.

"No wonder you love it," she said. "It's breathtaking."

"Then come on outside and really breathe," he said. And they went and stood on the deck, inhaling the cold crisp salty air, hearing the wind tearing through the trees and the surge of the great ocean.

"Yet just down the beach there's the river and the calm backwaters and the marshes," Sam told her. "There's the reeds where the ducks nest and the mangroves with their gnarled roots dug deep in the mud, and dripping with Spanish moss like cobwebs on Halloween. And in summer it's a different world, sun-filled, with white-sailed little boats skidding across the horizon, and an entirely different light, more golden and blue."

"I'll bet it's humid," Preshy said, thinking of her hair, and succeeding in making him laugh. That was better she thought. At least he could laugh even though he'd just spent a couple of hours with the cops answering questions about his wife's disappearance. She still didn't ask him what had happened though. She knew if he wanted, he would tell her.

While Sam built a fire she heated up the gumbo and sawed uneven chunks off the loaf of bread. He brought out a bottle of wine and two glasses.

"The Carolina red?" she asked, tasting it suspiciously.

"So?" he replied, one brow raised in a question.

"Well, it's no Bordeaux," she said, and then she laughed. "But it's pretty darn good, especially on a cold windy afternoon after a long and grueling journey."

"And a grueling questioning," he said wearily, sitting next to her at the white-tiled kitchen counter.

She took a sip of the wine and waited for him to go on.

"They found Leilani's jacket," he said, "washed up on the beach not too far from here. A padded red winter jacket. 'It was summer and the night your wife disappeared was warm,' the detective said to me. 'Why do you think she would have been wearing such a jacket?' I said I didn't know, it was a puzzle. 'Perhaps it was because, with the padding, it holds water better, makes it easier to drown someone,' the cop said."

Preshy drew in a sharp nervous breath.

"I said I supposed it did." Sam took off his glasses and rubbed his eyes. " 'I'll remember that for my next book,' I said. And then they showed me what they had found, zippered in the pocket." He held out his left hand to show her. His eyes met Preshy's. "Leilani's wedding ring. Exactly like mine."

She covered his hand protectively with hers. He was a man being destroyed before her very eyes. "She must have taken it off before . . ." She stopped, not wanting to say it, watching as Sam got up.

"I'm going out for a walk." He rummaged in the closet for a jacket. "I'll be back later," he said as he closed the door behind him.

Worried, Preshy called Daria. "I'm here with Sam," she said.

"I know, Sylvie told me." Daria sounded upset. "So what is it this time, Presh? Is it love?"

"I'm still nervous when I think about 'love.' But I've never felt like this before, so . . . sort of caring, concerned, so *involved* with a man. Can this be love, Daria?"

"Maybe. And now what?"

"I have to help him. Oh, Daria, you never saw a man more devastated, and now the cops are hounding him because they found his wife's jacket on the beach with her wedding ring in the pocket. They think he killed her, and Sam knows it. And I don't know what to do."

"Why not just go home, sweetheart," Daria said gently. "Work out your own emotions and let Sam work out his own fate."

But Preshy knew better than that. She knew what she was feeling was real. "I'll stick with him to the end," she said. Because that was what he had done for her.

And she knew he would do it again. He was her savior, her hero. And she wished he was her lover. But that might never be.

SEVENTY-FIVE

SAM strode along the hard-packed sand at the very edge of the sea where the waves foamed over his boots and the sandpipers scattered in front of him. He was alone with the roar of the ocean and the plaintive cry of the birds wheeling overhead, with the boom of the surf on the sandbanks and the creaking of the leafless trees. And always the roar of the wind. It was wild, elemental, all noise and power. The power of the ocean.

Turning up the collar of his jacket, he strode on. Leilani was gone. He would never see her again and his heart would bear the scar forever. No matter what happened, he would have to leave this place he loved. It could never be the same without her.

The Shanghai temple fortune-teller's face came into his mind, clear as a photograph. "I'm searching for two people," Sam had said to him. "I want to know if I'll find them." The fortune-teller's words rang in his ears once again. "The first person you seek is a woman. And the answer lies in your own soul," he had replied. Sam had been asking about Leilani. And he knew in his heart that what the man had said was true. Now he searched his own soul, asking where he had gone wrong, how he had let her down.

Thrusting his hands deeper into the jacket pockets, he emptied his head of all thoughts until he seemed at one with the elements, adrift on the wind and with only the roar of the ocean for company. His left hand closed around something deep down in the crease of the pocket. A piece of paper.

Some old receipt, he thought, taking it out and crumpling it, ready to be thrown away. But then he saw it was a piece of green paper, the kind Leilani always used. Green was Leilani's favorite color, she said she found it soothing. He also saw she had written something on it. His name was at the top.

"Dearest Sam," it began,

I'm looking at our beloved dog lying here next to me as I sit on the upper porch, trying not to look at the ocean where I know you are tonight, and which, from your love of it, your knowledge of it, you can almost claim as your own. Your dog is old now, Sam. His eyes are faded, his breathing shallow. He has not much longer for this world and you cannot know how I envy him.

I can never "love" the way your dog does, the way you do, so direct, so uncomplicated. So easy. I wait for my heart to show me how, but it is frozen inside my chest, a lead weight, dragging me down. I wait for those feelings to happen to me, to send me soaring with simple happiness, the way you were this evening, whistling as you prepped your fishing tackle and cleaned your little boat. Why, I asked myself, can't I be like that?

All my life I have tried, and all my life I have failed. Sometimes I was able to lose myself in my painting, and that was the closest I could come to "happiness," or what I believed happiness to be. But mostly, Sam, I was just lost. And now I know I will never find myself.

I don't "own" me. I don't own you, Sam. I don't even own the dog. I can't bear it any longer. All I want, dear Sam, is to be "nothing." And tonight I will finally achieve my goal. In a few minutes I'll take a walk to the small inlet and the sandbank that's uncovered only at low tide. I'll sit there and watch the sea come for me. Only you know how afraid I am of the ocean. They say it's a coward's way out, but this is a brave thing I'm doing, Sam, isn't it?

And then, my dearest, I will finally be free. We will both be free.

I'm thinking about our happiness on our honeymoon in Paris. That was happiness, wasn't it? I used to remember how it felt but it's lost now under all the darkness.

Do not grieve for me, or for your beloved dog, who will, I know, soon follow me.

You must go on, Sam. Be "happy." I know you have the capacity for that, and for love. And believe me, if I knew how to love, it would have been you.

She had signed it "*Leilani Knight.*"

Sam folded her note carefully. He put it back in his pocket, where she must have left it, expecting him to find it right away because he always wore that jacket when he took the dog for walks along the beach. And she would have wanted to make sure only he found it and read it. Her message was meant only for him.

Hands thrust in his pockets, he strode along the beach where the wind dried his tears. When he came to the place Leilani had mentioned, where the sandbank was uncovered as it was now, at low tide, he stopped to look.

The tide was turning and as he watched the first wave powered over the sandbank, then retreated again, leaving it clean and empty.

Tears stung his eyes. "I loved you, Leilani," he shouted into the wind. "I will never forget you."

SEVENTY-SIX

PRESHY saw from Sam's face when he walked in the door that something had happened. She watched anxiously, as he took off his jacket and threw it onto a chair. He took the folded piece of green paper from the pocket and stood with it in his hand looking at her.

"This was meant only for me," he said quietly. "But I think you are owed some explanation."

She took the letter, still looking at his weary face. All the life seem to have drained out of his eyes and suddenly she knew why. "It's from Leilani, isn't it?" she said.

He nodded. "She left it in my jacket pocket, thinking I would find it right away. It was crushed into a fold and somehow the cops missed it." He walked to the fireplace and threw on another log, kicking it until it sparked. "Please, read it," he said.

Preshy walked to the window and began to read. When she had finished, she stood for a long moment, struggling with her emotions. "But why? *Why?*" she said fiercely at last. "She had everything to live for."

Sam threw himself into a chair. "Manic depression is a serious illness. Leilani told me she was taking her medication, but . . ." He shrugged. "It seems she was not."

Preshy went and knelt at his feet, looking anxiously at him. "You have your answer now, though. The police won't ask any more questions once they read this."

"But they never will read it."

"What do you mean? Of course you'll show them her letter."

"No!" His response was fierce. "I won't have them reading Leilani's last words. They were meant only for me."

She leaned her head tenderly against his knee. "It's the only way out, Sam," she said gently. "You have to do this."

Shrugging her off he got up and began to prowl the room. "I didn't expose Leilani's illness, her vulnerability to the cops before, and I won't do it now."

"But you must," she said stubbornly. "It's serious, Sam. You saw *how* serious this afternoon when they questioned you. If you don't show them the letter then they'll arrest you for her murder. And that's not what Leilani meant to happen. You *know* it isn't."

Their eyes linked for a long moment, then he sighed and said of course she was right.

She walked to the kitchen and filled two wineglasses with the Carolina red, then went back to him.

"We're going to drink a toast," she said as he took the glass from her.

He knew what she was going to say and he said it for her. "To my beloved wife, Leilani," he said. "A graceful presence in my life."

And they raised their glasses to her, and drank.

SEVENTY-SEVEN

SAM called the police. He showed them Leilani's letter and they checked it against other samples of her handwriting. They gave him back the red jacket and the wedding ring, said they were sorry for his loss, and that the case was now closed. It was over so quickly, it was almost as though it never happened.

Preshy stayed on at the beach house with Sam. They were comfortable together, friends, bickering gently as they always did, but easy now, no longer sparring partners. They took long windy walks, cooked simple meals, drank wine by the fire and talked endlessly into the night. She told him stories of her life, and listened to stories of his. It was as though they had known each other forever, linked as they were by tragedy.

Time passed, a few days, then a week . . . More. But Preshy

knew she couldn't stay here, in limbo, a friend but not a lover. She must go back to Paris.

Then late one afternoon, Sam grabbed her by the hand and said, "Let's take a walk, catch the sunset."

For once the wind had dropped and all was calm. Even the sea murmured now, instead of roaring the way it always had. Terns swooped over the waves and the air carried a hint of brine and of sea pines. Sam's hand still clasped hers, and she felt its comforting warmth as they climbed the sand dunes until they came to a sheltered hollow. He let go of her then and flung himself down, lying, hands behind his head, looking up at her.

"Come join me," he said, smiling.

And so she did, lying next to him, matching her length against his as they lay together, staring up into the golden evening sky, tinged with coral from the setting sun. Too soon it was over. The sun had gone, and so, Preshy knew, had her time with Sam. She would have to return home.

"Rafferty?"

She turned her face to his. "Yes?"

"You're a good friend."

She nodded. "I'm glad."

"But . . ."

She waited, but he didn't go on. "But—what?"

"I'm afraid to say this—in case I spoil our friendship."

She sat up now, staring at him. "Say . . . what?"

"I think I'm in love with you, Rafferty."

"Ohhhh . . ." Her face lit in a smile. "And I think I'm in love with you too."

"Could it be the real thing, do you think?"

She shrugged. "I don't know." Then she grinned. "But I don't care."

He grinned back at her. "Nor do I. I was just testing the water, leaving myself a way out in case you said no. Because you see I know I love you. You're unique, one of a kind, a girl in a million. Don't leave me, Rafferty, I'd never find another like you."

"Ohhh," she murmured again, but by now her lips were only inches away from his. And then his arms were around her and he was kissing her, and she was kissing him back. The cold sand trickled down the neck of her sweater, but his warm hands were underneath, as he pulled her even closer. She didn't even mind the sand in her hair. Because this was what it was all about. The tentative beginnings of "love."

They made love for the first time under the starry evening sky, with only the sound of the sea and the breeze brushing their naked bodies and only the first stars to watch over them. It was, Preshy thought, a fine beginning.

Later that night, they sat out on the enclosed porch, glasses of wine in their hands, watching the great gray waves rolling endlessly in, while the softer wind rustled through the tamarisks. "I have a confession to make," she said worriedly.

"Oh? And what could that be?" He was smiling as he turned to look at her.

Shamefaced, she said, "I suspected you had something to do with Lily's death. I thought you might even know Bennett, be involved. Of course I didn't really know you then," she added hurriedly, making him laugh.

"So just don't do it again," he said.

"I won't," she promised.

"Is that it?"

"My confession, you mean? Yes, that's all."

"Okay. I'll forgive you. Under the circumstances," he said, and then he laughed. "Come on, Rafferty. It's okay. You had every right to wonder what I was up to. But now it's over."

"Yes," she agreed, feeling relief sweep over her again. The past was truly the past now, and life must go on.

"What will you do now?" she asked.

He thought about it. "I'll sell this place. I'll move on, maybe get another boat, another dog . . . try my hand at writing again."

"Sounds good to me," she said.

He turned his head to look at her.

"What about you?"

"Oh." She lifted a shoulder in a nonchalant shrug. "I guess I'll just go home. Back to Paris."

"The most beautiful city in the world." Their eyes linked. He reached out his hand, took hers. "Don't leave me, Rafferty," he said, quietly.

"Why not?"

"Because I'm in love with you."

The words made her spirits soar. "Funny way of showing it," she said with a sparkle in her eyes. "Why not come over and kiss me?"

And he did. And one thing led to another, and all in all it was another week before they finally headed "home" to Paris, and a new life. Together.

SEVENTY-EIGHT

PARIS

PRESHY had been gone a long time and Maow was alone and bored. She sat in the exact center of Preshy's bed, feet daintily together, a stern look on her narrow face, as though she were plotting something. After a while she got up and stretched one long svelte chocolate leg all the way out in front of her, then she did the same with the other. After that, she went in search of action.

Her first stop was the kitchen where she sniffed the food the concierge had left that morning and decided against it. She hopped onto the counter and prowled its length, daintily crisscrossing her legs as she negotiated the stove top, until she came to the small cardboard egg carton the concierge had left out, along with a loaf of bread, for Preshy's return.

Maow found it interesting. Sniffing and poking her paw at it she soon had it open. Six brown eggs, like balls she could play with, awaited her. She scooped one out, and rolled it across the counter. Sticking her head over the edge, she watched it fall with a satisfying plop onto the tiled floor. She stared curiously at the little ball that had now turned into a yellow blob, then went back and got another egg. She rolled that to the edge, watched it plop. She trotted back to the carton four more times, until six eggs lay scrambled on the kitchen floor. Then she looked for something else to do.

Tail up—Siamese tails are always up—she stalked into the dining room, a little tired after all that activity. The nice big antique glass bowl in the center tempted her. It was just the right size to curl up in. She put tentative front paws on its edge, then aimed her jump. The antique bowl tipped, crashed under her weight and smashed into a dozen pieces. Maow looked at it puzzled, then she picked her way carefully through the shards, jumped down again, and went to see what was doing in the living room.

She stood on the window seat, looking out at the traffic and the people. Bored, she scratched a tentative paw at the glass, looking for an escape route. Impossible.

Filled with a sudden ferocious energy, she spun round into a crouching position. Then she took off across the room, over the sofas, up the back of the chair, into the bedroom, flying over the bed in one giant leap, spinning round, mashing the coverlet into a tangled heap, hurling herself back again, over the bed, over the sofa, up onto the shelves, scattering photographs and artifacts.

She sat on the shelf, paws together, the graceful wrecker, looking very pleased with herself. She rested her head on the terracotta statue of the Xi'an warrior, rubbing her ear against it. She leaned harder. The warrior tottered for a moment, and toppled. It lay hanging over the edge. Then it slid slowly forward. Interested, Maow leaned forward also, just as it slid the last few inches. And then fell. She stalked to the edge of the shelf looking down at it, smashed into a hundred pieces on the floor.

It was odd but like the eggs that started out as nice brown balls and ended up as yellow lumps, the statue was not all it seemed either.

Bored again, she went back to the window seat, curled round and round a few times, then finally settled down on her favorite cushion to wait for Preshy to come home.

SEVENTY-NINE

EN ROUTE TO PARIS

SAM slept most of the flight "home." It was the sleep of a relieved man, Preshy thought, watching him tenderly. She'd bet he hadn't slept like this in years. But now, with a new start, and the two of them beginning their lives together, and the horror of being a murder suspect and the sadness of Leilani's death finally behind him, and with Bennett finally eliminated, she knew life was about to change for both of them.

The word *happiness* danced before her eyes. Would she finally be *happy*? Would Sam? Glancing again at him, she believed she would.

Paris swam into view beneath them, still scattered spottily with snow, and still the most beautiful city on earth.

The pilot informed them they were coming in to land and she

nudged Sam gently. "Almost home," she said, smiling as he rubbed his eyes and looked groggily back at her. "Tell you what," she said, inspired. "Tonight I'll cook you the best omelet you ever had in your life."

"Sounds good," he said, smiling.

THERE'S NOTHING QUITE LIKE COMING home," Sam said as, a while later, she unlocked the door. Outside was sleeting and cold, but in Preshy's home the radiators were hissing with warmth, and there was a delighted cry from the cat, who launched herself out of the darkness at them.

"Maowsie, Maowsie." Preshy clasped the cat in her arms,laughing while at the same time joggling her elbow at the light switch. The lamps sprang to life, and the two of them stared, stunned, at the scene of destruction.

"Looks like the demolition derby was here," Sam said, awed.

Oh, Maow, what *have* you done?" Preshy stared horrified, at her expensive antique glass bowl now lying in shards on the table, and at the photos and the smashed artifacts. In the bedroom the coverlet was trampled into a muddled heap and there were eggs all over the kitchen floor.

"So much for omelets," Sam said from the kitchen.

But Preshy was surveying the destruction in the living room. "Sam, come here," she said urgently.

The necklace gleamed up at her from the piece of scarlet silk it had been wrapped in. "It's Grandmother's necklace," she said, awed. "Lily must have hidden it inside the statue and sent it to me for safekeeping. Look, Sam, it's magnificent."

Picking it up, she ran a tentative finger over the giant pearl. It felt cold, and remembering where it had come from, she put it hastily down on the dining room table. They stood, looking at it.

"This is what Bennett killed Lily for," Sam said. "It's probably worth a fortune. I'll bet he also killed his wife for her money, and when he didn't get it, he had to find another source of income. Unfortunately, Rafferty, that was you.

"When that fell through," he added, "Bennett latched on to the necklace, but Lily stood between him and it. When she didn't hand it over to him, he killed her. But he still didn't have the necklace. And the trail led, via Mary-Lou Chen, back to you."

"And now what?" She looked at the sinister corpse pearl, gleaming like moonlight on the black glass table. Picking it up, Sam clasped the necklace around her neck. The jewels gleamed somberly. "It's magnificent," he said, awed.

Preshy shivered. "It doesn't belong to me. It was stolen from a dead empress. It's part of history. It should go back where it belongs, back to China. I'll donate it to them. Maybe they'll put it in a museum."

He nodded. "I'll contact the embassy. I'm sure they'll be thrilled with your gift."

She picked up the cat. "If it were not for naughty you, Maowsie, we would never have found it," she said, kissing the cat's smooth chocolate ears.

Maow hooked her paws onto Preshy's shoulders and peeked triumphantly at Sam. He could have sworn the cat was laughing at him. He went into the kitchen and began to clean up the eggs. There would be no omelets tonight.

Preshy followed him and he turned to look at her. A smile lit his lean narrow face. "Put down that cat and get over here, Rafferty," he said, holding out his arms.

Maow watched from her place on the countertop as Preshy walked right up to him. And then their faces blended in a kiss.

Life was going to be a little different here, in future.

Turn the Page for a Sneak Peak
At Elizabeth Adler's
Upcoming Book

One of Those Malibu Nights

Coming in July 2008

ONE

It was not the kind of night, nor the kind of place, where you'd expect to hear a woman scream. It was just one of those Malibu nights, dark as a velvet shroud, creamy waves crashing onto the shore, breeze soft as a kitten's breath.

Mac Reilly, Private Investigator, was walking the beach alone but for his dog. His lover Sunny Alvarez had taken off for Rome after a slight "disagreement" concerning their future. But that was an ongoing story.

Mac lived in the famous Malibu Colony, habitat of movie stars and showbiz moguls and megabucks persons of every sort, each one richer than the next, give or take a couple of million, or in some cases billion. Their fancy beachside mansions didn't look so fancy from Mac's angle, but then the beach was also not an angle from which most people ever got to see them. In fact, the public rarely got to see them. The Colony was gated and guarded, one entrance in or out, and though the beach had free access, it was only along the water's edge with no loitering. Any unknown caught prowling along it at midnight would be in for some tough questioning.

The Colony's mansions were mostly the simple second or even third homes of rich people, understated in their beach chic and with the narrowest bit of oceanfront deck known to man, at a cost per square foot that boggled the accounting.

Mac's own place was a more modest dwelling, a forties bungalow he had bought cheap years ago in the big real estate slump and which had once been owned, or so he'd heard, by the old-time movie star Norma Shearer. Or was it Norma Jean? Norma or Marilyn, it made no difference. A shack was a shack whichever way you looked at it.

The house's saving grace, apart from its ritzy location and the view, was a small wooden deck with steps that led directly down the beach. It wasn't unknown in a winter storm for the ocean to come thudding at the wooden pilings under that deck, slapping over the rails until Mac felt as though he were on a boat, but he liked the excitement and even the possible danger. He was happy in Malibu, he wouldn't live anywhere else if you paid him. Except maybe Rome for a week or two, in the company of Sunny.

Mac kind of looked the P.I. role, six-foot-two, longish dark hair—still thick on the head, thank God, even though he was forty. Dark blue eyes, kinda crinkled from too many days on the beach and too many nights spent propping up bars in his youth.

No facial hair—Sunny didn't like it. A lean athletic build, which since he was a lazy guy gym-wise, was mostly earned from jogging along the beach with his rescued three-legged, one-eyed mutt of a dog, Pirate, who was pretty fast when he had the wind behind him.

Pirate was Mac's best buddy, and you've never seen a more perky little tyke. With his long spindly legs and ragged gray brown fur, plus a severe underbite that left his bottom teeth exposed in a perpetual grin, he'd win Malibu's Ugliest Dog contest easy.

Of course Sunny adored Pirate, even though she wouldn't let him near her chihuahua, Tesoro. Strong on the claws and quick with a bite and weighing all of three pounds, Tesoro outsmarted Pirate at every turn.

Sunny believed it was the animosity between their dogs that was preventing their marriage, but Mac was not quite certain on that score. I mean, why spoil a good thing? Sunny and he were *good* together just the way they were—i.e., unmarried.

Sometimes Mac thought maybe it was his alter ego that appeared on your TV screens Thursday nights, in real-life documentary-style reinvestigating old Hollywood crimes, of which there were more than you might imagine. His show was titled *Mac Reilly's Malibu Mysteries,* with yours truly looking extra cool in the Dolce & Gabbana black leather jacket Sunny had bought him.

When she'd told him it was a "Dolce," Mac had no idea what she meant. It sounded like Italian ice cream to him. Later, he'd discovered it was an Italian designer and the jacket was without doubt the coolest garment he owned. Soft and pliable as wet putty, it had become part of his on-screen image, though God knows he was more usually to be found in sweats slouching up Malibu Road to Ralph's supermarket in search of beer and dog food, or breakfasting in Coogies coffee shop in a T-shirt and shorts rather than decked out in black leather.

Anyhow, the show, which took old murders and reckoned to solve them, had given him some kind of fame. It was all relative, of course, because as everybody knew in Hollywood, once your show went off the air you were as forgotten as last week's dinner. And now it looked as though Mac's time had come and gone, and the show was likely not to return for another season. Too bad, because the income had come in handy and he'd gotten to keep his day job, investigating for all those nice rich folk. And surprisingly many of them were genuinely nice. Plus they had the same troubles as everybody else. Sex and money. In that order.

He gave Pirate the low whistle that meant get the heck back over here, and the dog came running from whatever exciting secrets he'd found on Malibu's most expensive bit of shore. Together, they turned and headed for home. They were strolling along, minding their own business, listening to the crash of the waves, breathing in the salty ocean air and keeping an eye out for shooting stars, all that romantic stuff. And then they heard the scream.

High pitched. Quivering. *Terrified.*

It didn't take a P.I. to figure out that the screamer was female. And that she was in trouble.

TWO

MAC quickly scanned the houses. All were in darkness save for a glimmer of light on a deck a couple of houses back. He stumbled through the soft sand toward it, followed by Pirate.

He paused at the foot of the wooden steps leading to the house, listening, but there were no more screams. What he did think he heard though was a sob. Muffled, but nevertheless a definite sob.

Telling Pirate to stay put, he inched his way up the steps onto the deck, which was only about ten feet deep, a usual size for the acreage-tight Colony. The house loomed in front of him, a glass and limestone cliff that was more modern than the millennium and more stark than the architecture of Richard Meier, famous for the design of the L.A. Getty Museum, among other things. It was also as dark as the night outside.

Suddenly a lamp was turned on. Through the window he glimpsed a woman. A redhead wearing a sheer black negligee and, if he was not mistaken and even though it was at fifty paces, very little else. Now contrary to the popular belief, this was not your normal bedtime attire in Malibu, nor was midnight a usual hour to retire. Most everyone in the movie biz had an early call and was in their flannel PJs, curled up in a bed, learning the next day's lines by nine.

Mac knocked on the window but the woman didn't seem to hear. She just stared down at her feet as though there was something fascinating there. Like maybe a body, Mac thought.

She was young, maybe twenty-three, and beautiful, with everything in the right place as revealed by the sheer bit of black chiffon and lace she wore. Plus she had the face of a naughty angel. Mac felt glad to be of help. He checked, saw that the glass doors were unlocked and in his knight-in-shining-armor role he slid it open.

Her head shot up and he flung her a reassuring smile. "Hi," he said, "I'm Mac Reilly, your neighbor. I thought I heard a scream. Are you in some kind of trouble?"

The woman tossed her long red curling hair out of her tearful green eyes, lifted herself to her full statuesque height and pointed a gun at him.

"Get out," she said in a throaty whisper.

Mac eyed the gun. It was a Smith & Wesson Sigma .40, and definitely not to be messed with. He paused long enough to wonder why she was not pressing the button to summon security from the gate instead of threatening him. And then the gun went off.

The bullet ricocheted from the polished concrete floor near his foot, shattered a crystal vase, then buried itself in the back of a nearby sofa.

Mac didn't wait around for a second shot. He took off down the steps, sprinting back along the beach a couple of paces behind the cowardly dog.

"Oops, sorry, my mistake," she called after him, her voice floating eerily on the breeze.

THREE

SUNNY Alvarez was lying on the bed in her room in the Hotel d'Inghiliterra in Rome, dialing L.A. every ten minutes and wondering where on God's earth Mac Reilly was. I mean, it was nine a.m. in Rome, which meant it was midnight in Malibu. Could Mac be out on the town the minute her back was turned? When the truth was she'd only come here to stir him up a little. She'd figured a little jealousy wouldn't hurt. They'd always said absence made the heart grow fonder. Now she wasn't so sure.

Restless, she got up and began to pace, running her hands distractedly through her long hair that swung around her shoulders like liquid black satin, with just enough wave in it to give it bounce. Sunny's eyes were amber brown and fringed by lashes so thick they were like miniature shades on the windows of the soul.

Her skin was golden, her legs long, and her skirts usually short. She was, as Mac often told her, in between kisses, a knockout.

"Even though you're ditsy enough to drive any man mad," he'd once said to her, causing her to swat him with a handy cushion, which in turn sent Pirate into a barking frenzy because nobody—not even Sunny, who he loved—was going to harm his "father."

The only positive news Sunny had were the postcards Mac sent her daily. At least she believed they were from him, but since there was no signature she couldn't be absolutely sure. Except she knew nobody else who would be FedExing pictures of Surfrider Beach, and Zuma, and Paradise Cove with the anonymous message, *From Malibu, With Love.* Sunny was saving those postcards. She planned to stick them in her "Memories" book to look at when she was old and gray. And also, unless she could get Mac to the altar soon, still single.

Her room looked as though a typhoon had hit it. Her method of unpacking was to take everything out of the suitcase and toss it over chairs and the bed, then sort out whatever she needed from the various piles. Her apartment was kept mostly in the same state of chaos. It was a leftover from her college days when it had seemed the easiest—and quickest—method of getting dressed, and it drove Mac crazy. To compensate she would point out her kitchen to him, immaculate as an operating room, where she would cook him delicious meals—plus she always did the dishes afterward. Food was her first passion. The second was clothes, as evidenced by the shopping bags from Rome's boutiques scattered around the room. The third was her Harley chopper, but that unfortunately was back in L.A. Rome was a city full of Vespas, but they were definitely not the same thing.

She picked up the phone, got Mac's voice mail one more time, slammed it back down again, and lay back on the bed contemplating her coral pink toenails and her life.

Of course her name was not really Sunny. That's just what Mac called her. Her real name was Sonora Sky Coto de Alvarez. Quite a mouthful, as she was only too painfully aware. In fact she was truly grateful to be designated as "Sunny." At least it let her off the hook of constantly explaining those names, which were the direct result of having a hippie-style mother who'd communed with nature as well as with the spirits, in the desert around their adobe-style ranch outside of Santa Fe, New Mexico.

Sunny's mom was still dreamy and off-beat beautiful and still prone to wearing floating shapeless garments with long strands of crystal beads, and often flowers in her smooth blonde hair. Yet, oddly enough she'd always been a terrific mom, even if her daughters did have to spend nights with her out in the desert, communing with nature while keeping a nervous eye out for rattlers. Mom didn't even think about things like snakes. Her mind was on a higher plane, one which sadly Sunny and her sister never reached.

Their feet were more firmly planted on this earth. As kids they loved riding horses, chasing boys, and raising hell. Later, they'd graduated to riding motorcycles, chasing boys, and raising hell. That is until their father took them in hand, straightened them out, and packed them off to college, where he hoped real life would not deal them a killer blow between the eyes after the gentle ministrations of their otherworldly mother.

Sunny's Papa was something else again. Handsome? You don't know what that word means if you haven't seen her dad. He's Mexican, with that polished-tan skin, thick silver gray hair, soft brown eyes, and a trim mustache. Kind of like Howard Keel used to look on *Dallas*. Astride his black thoroughbred he was the epitome of the Mexican ranchero.

He'd thought Brown was the perfect college to tame a Harley-riding, boy-mad eighteen-year-old, and true, it opened up Sunny's world to a kind of life she had never seen. But she'd missed her family, and she'd cried thinking of her beloved *abuelita,* her Mexican grandmother, and of her tamales, cooked the way only *abuelita* knew how to cook them. The tamales were a Christmas Eve staple at the ranch and everyone from the workers and the cowboys and the local families gathered to enjoy them, along with a large amount of tequila and Corona beer and Mexican music and dancing.

Of course Mom also cooked the traditional turkey, albeit, in her usual haphazard way. Sometimes its wasn't quite done and had to go back in the oven for an hour or two; and sometimes it was too well done and Papa said you needed horse teeth to get through it. Either way it was fun.

At college it hadn't take long for the golden-limbed raven-haired Latina in black biker leathers zooming around on her Harley to get noticed. Soon, she was cooking tamales and handing out the Corona at her own parties. By the time she graduated, magna cum laude, with her proud parents and her sister beaming in the audience, Sunny felt almost ready to tackle the world. But before that came the Wharton School and a master's in business.

Later, she'd found herself a job in Paris, working for a fragrance house. After a year there she moved on to Bologna and a job with the Fiat Corporation. Then back home and on to California, where she'd opened her P.R. business, which was doing very nicely, thank you.

She'd met Mac at a press party for his TV show. He told her he'd noticed her across the room. "How could I miss you, in that outfit," was what he'd actually said.

It was winter and she had on a tiny white miniskirt, her tough-girl motorcycle boots because she'd driven there on her Harley, and a black turtleneck. She was all long golden legs, sexy curves, and tumbling black hair. She was always careful about drinking and driving and was sipping lemonade when he'd come up behind her and tapped her on the shoulder. Swinging around she found herself looking at this rugged guy in jeans and a T-shirt, whose deep blue eyes were taking her in like she was the best thing he'd seen all night.

It's him, she'd thought, thrilled. *The man I've been waiting for all my life.* Of course she was smart enough not to tell him that and it was true, they were total opposites: Mac, dragged up by his bootstraps from the streets of Boston and the Miami crime scene to the P.I. and TV personality he was now. And she, the wild child brought up on the ranch, beautiful and brainy and ditsy, but with the determination to be her own woman.

In fact, life seemed set, romance-wise, until she'd invited him for dinner at her smart high-rise apartment a few miles from his home in Malibu in Marina del Ray. Even her home-cooked tamales were no match for that first disastrous encounter between Tesoro and Pirate.

Let's face it, Sunny thought, sighing, *Pirate was willing to be friends. Tesoro was not.* And rather than have his dog harassed, Mac had departed, leaving the tamales uneaten. "Next time I won't bring the dog," he'd said, shielding Pirate from the marauding chihuahua.

And that was how things now stood. She went to his Malibu house without Tesoro. He came to her Marina apartment without Pirate. "And never the twain shall meet," was Mac's motto. Which, of course, left them in their current uncertain limbo.

Sunny checked the time. It was after midnight in Malibu and Mac still wasn't home. She should get off this bed right now. Get out there in the vibrant bustling streets of Rome, pick up a charming handsome Italian and let him sweep her off her stilettos.

Heaving a sigh that this time came from her gut, she decided that she would call Mac no more. The hell with the diet. She could practically smell sugar and cinnamon as she ran her hands hastily through her long dark hair, pushed her feet into black patent sandals, and headed for the door.

The phone rang. She swung round, staring at it.

It rang again. Of course it wouldn't be *him*. How could it? Hadn't she been calling him for the past hour, damn it?

She picked up the phone. "*Pronto?*" she said sulkily.